Isis, Vampires and Ghosts — Oh My!

I0589808

Janis Hill

—————⊖—————

Book 1 of the
Other World series

ISIS, VAMPIRES AND GHOSTS – OH MY!

Book 1 of *The Other World seriese*

The moral rights of Janis Hill to be identified as the author of this work have been asserted.

Copyright 2018 Hague Publishing

Hague Publishing
PO Box 451
Bassendean Western Australia 6934
Email: contact@haguepublishing.com
Web: www.haguepublishing.com

ISBN: 978-0-6480503-4-6

Cover Art: 'Isis, Vampires and Ghosts — Oh My!' by Jade Zivanovic
http://www.steampowerstudios.com.au/

Typeset Garamond 12/14

Dedicated to those who have touched our lives but are no longer with us, you will be remembered.

Chapter 1

IT LOOKED like one of those old Christian churches that had run out of funds and been sold off to the highest bidder. I'd seen it happen before. Some became high-class antique shops, others turned into seedy nightclubs. The unluckiest of all, as with this one, became 'new' places of belief and worship for those who needed to believe in something, but who felt the top religions were all too mainstream.

And so I had found the Temple of Isis, lucky me. Even in my depressed state of mind, my sarcastic sense of humour scanned its front bulletin board for another reason to pick on it. I half expected it to have a timetable at the bottom stating it was only the Temple of Isis on certain days, and some other half-arsed, made-up faith at other times . . . But there was nothing. Ah well, sarcasm can only comfort you so far.

Wrapping my mind in its full sceptical cloak, I braced myself for what lay ahead and stepped over the threshold into the darkened entrance of the Temple of Isis, preparing myself for my sister's funeral.

Yes, I'd had better days, but when it came to my sister, not many. We had been estranged for several years, and before that she had only been a sporadic visitor in my life since the time she'd been old enough to flee the family home without being brought back by the authorities, kicking and screaming all the way. It's not as if we'd had a terrible childhood. Our parents had loved us, fed us, provided us with an education, and given us the freedom to determine our own beliefs and activities within legal boundaries. You really couldn't have asked for more. Sadly Estella — said sister — had been wired oddly and saw our upbringing as overly restrictive, and held a great need to rebel against it at every turn. I had always felt that if she had been raised as a wild child, free to do as she liked in a Hippy commune, she would still believe it too restrictive and have found an excuse to rebel against its carefree nature. The really deep-down dark part of me had actually been relieved to hear she'd died. Finally Estella had stopped being a problem for me, or for anyone else.

"Welcome dear daughter and sister of Isis, to our Mother-sister's holy house of order!" The sunny greeting and enormous smile on the bright faced woman in white approaching me was enough to make me want to scurry away. However, I do have some pride, and rarely scurry. Well, not once eye contact has been made.

"Uh, Hi?" My stammered reply was the best I could manage in my 'playing nice with others' tone and expression. I was raised to believe everyone should have their own personal beliefs; I just really hated it when they tried to thrust those beliefs onto me personally.

"You must be Stephanie Anders? Beloved and devoted sister to our newly departed Estella, sister and Priestess of the fifth order."

I smiled — slightly manically — and dumbly nodded back, hoping I appeared overcome with sadness, and that she couldn't tell I was gritting my teeth and madly biting back what I really wanted to say about the 'dearly departed' Estella. But I didn't have any choice; I was the executor of her will and had to preside over her funeral. It had all been prearranged and paid for — which was unusual for Estella. All I had to do was show up and play nice with her weirdo new-age friends for a few hours.

So here I was. It wasn't going to be an afternoon of my life I'd ever get back, but she had been my only sibling and I had sort of loved her — despite her annoying, frustratingly 'intolerant of other people's feelings' way — at one point in my life. This was probably the least I could do for her. The dark bit of my mind piped up it was also a good way to make sure she really was now dead and buried, and out of my life for good.

The woman in front of me seemed to fit into what I'd expected at such a place. She was medium to short in height, dumpy, and a little older than myself, with long, dark hair hanging loosely down her back. She appeared to be wearing someone's white bed sheets and lace curtains that she'd cut a hole into for her head to fit through. Or that could have just been me being a teensy bit sceptical.

"Greetings daughter-sister. I am Jasmine, Priestess of the fourth order to this glorious Temple of Isis." The woman went on to say, so I smiled, nodded some more and kept silent. "High Priestess Roxanna is awaiting you within the central chamber, with your sister."

I went a little cross-eyed by trying to change my desired look of hor-ror into intense interest at this news. I had no problems meeting this

High Priestess chick, but I'd been rather hoping to avoid looking upon Estella so soon after lunch. I mean, although I'd had to identify her from a post-autopsy picture — head and shoulders only — I was still a little unsure on the details of her death. So wasn't too sure how gruesome or, erm . . . bloated and decayed, the rest of her looked. And we just won't go into how bad she could smell.

"My poor daughter-sister, you appear overcome with the sad emotions we all share right now," Jasmine went on to say, rushing forward to drape a bed sheet and curtain-clad arm around my shoulders. I didn't flinch, much. "Let me take you to the High Priestess right away. There is much to do before we can assist you to release your sadness and move into the purified Light of our beloved Mother-sister Isis."

I let her lead me away down the aisle towards the inner chambers of the church, hoping she was as blissfully unaware of my tension as she appeared to be about my complete and utter dislike of pretty much everything she'd said so far. Then again, I was fairly certain I could set fire to her robes and she'd have been blissfully unaware of that too, if it didn't have something to do with Isis. She had that kind of vacant, happy, sunny-side-of-life look to her. Poor thing, no wonder Estella had ended up here, if Jasmine was anything to go by. It was obviously a place that attracted the strays and dregs of life that had no self-worth and needed someone to tell them what to do and how to think. Catty, me?

At the end of the aisle was the typical raised dais found in all churches of this architectural type. Above the dais, where a crucifix would have usually hung, there was a huge tapestry depicting a woman in white watching light and smoke swirl around a pool of water within a cave. Isis, I presumed? Despite my sceptical nature being in overdrive, I had to admire the beauty of the tapestry and the artistic dedication that had been put into it. I was no expert, but the roughly five by three metre cloth appeared to have been done by hand. Upon the dais itself was an altar. But the typical golden eagle or plain wooden stand usually found within old churches was gone. In their place was another astounding work of art of hand-carved wood, depicting entwined branches of ivy. It seemed to organically have sprouted from the dais, winding around and over itself until it was of the right height for a person to stand behind. There it opened into a flat, smooth table, holding a large candle inlaid with dried flowers and herbs. There were spaces for other items upon the top of this altar that were obviously kept elsewhere, when not in use during a ceremony. The candle, though unlit, seemed to shimmer in the darkness of the converted church. A lot of time, effort, and money had gone into this place. Despite the wittering Jasmine next to me, some of my initial distrust and scepticism started to thaw.

Beyond the dais was a wooden screen created with the same theme of entwined branches and ivy, obviously made by the same hand as the one who had carved the beautiful altar. The screen had been designed to hide the doors to the back chambers, from the front of the church. As we approached a row of three doors hidden behind the screen, the one to the left opened and I was surprised by the vision that walked out. She was an elegant, mature aged woman in a neat sleeveless, short, spotless white dress, over which a tailored near-transparent white chiffon robe sat almost regally. Her silver to white hair was cut short, but was of a well-maintained cut in an expensive-looking, elegant style. She wore no jewellery apart from a torque of gold around her neck and a thin circlet of gold around her head. Everything about this woman clashed with Jasmine; from the clothes to the hair, to the way she held herself. Her expression was one of someone who appeared to know her place in the world and, in a not too demeaning manner, knew it was on a few pegs higher than the rest of us. As our eyes met, my pent-up hostility and final shreds of scepticism drained away as if she'd pulled the plug. There was just something about her that made everything in this place seem justified and right. There was also a glint in her eyes that seemed to dare me to prove her wrong.

"Stephanie Anders?" she said in a calm, level voice. I felt her eyeing me over, but not in the critical, assessing way others with money and higher life status usually seemed to. I mean, I had worn my best conventional black dress for Estella's funeral. It was almost as if she knew I'd made my best effort and that was good enough for her.

"High Priestess, I've brought our beloved dearly departed Estella's sister for your blessing." Jasmine wittered on happily, in obvious awe of the powerful matriarchal figure before us.

"And that was very kind of you, Jasmine." The High Priestess said, in the patient tone often used by a mother to a child. "And I thank you. Please leave us now and get back to your normal duties." As Jasmine did a poorly executed genuflect to the older woman, I actually caught the expression of mild annoyance and embarrassment in the High

Priestess' eyes as she glanced at me. We stood there in silence, sharing neutral glances, while watching Jasmine wander off back into the main area of the church.

"Sadly, yes, we do get all sorts here." The High Priestess remarked, shocking me into an almost hysterical giggle. "But if their hearts are pure and their efforts can be turned towards good, the Temple of Isis welcomes all such creatures." She glanced over my shoulder to ensure Jasmine had truly left us alone. "I mean, they all need love, a place to feel they belong, regular meals, and a warm home. How could we not provide what we can? I do hope to have her out of that mother, daughter, sister rubbish soon though." Wow! I had never heard anyone sound so catty, while still seeming to be the nicest person in the world. I simply had to learn how to do that.

"I am Roxanna De Vries, fourteenth High Priestess of this beloved Temple of Isis," she went on. "I am aware that there are many different Temples to our beloved Goddess around the world and I really can't say which one She smiles upon the most. But we've been here over one hundred years and seem to be doing okay. Still standing, and the drains haven't caused us any issues in oh, twenty years now."

I was stunned to silence by her matter of fact calm tones as she spoke and barely noticed that as she was speaking, she had been ushering me through the door she'd just emerged from.

The room I was guided into appeared to be her office come High Priestess inner sanctum. There was a large wooden desk obviously created by the same magician of a carpenter who had made the altar and screen. Behind it was a throne-like chair for the High Priestess to sit on. Smaller, simpler works of intricate woodcarving in the shape of chairs occupied the other side of the desk. While one wall of the room was taken up with filing cabinets and other office and managerial looking items, the other was hidden by another gorgeous hand sewn tapestry of Isis. This tapestry showed the Goddess appearing to hold the moon in her upraised hands on a starry, deep indigo night. A smaller altar was set up in front of this wall hanging, its candle lit and filling the room with the scent of peppermint, lavender and rosemary.

The High Priestess gently urged me into a seat, before settling upon her throne on the other side of the desk.

"You're not exactly what I expected Estella's sister to be like," she said pleasantly enough, though her eyes continued to assess me thoroughly.

"If it helps, you're not exactly what I was expecting for the High Priestess," I replied, noticing I'd lost my 'playing nice with others' tone. Hey, she started it.

"We are not all peace, love, mung beans, flowing hair and curtain-like robes." She smirked at me, her head tilting to one side slightly as she said it. Almost uncannily describing not only Jasmine, but my original belief of what they'd all be like.

"Yes, well, my parents only produced one child whose wiring was so cross-circuited she never knew how to appreciate what she had, or realised we weren't all just there for her entertainment, bail money or hotel service." I hadn't meant to sound so narky about Estella, but after being in this room under Roxanna's cool gaze, it just happened. The High Priestess studied me for a silent moment longer, then gave me a small smile.

"If it helps, once Estella felt the Light of Isis fall upon her she did become repentant for most of her actions and choices in life." Roxanna was starting to remind me of a cat, the way she'd say something then pause, waiting for my reaction, to see how she would toy with me next.

"And yet she couldn't even scribble that on a postcard and send it to me." There was scorn and anger in my voice. It was mostly due to Estella, but also Roxanna. As her initial glamour wore off I had started to see beneath her pleasantly neutral manner. Yes, she still did seem a nice person, but she held some sort of power that I could feel as a slightly threatening undertone. It almost made me feel that if I fell off the wrong side of the fine line she had me walking upon I might not survive the consequences.

Roxanna stared at me in passive silence a moment longer, then gave me another smile.

"It seems Estella knew her burden upon you better than you think, and I can say she was truly thankful. Within our faith, being the person in charge of our dispatching to the next life is one of the greatest honours to be given. I can understand your animosity towards your sister, being treated as a safety net and doormat by your own flesh and blood can be one of the worst relationships to have." She paused as her face clouded a moment, and I wondered if she was deliberately showing me she knew exactly how that felt, or if it was an unconscious grimace at people who acted that way.

"And I am very thankful you lived up to your sister's expectations and have come here today." Roxanna then smiled again, her face once more hiding her emotions.

"Estella will be relieved to know you made the effort. I feel it will help the completion of her passing from Isis' Light and into the New World so much smoother." Alarm bells started going off in my mind as I watched her watch me run through the strange choice of words she'd just used. Knowing she was waiting for me to take the bait, I jumped in, boots and all.

"Look, no offence here towards all your faith and Goddess Hoo-hah, but my sister is dead. I'd appreciate it if all statements on how she might feel could be done using the past tense, so as not to muddy our already cloudy conversation. 'Kay?"

Roxanna had the gall to look triumphant and amused at the same time. Still, I guess it was better than being angered at my total disrespect for her belief system.

"And how do you know that talking in the past tense about her is what she would want?"

Cue the eye roll and scoffing sound I'd been ever so good at holding at bay til then.

"Because she looked pretty dead in the pictures I was given to identify her by, if you must know." I was terse, but still in the realm of polite tone and volume. "And I'm yet to know of anyone proven dead by autopsy to sit up and request everyone speak of them in the present tense, until we set a match to their pyre." Why the hell were we even having this conversation? Was she trying to strip away my sympathetic padding, and have me give Estella a send-off in the best bitchy sister mood I could muster?

"I can assure you it's not always the case. And this is from experience in my circles of 'Goddess hoo-hah'." Roxanna smiled at me before continuing. "Were you ever informed by police how it was she died? Or just that she was dead?"

I sighed, letting it shudder through me with the suppressed sob and sudden rush of sadness. "My parents may have been told, as they were the ones who drew the short straw to personally identify her. I was just the lucky family member to be asked if I recognised the picture of her laid out on a slab." As I watched, I noticed all amusement and challenge leaving Roxanna's expression, as she moved back into her more passive to neutral state. "And I can assure you here and now my parents would have told me if they felt it noteworthy. I had honestly assumed it was a death by misadventure, with some stranger she picked up in a bar. I'd rather not delve into it if it's anything worse."

"Stephanie, I truly am sorry your family has been affected by a loss in such a way. Especially when it appears Estella was more estranged from you than I was aware. However, I do feel you should be advised how she died, because it does affect whether she should be spoken about in the past or present tense."

Dear Lord, I had just about had enough of all this hokum! I must have shown as much in my expression, as Roxanna rose elegantly and moved to the door, beckoning for me to follow.

"Come, I think it's now time for you to see your sister," was all she said, before moving back through the doorway. It was the last thing I honestly wanted to do. Really, all I wanted to do was get the damn ceremony and other necessities over, and disappear before they brought out the cheap sherry and stale sandwiches at the wake — assuming they did wakes like that in the presence of their precious Isis. Somehow, I found myself rising and following her out. We moved to the far right door, and she opened it to reveal a darkened stone stairway leading down. There were lights below and the sound of quiet chanting. I took one last look at the church, feeling it was a pretty sane and safe view compared to what I might be about to see, then started down the steps with Roxanna behind me. The things I did for my damned sister. Surely this'd be the last one, right?

Chapter 2

THE first flight of stairs kept with the architecture I'd seen so far. So, the church had a crypt or at least a basement, nothing unusual. However, when it didn't stop there and the second flight past rough-hewn rock walls, rather than the neatly crafted grey stone blocks and mortar of the first, I started to wonder how old this place really was. By the fourth flight down, I was wondering how much of the city actually knew this church ran so deep. What sort of crypt needed to be hidden this far down? I guessed we were almost at the bottom, when the shadowy lighting of the stairs started to change to a soft, light blue glow that emanated from below. I will freely admit to stumbling down the last few steps, as the stairwell opened to reveal the chamber that was at the end of it all. A chamber that was the spitting image of the one depicted in the tapestry in the main area of the church, sans Isis of course. There was the cave, stalagmites, stalactites and all. There to the right of the chamber's centre was the pool of water among the rocks, shrouded in mist, and the source of the light blue light — my mind of course already trying to figure out how it was all wired to give off those effects. Scattered about the chamber were women of various ages, shapes and sizes draped in white robes that were almost as varied as they were. The source of the quiet chanting I'd heard as I'd descended also came from them. And there, on a raised stone slab in the middle of the chamber, bathed in a crisp, white light shooting down from the rocky ceiling, was Estella, my sister.

I felt I was holding it all together really well, seeing the chamber with all its put on mysticism, devotees, and the peacefully reposed corpse of my sister. I really did feel I was handling the whole situation quite well. However, when Estella sat up, autopsy scars showing above her death shroud, and said, "Hey sis, 'bout time you showed up." I was out of there. The High Priestess herself could not bar my exit, although I swear she'd been preparing to do just that. Roxanna was almost thrown down the stairs in my retreat. I will say, however, that I didn't run screaming from the building, no matter how much I had really wanted to.

***

I cursed my knees when they gave out beneath me, as I stumbled down the stairs two at a time outside the church. At least I managed to turn the fall into a deliberate looking and slightly more graceful sitting down on the bottom step. I just wished I could have made it at least a few blocks away before it had happened. That way, Roxanna — High Priestess of some pretty freaky stuff — wouldn't have found me so easily. I knew it was her that I felt sit down beside me, even though my head was neatly buried in my arms, crossed over my knees. It smelt like her office, it had to be her.

"If you so much as try a smug 'I told you she wanted to be spoken of in present tense', I'm taking your torque and cramming it as far down your throat as I can." What can I say; my tone had been stable, even if said through very clenched teeth.

"Peace, Stephanie," Roxanna said. "I was actually going to say you handled that better than most would have."

I laughed; admittedly it started more as a barking cough until hysteria lightened it and gave it wings. Thankfully those wings had been clipped and it didn't fly away. Instead it flapped about a bit then died in my throat shortly afterwards, as I fought off tears.

"And you see this happen a lot, do you?" I asked, finally looking up at her. She sat stiffly reposed in the midday sun, looking out of place while still seeming part of her surroundings.

"Only some of our more interesting deceased, such as Estella, are cared for in the Light of Isis. I have seen worse reactions than yours from a simple open casket on the central dais, however." she smiled sympathetically at me. "It is a lot to take in, I know. I am the keeper of some rather old secrets and am relieved you're handling this one so well."

Was she serious, I mean about how I was handling it? Because, despite my card carrying scepticism of all the mystical mumbo jumbo, after what I'd just seen in the crypt of her church, there was no doubt she had a lot of secrets. I looked at her and saw the serious expression on her face, saw the deep truth within her eyes. All thoughts of her and her church being some scam were gone. Just seeing Estella had convinced me of that — she had been dead. I felt it in my bones she had been dead. So why the hell had she sat up and spoken to me?

"Please tell me you have a lot of holy spirits we can imbibe while you tell me what the hell is going on around here," I said plaintively. I may not have believed in a lot of the things religion was blamed for, but my mind wasn't closed off to it entirely. And the bigger the new thing to believe in, the bigger the beer please!

"I am more than happy to share some of our fine Damsel and Thistle wine with you . . ."

"Damsel and Thistle?" I broke in, unable to help myself; there is only so far I will go in experimenting with new things.

"It's the winery's name, not the ingredients," Roxanna answered soothingly; apparently relieved I was still taking it all so well. "However, before we breach the bottle, I really do feel you should stay sober a little longer so we can go back down to Estella, and we can explain everything to you."

I whined loudly at this, I really did. It was my best impression of a three year old being asked to eat their broccoli.

"Really? Sober?" Damn. Part of my brain still just wanted to get the damned day over and done with. That part of said brain was ignoring another bit of my brain that was laughing near-hysterically and saying it was going to take more than a day to get over this.

"Fine." I said, shooting to my feet and dusting myself off. "Just because Estella is dead, why the heck should this stop her from screwing me over all the time? Hey, she is the gift that just keeps giving after all."

Roxanna gracefully rose next to me, smiling in a noncommittal way, before leading the way back up the steps and into her church.

"Thank you for seeing this through, Stephanie," she murmured as we slowly made our way back down the aisle to the doors at the back of the main chamber. "I can assure you that the majority of followers of Isis do tend to pass away like everyone else. They die, they stay dead, and their remains are disposed of in the usual dignified way like so many others of varied faiths."

"But Estella had to go cock it up, like she's done with so many other things in her life." I had only meant to think the thought, but somehow it escaped. I gave an apologetic look to the High Priestess and her surprised expression.

"Not exactly." She paused at the doorway, appearing to be considering how to put her next few sentences. "Admittedly, Estella was a bit of a wild child when she first came to us, but upon bathing in the Light of Isis she really did see the error of her ways and had started to reform herself. She has become a better person."

"So what went wrong?" it was an innocent enough question, I simply couldn't help but say it in a tad too bitchy a manner.

"Nothing that was due to her own fault or error." Roxanna assured me as we reached the door that led back down the many stairs to their secret grotto. "She was assisting in the banishment of evil from a house of ill repute."

Perhaps I had the wrong idea as to exactly what a 'house of ill repute' was as mental images of Victorian whorehouses or ghetto crack dens flashed through my mind. I really couldn't see these white lacy curtain-clad ladies taking either place on successfully. And obviously it hadn't been successful, or there wouldn't be a corpse of sorts in their deep basement.

"Again, I cannot speak for all Temples of Isis." Roxanna said, breaking into my rather bizarre thoughts, "But part of our duties under the Goddess' Light is to protect the unsuspecting from the Darkness." I really do feel my blank look said it all. It was better than scoffing and doing the loony sign at the side of my head. Roxanna opened the door, and we slowly started our descent once more. This time she took the lead.

"Stephanie," she was obviously starting again, trying to find the best way to approach the subject. "I know the world is full of a lot of lost people with a thin grasp on reality, who find it hard to differentiate between reality and fiction. We see it all the time from both sides. From those who want to join us, despite feeling our faith in Isis is probably a complete fabrication, and only come because we offer a warm bed and regular meals. Through to the disbelievers who would rather lock us up for desecrating what they see as a Christian church and for corrupting the gullible."

I wondered at which end of that varied spectrum of disbelief I fitted. Instead of deciding, I just made a sound that showed I was still listening. I really couldn't trust myself to do much more. Roxanna glanced over her shoulder at me and sighed. Obviously I wasn't responding in the way she had hoped.

"What people need to understand, is that a lot of what is seen as fiction and fantasy really is based on reality." She had stopped on the first landing and was staring at me as I joined her, studying my expression.

"O-kay." I said with a half shrug. "Look, I was raised to let people believe in what they will, as long as they intentionally harmed none." What did she want me to say? That yes, Santa really was real, and if she was a good little High Priestess this year she was going to get a new shiny red bike?

"I'm really not here to judge you or your belief in Isis." I tried to sound reasonable as I said this, "I just want to know why, when I've come to bury my dead sister, she's sitting up and talking to me." Roxanna was giving me a studying look so I went on. "I am here with as open a mind as I can manage, honest. So just hit me with it. Tell me what the hell happened, what the hell is going on, and how the hell I can get it all sorted out, and back to my boring white-bread-with-no-crusts life." From the expression she was now giving me, I wondered if I'd gone too far. "I can say hell, can't I?" Was it too late to attempt an innocent and doe-eyed expression?

"Doesn't everyone?" she answered, with an air of mild amusement mixed with relief. "And all right, if you want the truth, I'll stop waffling and get to it." She then turned and kept walking, taking a deep breath before continuing:

"The house of ill repute we were banishing was the home of evil in the shape of Branwyre, eighteenth vampire Lord of the Aegean." She stopped, hearing my own step falter as I tripped a little on the stairs, as well as the words, as they sank into my brain.

"Of course it was." I replied, trying to keep face and tone as neutral as possible.

"We had already slain the body of Branwyre just before the last new moon." Roxanna went on determinedly. "But we obviously missed cleansing this world of all of his Dark soul, as the night we shut down his house of evil, they were performing a ceremony to instil his essence into a new body."

"Oh, for sure." I said in neutral 'yes, I am still listening' tones, forcing my body to continue down the stairs, rather than letting it loose to flee back up the way we came, as it so wished to do. Roxanna had seemed so nice, completely unlike the fruitcake-short-of-a-few-nuts she was coming across as now. We reached the next landing and she turned to look at me, frustration clear on her face.

"Stephanie, I really do appreciate your near-silent cynicism, but I hate to break it to you: What I am telling you is all real." I stopped too and met her look with my own.

"I'm sure you really feel that way." I began, caught the look in her eye and snapped. "Look, okay. I'm freely willing to keep an open mind towards your religious belief, but vampires? Puh-lease! So tell me, are they the dinner jacket and slicked-back hair type? Or the pale, youthful and moody ones?"

Roxanne blinked a few times, as if shocked I'd say such a thing, then actually smiled. "Oh thank Isis you've finally gotten over your 'let's be polite to these religious loonies' mood!" She shook her head. "Vampires are real, but I can assure you that they are neither of the sad and silly things you mentioned. They are an evil disease that infects the Darkness of this world. And, our Temple of Isis is there to shed some of Isis' Light onto them. To dispel them to the beyond."

Oh to be able to sigh deeply and looked resigned and disappointed in what she'd just told me. What the hell, I did it anyway. I was then shocked to see Roxanna do the same, before turning on her heel and continuing down the stairs.

"As I was saying, they had his essence and were performing the ceremony of instilling it into a new body, when we broke it up. And although we defeated his followers and prevented the ceremony from completing, it wasn't without casualties on our side. We lost two Priestesses, besides Estella. They were the lucky ones." I continued to follow her down as she spoke; I have no idea why, but I felt almost compelled to hear the end of her tale.

"So you mean two more of your Priestesses died, but they stayed dead?" What can I say, it was one of those situations I felt the need to state the obvious to ensure I wasn't misconstruing any of the story.

"Yes." Roxanna glanced back at me at the third landing, but didn't stop this time. "Estella was a little zealous in her vanquishing and unfortunately got caught between the essence of Branwyre and his new body. In the crudest terms, she copped some splashback." My mind started tingling in the background; there was something in her words I was understanding, but not quite getting. Splashback? Essence? New body?

"Why in the hell would a vampire need a new body? Aren't they just some sort of undead hunky fellow trying to take over the world one virgin at a time?"

Roxanna sighed in what almost seemed like frustration. "The vampires of stories are not real vampires Stephanie." She stated this calmly enough, but there was an edge of frustration to her voice. "As I explained, they are a disease . . ." She seemed to be grasping for a better explanation. "They are a virus that lives in the blood and holds the soul, the essence, of the vampire. It turns their carrier into a subhuman creature of superhuman strength. Vampires are the smear of a vanquished demon left behind long ago during a battle. Those who destroyed the demon had their blood tainted with the Darkness of its own soul and, from that stain, the vampire essence arose. They can only exist in human form if the host body is infected with enough of this ageless virus." I freely admit to stumbling on the steps behind her again, as I took this all in. We were just above the cavern now and Roxanna had dropped her voice to a hushed tone that was hopefully drowned out to those below by their own chanting. Unfortunately, what she had just told me scarily held some merit. It seemed I could believe in a viral-based evildoer more than I could in the opera cloak, dinner suit and smouldering eyes.

"And the virgin part of the myth comes from the host bodies having to be virgins?" I asked hopefully, trying to show I had been not only paying attention but was trying to accept her story. She actually snorted in contempt. The High Priestess of Isis spinning me this grand tale snorted at me!

"Hardly!" she quipped, "Host bodies usually come from the followers of the vampire and, due to their following the values of a creature born from Darkness, I can assure you they are far from pure or virginal. But nice try." Oh bite me Roxanna.

"Well, I was basing it on why it didn't seem to effect Estella. She's not exactly vamping out down there." Was what I did end up saying out loud.

"Although we're unsure of exactly what happened with Estella, the reason she isn't 'vamping out' is she was not the intended host. The real power in a ceremony — both for Darkness and for Light — are the words, especially names. They are invoked to hold the magic in place. The essence had been invoked to take host in a body that was not

Estella's. Plus, she only received a small smear of the vampire blood as she beheaded the Master of Ceremony." Yes, I freely admit to stumbling again at those words. As much as I remembered Estella as a wild child, I'd not once imagined beheading was one of the things she got up to.

"Ah, the splashback effect. Never a good thing." I muttered, trying to lighten the conversation before I ran screaming again. Roxanna just raised a questioning eyebrow at me, but seemed to sense my flight risk and left it at that. Although the last set of steps had been taken slowly to finish our conversation, we were finally at the bottom again and I was staring out at my deceased sister propped up on her elbows, watching the women in white robes pacing around her chanting. My life was about to get a little more interesting than a funeral and stale ham sandwiches at a wake. Damn it!

Chapter 3

"ABOUT time!" my dearly departed sister called out in her usual carefree manner. "So, has our High Priestess had a chance to bring you up to date on my latest pickle?" Only Estella could make such an understatement.

"Not quite." I said, feeling the whirl of emotions building up to fever pitch, as I eyed her over. Hate, sadness, loss, confusion, worry; all the good ones were stewing away. She was indeed paler than usual and not looking all that healthy; dark shadows around her eyes, straggly looking hair. My own eyes were drawn to the V-shaped stitched autopsy scars on her chest above her death robes. She followed my gaze and shrugged.

"Oh that." She pointed to her scars, "I can't remember exactly what happened, but the police busted our raid shortly after I'd done away with the Master of Ceremony. The backlash of his invoked magic cut short apparently dropped me stone dead, and when my sisters had to disperse before the cops got the wrong idea they had to leave me behind."

How could she call these strange women her sisters? And what the hell did that make me? Just the poor schmuck who was born into the role and didn't get a choice?

"You were technically dead, dear child, along with Priestess Fiona and Priestess Meredith." Roxanna spoke up, stepping closer to Estella and trying to encourage me to do the same. Oh, fat chance!

"Your time in the state morgue appears to have given the virus enough time to replenish itself and bring forth your new life after death."

This really was all getting too much for me, especially as they all seemed so confident in it all being true.

"Oh, come on!" I couldn't help it, I'd finally snapped at the ludicrous ideas they were spouting. "If she had been dead, how on earth could a virus have started working its way through her body? They need healthy cells enriched with oxygen from working lungs, and healthy blood being pumped around the body by a beating heart. Neither of which could be happening if she was dead!" How dare they both give me such an exasperated look? At least the other women seemed fine at ignoring me as they continued their pacing and chanting.

Roxanna turned back to me, ready to try and explain, when she was interrupted by Estella. "Lighten up to the real world, Stephanie. Look into the Light of Isis!"

"I did say she was technically dead, Stephanie." Roxanna tried soothingly, but sensing my turmoil didn't push it. "To modern medicine and science, blind to the Other World we walk in, she did indeed appear dead. When she killed the invoker of the spell, it didn't drop her 'stone dead', merely stunned her to her very soul and slowed her life force to the point she appeared dead to those not in the know." I gave Roxanna my best sceptical look, I really couldn't help it. As if the doctors who examined her and dissected her for autopsy hadn't ensured she was well and truly dead. If not before they started, what they'd then done to her would have done the trick. Again, as if sensing my train of thought, Roxanna of course had another answer for me.

"The vampire virus, due to its demonic origins, doesn't just infect the body but can also entwine the victim's soul, hence its insidious nature. It appears that by the time they were scooping her organs out for examination, the virus had infected her enough to bring out the undead aspect in its new host."

This caused another eye roll to be added to my sceptical look, followed by a sigh.

"If you can get the undead side of the whole vampire thing, how was the original vamp host killed so that the blood needed a new body?" It was a simple enough question, a pity about the amount of scorn that ended up in it.

"As you do with any vamp," Estella piped up from her spot on the stone slab. "You chop their fricking head off. I mean, duh, Stephanie, haven't you been taking in anything our High Priestess has been saying?"

Yup, she may have been dead and brought back to life, but my sister was still a royal pain in the arse, no matter how you looked at it. We were standing close to the raised slab she lay upon now and I exchanged my usual pained, world-weary expression with Estella. It was the one I always had when having to deal with her and cleaning up her messes.

"And so my sister is an undead vampire who you want me to behead, in this holy-of-holies place of yours?" And if there was mild sarcasm in my voice, could you really blame me?

"I'm not a damned vampire, you silly cow!" Estella exclaimed, about to get up off the slab when Roxanna raised a hand and sternly shook her head at her. "Geez, Steph, I thought you were more loose and easy going than the rigid people who got to be our parents. Haven't you been taking any of this in?"

I closed my eyes and gritted my teeth, doing the mental countdown I'd for years hoped would help lower my anger at her glib tongue and total lack of respect for our parents.

"Estella, you may want to lie down and rest a little longer." It was Roxanna, not oblivious to my current state of mind — unlike my sister — and I assumed it was her hand that led me to a quiet corner of the cavern. I opened my eyes as we walked, turning my head to look back at Estella who was settling herself back down into her own death repose. I mean, how messed up was that?

"I am starting to see where your hesitance to assist your sibling comes from." Roxanna soothed as we moved into the shadows away from the chanting. "I must admit, she isn't as glib towards us, and I apologise for her behaviour." I grunted and shook my head, calming myself down from my conversation with Estella. Her being alive and just as blasé about the world around her, after the week of mourning I'd been through, was bad enough. Having to take this vampire rubbish into account with it, was just too much for me. I wanted out, and I wanted to go home to my safe, boring, drab apartment and I wanted to have a nice big glass of wine.

"You should never apologise for my sister. It gets you nowhere and makes you look all the more foolish for sticking up for her when she screws you over too." My tone had been bitter, but held more sadness to it than I'd expected. I glanced at Roxanna and watched her studying me, obviously calculating how to proceed. I sighed again and rubbed my temples with the tips of my fingers.

"Okay Roxanna, let's just cut the crap." I then began, knowing I needed to get this whole mess over with. Having 'Big Sister' responsibilities to consider, and all that. "Let's just pretend for a moment that all of what you've told me is true. Vampire blood, beheadings, blah blah blah. What in the hell am I here to do about it? I was meant to preside over her funeral, so what am I doing? Staking her?" I started to lose any real train of serious thought and felt another huge sigh surge through me. "Just tell me what the hell I am meant to do to clean up her latest mess, so I can get back to my version of a normal life, okay?"

Roxanna gently patted my arm; I let her, feeling some small comfort in it.

"Your sister is in a lot of trouble, Stephanie," she begun. My grunt and dark expression pretty much showed my unspoken 'so what else is new'. She smiled but it was tight, and she was starting to look as tired as I felt.

"She is not a vampire, but she has been infected by one. For now, that just means she is a carrier of the virus, with only mild side effects. But soon, if nothing is done to save her, she will be taken over by the virus and become possessed by the vampire." She then stopped speaking to allow what she'd just said seep in. If being able to survive an autopsy and death itself was a 'mild side effect', I was wondering if I really wanted to know how bad it could really get.

"Being undead is a mild side effect?" I couldn't help but voice that concern. Something seemed to change in Roxanna, as she realised at about the same time that I did, that I was starting to really accept what was going on.

"There are others, but yes." She replied. "It is only a small thing for now. We don't try and remove vampires and other such creatures from the world simply because of some sort of Girl Scout complex. They are evil, nasty, and will be the death and destruction of our planet if we don't try and wipe them out. They walk in the Darkness, while we walk in the Light." Roxanna was still watching for my reaction, and no doubt noticed in my expression the fear and concern at where the conversation was going.

"We may look like a bunch of women wearing their grandmother's lace curtains and growing our hair long, but Isis is real. And our faith in her and the other Goddesses and Gods of the Light that watch over the planets, isn't just for show. We respect and honour them; they appoint us as the guardians come warriors to watch over their Earthbound flocks." This just caused another sigh from me at this holier-than-thou pep talk. Though it wasn't a sigh of disbelief, simply of not understanding the passion and sincerity in her voice when describing such things.

"Your sister is very sick Stephanie," she went on to say, seeing I was ready to pretty much hear anything she now had to say. "Praying for her soul while she is within the Light of Isis right now is keeping that virus at bay. But she will need to leave it soon, and will need your help and protection, as well as our own."

"Why me? If all this is so important, and you've been given the green light to do it by those up above, why me?" I had to ask, I had to know why the hell I needed to be dragged into all this weirdness; me, with barely a grasp on the basic, better-known religions.

"The vampire virus attacks the blood, and the blood ties to the soul. As her closest blood relative, her sister, you have within you a blood tie just as powerful as the one the vampire forges. One that we hope will give you the ability to destroy the virus and free your sister." I blinked at this; I had to save her, again? Unfortunately, I had a bad feeling where that would leave me at the end of it all.

"Once the virus is removed, unlinked from her soul . . . ," I began, looking hesitantly back to where Estella lay twiddling her thumbs, then returning my gaze sadly to Roxanna.

"She will cease to be. She will reach her final death and be welcomed fully into the Light by Isis." Roxanna nearly whispered this news sadly, following my gaze before returning to mine. "I am sorry Stephanie, but Estella really is dead already. We just need to rid her soul of the demon's stain that is keeping her here, so she can rest in peace."

I closed my eyes, wondering where the sudden tears welling up had come from. Yes, I had cried for my sister on the news of her death. Angry, frustrated tears of how unjust and unfair the world had been, and how stupid she was to have gotten herself killed before we could . . . Well, before what had caused the estrangement could be resolved. When I had stopped crying, I had continued to mourn her in my own self-contained way. Things were slowly stuffed deep-down inside me where all the 'too painful to deal with' emotions and memories lay. Then I had started to move on. These new tears were an indication I would have to go through all that again, and I really didn't know if I wanted to. This just wasn't fair. Why the hell was I the one to suffer? The one to have to clean up after another Estella stuff-up?

Roxanna's patting of my shoulder became a gentle rub, as she tried to give as much comfort as I would allow.

"Damn her," I muttered, angrily wiping the tears away while looking over my shoulder to check Estella hadn't noticed them.

"Sadly, she already has been." Roxanna whispered softly. "We are hoping you will rescue her from that damnation and set her free." Another sigh shuddered through me, I had known I was going to have a bad day, but damn. I took a moment to collect my thoughts and clear my head, before looking back into Roxanna's soothing gaze.

"So what do I need to do?" I asked. "If you want me to dress up in lace curtains, I have to stop you right there." It was her turn to close her eyes and sigh. This time though it was a sigh of relief.

"You have to find the ceremonial crucible used to extract the blood from a dying host, and use it on Estella before the next new moon." Oh sure, nothing too hard then I see.

"Uh . . ." I started, not knowing which of the dozens of new questions in my head I should ask first.

"The new moon is in a week's time." Roxanna answered one of the more important unasked questions.

"And where am I meant to get the crucible from?" I still felt slightly insane, to actually be agreeing to all of this without any real proof. Well okay, maybe Estella counted as proof, but the whole thing still felt pretty messed up.

"From Branwyre's private rooms." Roxanna replied, visibly bracing herself for my next question.

"And how do I find these private rooms?" I asked, nervous fear rising in me as I started to get an inkling of what she was asking of me. "Being private, I'm assuming it's not something I can Google. Or something you'd have in your church address book, right?" I was trying to hide my fear and unease in my use of sarcasm. So what else was new?

"Branwyre will have to take you to it." Roxanna finally said, watching for my response. Which was to close my eyes as I felt myself crumble inside, as realisation of what she was saying actually meant. Damn.

"Branwyre is in my sister already, isn't he?" I may have gotten the original vampire thing all wrong, but I felt I was catching up quickly.

"Branwyre's soul is a part of the virus . . ." Roxanna began.

"And is why she is within your protective circle under the Light of Isis. She is being protected from him." I finished, amazed at how it all seemed to come to me. The small hope of Roxanna correcting my misguided thoughts died quickly as she just nodded. Double damn.

She'd not just been infected to become a vampire, but would become the vampire she had been trying to kill.

"As I said, Stephanie, she is showing only the mild side-effects of him right now. He is not powerful enough to consume her, and completely take her soul." I read between the lines of what she had just told me.

"So my sister can, when out of that Light, be possessed by Branwyre?" All emotion was seeping from my voice — what on earth had I gotten into here?

"Yes and no," Roxanna replied, then winced at my expression before resting a placating hand on my shoulders and turning me to face her. "Part of the cliché vampire is real, the bit where the undead evil can only come out at night." I shot another nervous glance over my shoulder at my sister. Who was still thumb twiddling while atop the stone slab. The enormity of what I was accepting as truth seeped further into my soul.

"The virus is weakest during the daylight," continued Roxana, "which has a similar effect to that of the more concentrated Light of Isis. And so while the virus is weak, daylight makes it near non-existent. Meaning Branwyre can only assert himself during the hours after sundown. In fact, until the virus strengthens, he can probably only assert himself during the darkest hours — from midnight til just before dawn." Oh great, I had never been much of a night owl, and yet was surprised my chaotic mind found that the thing to baulk at. What had I gotten myself into? Damn Estella.

"So," I started this next question slowly as I wasn't too sure where it was heading myself. "You're asking me to take Estella with me, wait until midnight when a really nasty vampire will possess her, and make her help me find the crucible?" Yeah, that sure sounded easy enough, once I said it out loud. I nearly flinched at the 'Yes and no' expression on Roxanna's face.

"I'm sorry, Stephanie," she replied in apologetic tones, "But it isn't going to be quite that simple. Branwyre isn't going to want to help you do anything that would result in his banishment and final rest." Yes, there was my sigh again. She studied me for a moment, obviously trying to find the best way to word her next sentence.

"Branwyre is evil, pure and simple. It comes from his origin in the Darkness and can never be changed. Although a female untrained in his

House's rituals and history isn't his preferred host, he is not about to give that body up until his people have a more suitable one already prepared to replace it."

I understood, even as the latest sigh — now more a quiet whimper — escaped me. So this wasn't going to be easy, but nothing ever was with Estella. That dear sister of mine who couldn't even die without rewriting my outlook on the world I had known.

"So he won't cooperate. Got it, so then what?" I asked resignedly.

"He won't just not cooperate Stephanie!" Roxanna exclaimed, seeming surprised I'd missed something in what she had said. "He's going to do his very best to stop you. He's going to keep Estella's body as safe as he can until the virus has made his parasitic soul strong enough to take over her body, and then he's going to seek out his House and have them help him get a more suitable host. Destroying anyone who has put him into this situation along the way."

"And presumably that would include . . . you?" More dumb questions from me, why not?

She nodded, actually looking a little worried. "We're definitely on his hit list. We've almost destroyed Branwyre twice now, and he's not going to be pleased with us and the tenuous situation we've now put him in. He is a very old and powerful soul who survives simply to inflict pain, death and disease on the world and everyone in it."

"So he's not simply going to come along quietly until I find out how to get his crucible," I replied, trying to show I still had some idea as to what I was meant to be doing.

"He is more likely going to try and kill you." Roxanna said brutally. "That is, unless he feels you have a stronger body than your sister's, then he will try and over-power and possess you." Ah, crap! Why was I helping my sister in this again? Blood ties, sisterly love, and all that rubbish. Got it.

"And this is where you tell me I'm going to be doing this alone, without the support of the church, right?" I had been wondering where Roxanna's sudden harshness had come from, and I had just got a feeling about it in my last question. It was her turn to sigh again as she lost some of her pent-up emotions.

"We're a Temple, not a church. And we will help where we can." Is what her mouth said, while her head gave a subconscious shake of denial. "You will, of course, have Estella with you to help where she can with her vampire lore. Though she is weak, and cannot be trusted to be left alone at any time. As for the other Priestesses of Isis, we tend to stick out in 'your' world, and so won't be able to come too."

"Surely the white robes can be ditched for undercover work?" I was surprised at how helpless I sounded. I wasn't liking the idea of this at all. From what she'd been telling me, I had to find the hidden rooms of an ancient, evil bastard. Find in those rooms a crucible that would then be used to remove said evil bastard from — and kill — my sister. Again. And while I was trying to do all that, I'd have my sister — currently mildly possessed by said evil bastard — along with me, sometimes helping, sometimes trying to kill me. Then to top it all off, the women who had caused all this couldn't, or wouldn't, come with me.

"We're fairly certain members of Branwyre's House have been watching for any sign he may have survived our attack by infecting one of our Priestesses, which is another reason we need to remain in the temple," Roxanna answered, shaking her head.

Oh great, just to make it more interesting. And all this had to be done in just a week. Right, well that would explain the sudden migraine threatening to crush my brain in. Good-o.

"I don't think I can do this," was actually what I ended up saying in a remorseful tone. There were far worse things on the tip of my tongue at that stage too, I might add. "I know she's my sister, and I know she once more needs my help, but I really don't think I can do any of that." I met Roxanna's eyes briefly, expecting disappointment. It was the sheer terror they actually held, that made me look away quickly.

"But you have to," she whispered intensely. "We cannot allow this disease to continue to live. Stephanie, please . . ."

I cut her off, pushing my arms up and away from her comforting grasp. I'd come to read a half-true eulogy and assist people with tea and cakes at a wake. Not discover that vampires, although vastly different to the stereotype, were actually real and that one was possessing my dead sister. And I had to get it out of her, alone, while people would be trying to kill me. My sister included. My sister . . . Damn, what about her in all this craziness?

"If I say no and walk away now, what will happen to Estella?" I asked, glancing briefly at Roxanna before looking sadly over to where said sister lay. "Will she be okay? I mean, if she stays in your Light long enough, will the virus die and her with it?" I turned back to Roxanna, hope in my eyes. It lasted only a moment before I saw the sadness and fear in her own.

"We cannot hold the virus back with the Light of Isis. Nor can we use it to cure her." Roxanna looked towards Estella amongst the chanting women in flowing white robes. "Soon the virus will be able to resist our prayers and the Goddess' Light, and it will grow strong no matter what we do. By the new moon Branwyre will be in control. He'll force his way out of here and any blood spilt in his escape will desecrate our Temple. Isis will leave us and we will be destitute without her, in a building on non-consecrated ground, open to any and all attacks from the other great evils who dwell in the Darkness out there." She tried to look away, tried to hide the tear that escaped the iron grip she had on her expression. "That is, if any of us survive the wrath of Branwyre. Simply, we are dead and ruined no matter what."

"Can't you behead her? Like you did to the other hosts?" I was grasping at straws now and feeling wretched inside, not only for feeling I couldn't help, but in suggesting they chop off my sister's head.

"That would be blood split." Roxanna murmured, regaining control over her tears and looking back at me. "And even if we moved off our grounds before completing the act, her soul would be lost to the Darkness. Never to return to the Light of Isis or allowed to be reborn in another life."

"Purgatory?" I knew little about religion, I think I'd mentioned that already. But from what she was telling me, some of my enforced public school religious instruction came back to me. My sister would be in purgatory.

"In a sense, yes." Roxanna said sadly. "Different faiths have different words and different interpretations of it all, but pretty much." Double frigging, triple-blasted, and damn it all to hell. She was my little sister. As much as she had always been a pain in my arse. As much as she had never been thankful for what she had, and had to rebel against everything. As much as I could never forgive her for what she had done to me . . . I just couldn't be the one responsible for her spending eternity in such a state. Why I suddenly deep-down really believed it would actually happen, I don't know. But it wasn't going to be me who put her there. Not when I had the opportunity to save her skinny little butt one more time.

"One last time." I murmured on an exhalation of breath. "I will save her and clean up her mess. One. Last. Time." I looked Roxanna squarely in the eye, matching her sudden happy shock and thanks with one of sheer determination. "I'm probably going to regret this, if I even make it out of it alive myself. But once it's done, so am I. If she doesn't go into Isis' Light and decides to stick around, she'll be someone else's burden to carry. I am done with her." Roxanna appeared taken aback by my sudden cold tone and expression, unaware it was hiding the sheer terror I was feeling by committing myself. She tried to stop me as I moved back over to where Estella lay. My sister shot me a bored look and was about to gripe when she noticed my expression.

"I am done with you and your stupid mistakes, Estella." I nearly growled at her. "And I'm telling you and that virus within you, that we are going to do this once and do it right. This is the last time ever that I will clean up after you." She looked a little sheepish, and turned to Roxanna to make it all okay. Roxanna stood next to me uncertainly, but silently backing me up.

"And if I'm going to be blamed for you ending up in purgatory," I added just as crossly. "I'm going to be the one swinging the sword and chopping off your head. Piss me off just once, sister dear, and it will happen. I promise." A final heartfelt sigh shuddered through me as I looked around the room. The women chanting seemed to waver at my angry words, but were still going. Estella looked afraid and was shooting a pleading look towards Roxanna. The High Priestess, however, was giving me one of her best studied looks, a hard smile on her lips. She then started slowly nodding. Good.

"Fine." I then said harshly to the room in general. "And now, if anyone wants me, I'll be in the High Priestess' chambers breaking out the wine."

Chapter 4

"YOU know, I find it really unfair that they actually gave you a sword to follow through with your silly threat." Estella's voice whined at me from the back seat of my car and I gripped the steering wheel all the tighter.

I'd not gotten the damned wine either. No. Instead, as soon as I'd agreed to the whole stupid mess, they'd whisked me away to gather Estella's belongings while they did some final secret incantations over Estella to help make her journey a safe one. Me? I got a pat on the shoulder and Roxanna's mobile phone's number. Proving you can not only be a High Priestess, but still keep up to date with modern technology. Go figure.

"If Mum and Dad knew, they wouldn't let you get away with being so mean to me. Not when I'm in one of my moments of need and all," she whined. Estella had always seemed entertained by the sound of her own voice, and it was obvious that hadn't changed.

"You keep our parents out of this you silly, self-centred little cow!" I hadn't meant to snap that at her quite so hard, but a moron in a red convertible had just cut me off, it was peak hour afternoon traffic, and let's just say it hadn't been a very good day for me either.

"Temper," she huffed, lying back down under the blankets and things arranged on the back seat as a way to hide her. Firstly, I didn't want to see anyone we knew catch me driving my supposedly dead sister around, and secondly Roxanna and the other Priestesses strongly felt Estella's leaving of their church should be done on the quiet. And thanks to the vampire virus, I wasn't even able to wait to the cover of darkness to do it in. So I found myself hunched and tense over my steering wheel, navigating traffic I usually avoided, trying to ignore the moaning from the back seat.

"I really don't know what your problem is Steph, I'm the one who died here," she quipped again, starting to sound bored.

"I would explain my problem to you Estella, if I thought for just one minute you'd actually listen to me and realise exactly what sort of trouble you're now in." I glanced in the rear-view mirror to ensure she was covered and out of sight. "This is worse than freeing the animals in the pet shop as a seven year old animal rights activist. This is worse than the time you tried to tattoo the amnesty international emblem on your leg in detention and gave yourself blood poisoning." Another glance as she gave a huff. "This is even worse than the time you splashed red paint all over my wedding dress, as you objected to the fact I had the audacity to wear our grandmother's white rabbit fur shoulder cape, as my something old and something borrowed!"

"At least I turned up! Despite not actually receiving an invite and all." She complained from under the plaid blanket.

"There was a very good reason you hadn't been invited Estella. And red paint wasn't it. My wedding, and you still had to make it all about you." I gritted my teeth; this was an old rant now and one I just wished I could get over, before it led to the really bad memories.

"But it wasn't even worth all the hype, glamour and money you wasted on the event. He left you two years later." Could she even hear exactly how selfish and pathetic she sounded?

"And you taking up squatters' rights in our spare room with a string of anonymous lovers, continual drug busts, and calls in the middle of the night to come and bail you out had nothing to do with it at all, I assume?" All I got in response was her pretending to snore. I was on the brink now, the very edge of the worst of my hatred for her and everything she had done. I didn't want to go any further, it would hurt too much. If I could have found a safe place to pull over, I was severely tempted to behead her already. Damn the peak hour witnesses, she was already dead after all!

"Seriously Steph, you need to lighten up and leave that baggage behind you. There's still some life in you, but that negativity is weighing you down and making you look so old. You're nearing your mid-thirties for heaven's sake, not your fifties!" Estella sounded like she was deliberately goading me now. I had nearly forgotten that was one of her favourite games when bored on a car trip.

As soon as I realised this was just another old game of hers, I found I was able to edge away from the brink. She had, however, wound me so tight that I nearly rear-ended the car in front of me. Knowing now it was just a game to her, I found the anger ebbing a little and concentrated on hardening a protective shell around myself before I caused an accident. It would have been her fault too, not that she'd ever see it that way. And even if she wasn't dead, it's not as if she'd ever be able to afford to pay for any damage her careless and self-centred remarks caused me to make. Estella hadn't in the past, even when a dented car wasn't the worst result of an accident she'd caused.

Those thoughts took me too close to the edge again. Damn her! Why was I doing this? Ah yes, I didn't want to let the cursed demon stain known as a vampire get loose, or for her to end up in purgatory. Seriously, the last twenty minutes in the car with her had me feel like I was there already.

When I didn't bite back at her last comment, Estella seemed to have the sense to see I wasn't going to play her game, and actually went blissfully silent for a few moments. Sadly, all good things like that tend to end far too quickly.

"Geez Steph, it took you a good ten minutes to put your defences up. You're slipping there, sis." As much as I had planned to keep my mind clear and my attention on the road in front of us, there was something in her tone that had my eyes stray to the rear-view mirror again. I could see her peeking out from behind the blanket. As our eyes briefly met, she smiled a smile very unlike any I'd ever seen from her before. As we were stationary thanks to a red light, I made a deliberate show of rolling down my window and looking up at the sun. Yup, still there, could she be possessed in daylight?

"I see what you're doing," came a nicer, calmer tone from the back seat. "And no, I am not possessed right now. The High Priestess told me to help you keep your guard up as protection against what we're about to face, so I thought we could use the car ride to practice."

"Wha—?" it was all I could dumbly manage before the traffic was moving again, and I had to concentrate on avoiding the pillock in the convertible as he changed lanes, without indicating, mid-intersection in front of me. Some people . . .

"Pretending to be like how I used to be made my skin crawl." She calmly remarked from the backseat, sounding more grounded and considerate than I'd ever heard her be.

"This is my first and final notice that I won't be speaking to you after this sentence finishes." I growled at her, using one of our childhood sayings that I'd had enough of her car games and wanted to be left alone. No expected laugh or exaggerated sigh or snort. Just silence for another good block or two. Then suddenly:

"I'm sorry, Stephanie." It was quiet and sounded surprisingly sincere. If Branwyre wasn't possessing my sister right now, someone else was, as that just wasn't her at all.

"For everything," she added softly. "From the first tantrum I threw that ruined your day, through to screwing up your marriage and leaving us not speaking for years."

Okay, so there was a park right here, time to pull over and get this done with before I caused an accident. Once we had parked, I whipped off my seatbelt and turned a good glare at her.

"Estella, what fresh hell are you trying to put me through now? I mean, I know you've had a bad day, but mine hasn't been all wine and roses either, you know?" There was a mixture of anger and exasperation in my voice, because I seriously didn't know where we currently stood. This was a new dimension to her mind games to me. She slid from the seat and sat in the well behind the front passenger's seat, blanket still over her head. She sighed, looking genuinely remorseful, an expression totally alien to what I was used to from her, as if she was trying to find the right thing to say.

"Look," she began. "I know you really don't believe in all that Light of Isis stuff, but it really is an amazing thing. I went to the Temple as, at the time, it looked like free food and board until I could hook up with my next sugar daddy." She looked embarrassed, she actually looked embarrassed. What the hell?

"But once I'd looked into the Light of Isis and saw exactly what I was, as if I was looking at another person, I recoiled from that personality. Had I really wasted all of my life in being such a selfish, pig-ignorant bitch?"

"Yes." It was an automatic response, and one I didn't even realise I was about to say until I had said it. She may have been my sister, but she had also been my worst nightmare. Still was, thanks to the vampire possession and the rest of it. Estella dropped her eyes and I'm fairly certain would have shed a tear, if being dead hadn't prevented her. What was with that? That wasn't like Estella at all.

I sighed and counted to ten in my head. This had been one mother of a day, and I was getting pretty sick and tired of each new turn of events happening at least half an hour apart. What was with her?

"Look," she continued. "I know you came in thinking this is just all a New-Age religion and a bunch of Hippy fru-fruisms', but the Temple of Isis is different."

"Yes, I did notice that with all the vampire slayings and dead rising from the grave." What can I say; sarcasm was better than slamming my head against the steering wheel and hoping a concussion would make me feel better.

"I know you've had a pretty shitty day," Estella remarked earnestly, noticing my expression and trying to assure me. Actually noticing these things was a first for her too, in my experience. "You got lumbered with burying a brat of a sister who you last knew couldn't care less about anyone but herself. And you had to do it in one of those nonmainstream churches I know give you the irrits. You then discovered I may have died, but wasn't exactly gone. Finally you're forced into helping save me one last time from something you thought was fictional garbage. And why? Because you've got the biggest heart I know, and don't want to see me suffer . . . despite our past."

"And you're sure no one is possessing you right now?" I asked agape, "Because as sure as hell that doesn't sound like anything the real Estella would say."

"It doesn't sound like anything the Estella who abandoned you several years ago would say, I agree," came the calm and quiet voice. It almost held the same peaceful inflections as Roxanna. "But as I said, that was before I stared daily into the Light of Isis, and meditated on what I was and how I should be. There is a lot of Darkness in our world Stephanie, and not just that created by the Other World evils Roxanna may have touched upon. We all carry around Darkness within ourselves, some of us more than others." Again she looked embarrassed, and I knew she was talking about herself and not me. She got that bit right too.

"And all of us need to take the time to allow the Light of Isis to shine in on that inner Darkness, and help us either control or dispel it."

I was still struggling, even after all I'd seen and heard today, to fully believe in this Light entirely, or in its opposite Darkness.

"So what was the bitch act as we left the church then?" I asked. Rather than confront and agree with her statement, it felt better to question what I could see and understand. She smiled faintly, again looking slightly embarrassed.

"Just that, an act," she replied. "As I explained, the High Priestess wants you on your guard at all times. After the day you've had and the tasks now set to you, we wanted to ensure you were ready for what lay ahead."

"And so Roxanna asked you to play the bitch until I either had a car accident, or found a convenient parking space to behead you in for pissing me off?" Incredulity could not cover exactly how I sounded and felt at that moment.

"Well, I hadn't realised you were so out of practice," Estella explained. "I had expected you to put up that good old hard-as-rock emotional barrier of yours within the first five minutes. I'm sorry, really I am. About all of it, and those horrid memories it brought back to us both." Again she looked close to tears. "All I could see, as I said it, was exactly how badly I had ruined both our lives, while you stood there steadfast and willing to help. Un-til . . ."

Here I just had to cut her off. What she had said and rehashed in both our memories was bad enough. Actually mentioning the trigger that had estranged us for so long was not the greatest idea.

"Okay, so I get the picture. You were a brat, you looked at the sun for too long, and now you're all peace, love, and mung beans. Got it." I turned away from her and looking out the front window of the car. A moment later I felt drawn to glance in the rear-view mirror at Estella. She had slipped back onto the seat with the blanket over her, with her face just peeking out from under the edge. She smiled faintly at me, though I could tell she hadn't liked the description I'd just used.

"Not exactly the way I would word it, but it'll do." She said, "At least it shows you've got your protective shell tightly wrapped around your emotions again. Atta girl." The last sentence sounded so much like the old Estella, I actually found myself flipping her the bird in the mirror. Then smiling at her responding grin. Damn it, had my sister really had to die before we finally got to see each other as real people, and not simply a brat and her dogsbody? Silently I put on my seatbelt and started the car back up.

"Steph, unfortunately being animated outside of the Light of Isis can be rather draining," Estella murmured from the back seat, as I pulled out of the parking lot and back into horrific afternoon traffic. "So I just need to . . . pass out for a while. I'm going to really look dead to the world, so let's not draw attention to ourselves until we have to, okay?"

Yup, no matter how long she stared into that miracle Light, she was still a self-centred cow. I was actually glad there was still some of the old Estella in there. Despite all the grief she had caused.

"Gotcha," was all I managed, trying to sound light and friendly, and hiding the fact my teeth were once more grinding against the bad driving of others. I mean, I know I am not a saint behind the wheel, but indicators were invented for a reason! The car grew silent and I suddenly had the overwhelming feeling I was alone in there, despite the shape I could just make out under the blanket. Another sigh, another muttered swear word at the world in general and more specifically at the cars around me, and I was on my way. Eyes and mind focused on the journey in front of me and not the body in the back, or the bigger journey ahead.

Chapter 5

———⟲———

PART of the very limited instructions I had been given was to find a hotel or motel in the western area of the city and wait for moonrise. I wasn't to return to my own home in case Branwyre's followers trailed us there. Heck that was fine by me, especially as a part of me didn't want Estella to know my new address either.

Another part of the limited instructions was how to restrain Estella until moonrise, then how to use its light to contain her and question Branwyre. If he chose to possess her tonight, that is. Well sure, what else did I have planned than to look a loony, tie my sister to a chair, encircle said chair in a ring of salt, and set up an array of mirrors to use the moonlight to encircle the chair. Then shine that light into my recently departed sister's face and ask the demon stain of a vampire possessing her where his damned crucible was, so I could kill him and have my weekend open for the more mainstream stuff. All the while ensuring we avoided attracting the attention of any followers of Darkness. No worries!

I must have looked the world's weirdest shopper as I piled the bags of rock salt, a dozen beauty mirrors (with swivel stands), white hemp rope and wooden stakes on the counter at the hardware store I'd found on my way to motel hunting.

I refused to meet the eye of the cashier as I paid in cash. She thankfully had the sense to do the same, and that little awkward moment passed quickly.

I'd left Estella in the car, as she really did appear dead at that time, no matter how much I poked her. Still, I'd cracked a window to be a concerned sister, and dumped my newly bought possessions in the boot rather than on top of her. I was still in two minds over it all and kept stopping to wonder what I was doing, and when the cameraman would pop out and say "Fooled you!" He hadn't yet, and unfortunately I was really starting to believe he wasn't going to. Still I refrained from sighing about it and that was a bonus, right?

Okay, so after that little moment of hysteria and the following coffee from a drive through, I felt more myself and started looking for a hotel or motel that would suit my requirements and the budget I'd been given by Roxanna. I'd gotten rather a large roll of dollar bills along with her phone number, and really didn't want to know how a church and charity came by the dosh.

Eventually I decided upon a motel that belonged to one of those large chains you find everywhere. It was my hope it meant the price was reasonable, and the room and facilities clean. It also meant I could drive my car right up to my door, which would hopefully allow me an easy getaway, if required.

I really don't know what was harder to explain as I unloaded the car: The weird items from the boot, the sheathed — but not concealed — sword, or having to lug my dearly departed sister from the car and literally drag her into our room. Talk about a dead weight. Still, there had been no witnesses that I saw, and after waiting several minutes for the angry knock on the door and eviction that never happened, I calmed down a little. Then, pulling the crisp note containing the instructions from my handbag, I got to work.

The bath was filled with water and then a good measure of the salt. Everything I was to use in the binding of my sister needed a good soak or wash in this liquid mix to purify it, or test my willingness to act stupid, or something. Heck, I did it okay? I can't say I was exactly comfortable with doing it, but I'd gotten a good mantra going that got me through it all.

"The sooner I do this, the sooner she's out of my life forever." How sweet and loving of me, I know.

So the rope, motel chair, and mirrors all got a good dip to purify them against the encroaching evil, or so my instructions said. I then took one of the complimentary hand towels and decided to even give the carpeted area of the bedroom floor I was to use a quick scrub with the salty water. You can never be too careful when dealing with matters of Darkness and vampires, while having absolutely no clue about it, right?

Once all the other items had had their soak, I tossed the half dozen wooden stakes in the bath for a jolly good soak too. Unlike vampires of fiction and television, I wouldn't be able to kill Branwyre with these, but apparently they'd work a treat on any of his possessed flunkies if they found me. My, wasn't that just a happy thought? Then again, my wild contemplations added, pretty much anyone 'normal' staked in the right spot is going to drop like a fly. Gosh that was a great comfort in itself!

Estella had the grace and timing to wake up just after I'd hauled her dead weight, literally, into the chair and balanced it there long enough the grab the rope.

"By the Light of Isis, what do you think you're doing?" Her tone was nearly petulant enough to be the old Estella asking me, not the new peace and love one.

"Following your High Priestess' instructions." I grunted while tying her hands behind her back as best I could, before continuing to wrap the rope around her and the chair.

"But why are you tying me to a chair now?" she asked, aghast to realise just how tight I had done it. "Branwyre can't take over until night-time. We've got at least another hour."

Ignoring her question for a moment, I snatched her right foot and tied it to the corresponding chair leg. Then, ignoring the attempted kick, did the same to her left one.

"Roxanna clearly states in her instructions here to gather the required items, purify them and set it all up, you included." I waved the note at her before continuing to wrap her legs, backside and chair in the rope. Yeah, I'd gotten a decent amount. Who says two for one sales are a waste of time? "Nowhere in her instructions does it say we should stop for coffee and a chat. When I've got as much of it ready as I can before moonrise, I can actually have a rest. You know, something even we non-undead need to do from time to time."

She went to protest, I even paused to watch the show I felt she was about to perform, but other than gaping a few times like a stunned fish, she stayed quiet. Wow, this Light of Isis was amazing if it could prevent the Queen of Whinge from speaking.

"Fine then," she finally managed, a slight sulky tone to her voice. "But how am I meant to eat dinner?"

I sighed; I hadn't honestly thought of that, going along the lines that she was dead. Yes she was an animated corpse right now, but dead was dead. You shouldn't have to provide meals for them.

"Nowhere in my instructions does it say I have to feed you." I muttered. Then feeling I should relent a little as she'd found it within herself to be nicer. "But how about I order pizza, and you eat it cold later.

Surely even the Light of Isis can't have cured you of your cold pizza habits."

She sighed, but said no more for a moment. Didn't even pout, which surprised me even more than the silence.

"I do wish you'd be more respectful of Isis and her purifying Light," is all she eventually said as I was adding a few more knots to the back of the chair.

"Uh-huh." I was more interested in making sure I'd done a good job, than listen to a lecture on appropriate religious respect. Especially from someone who in the past hadn't held any respect for anyone or anything.

"And no dinner is fine; I don't seem to have the need to eat that often anymore." She continued, trying to watch me over her shoulder. "I won't have you dissing cold pizza though."

"Sure!" I said, standing back and wiping sweat from my brow and then my hands on my dress. I remembered I was still in one of my best 'sombre but not kinky' little black dresses, not having had a chance to change. So Roxanna's wodge of cash was buying me a few clothes tomorrow, too. Why not! If I wasn't allowed to go home until this was all over, she owed me at least a pair of jeans and clean underwear. I checked the instructions again. Okay, so all items purified, sister roped tightly into chair. Salt time! Boy I hoped the motel's maid service wouldn't be too pissed at me, or at least wouldn't notice until after we'd left.

"So, how you been?" Estella suddenly asked. She may have turned over a new leaf and become someone able to think of others, but she still seemed unable to simply sit in silence.

"Well, you know, the usual. Having to rescue my sister again because she fell in with another wrong crowd, and was accidentally killed helping them slay vampires." I panted as I hefted the large bag of salt in from the bathroom. I then took one of the cups from the complimentary tea and coffee set and dug it into the bag. "Other than that, nothing special."

"Oh, ha ha, Steph. You do know sarcasm is a symptom of your inner Darkness? You need to let the Light of Isis into your life to help dispel it."

I made a scoffing sound, amazed it hadn't been a hysterical giggle. "No thanks. I'd rather take the other option and say I've got it under control. I mean, it's been my constant companion for so very long now and all." I gave Estella what I hoped looked like a cheeky grin to find she was giving me a stern, matronly look that didn't go so well with her overly-pale skin and autopsy scars.

"Estella," I sighed, trying to not get angry that she seemed to have gone from the extreme of no rules and regulations, to the other of religious fanaticism. "Something that I'm sure is covered under your religion's rules is that as long as people are harming none, we should be allowed to lead our lives the way we choose."

"How is tying me to a chair 'harming none'?" she asked aghast.

"Yes, but it's not my sarcasm that did it, so let it lead its own life with me and be done with it." I replied, relaxing slightly when I saw a smirk. Yeah, she could still be got with silly logic. "Besides, as I keep telling you, it's your High Priestess who instructed me to tie you to a chair. So how can it be harm if it's from her?"

"Fair point." She replied, and started looking bored again. As I scooped a cup full of salt out of the bag I really hoped her new Light of Isis restraint would keep her silent and not start another one of her petty word games.

"The line of salt has to at least be three centimetres wide and a solid, thick line." She piped up again a moment later.

"And you've done this before have you?" I asked as I poured the salt out the way she'd instructed me to.

"Oh yes, we're all taught how to create a protective circle before we're allowed to join in the fight against the Darkness," she replied so eagerly she gave me goosebumps. Breaking into a known 'bad guy's' place, beheading people, and being splashed in their blood should be said in a tone that at least sounded uncomfortable and afraid. Not as if all she'd done was handout pamphlets at a train station asking people to repent their sins.

"How comforting," I remarked, allowing my sarcasm to talk to her while the rest of me worked on the salt line.

"And you need to ensure everything is out of the circle that shouldn't be in there before you complete it," she went on, sounding eager to help.

"Already done," I nearly growled. I was trying to concentrate after all. I mean, have you ever tried to draw a circle free hand? They turn out a bit wonky at the best of times. And so you can imagine, it was bloody difficult trying to do it free hand using salt from a coffee cup on the floor of a hotel room, with your dead sister gabbling at you and you keeping an ear out for someone suddenly wanting to bust down the door and ask what the hell it was you were doing.

"You're trying to concentrate, aren't you?" she asked so innocently that I knew Estella was playing with me again.

"The sword is right there you know!" I snapped, pointing to the bed, within arm's reach. She sighed, looked about the room a bit while casually eyeing the proximity of the sword, then thankfully fell silent.

It meant I could concentrate better on my circle and concentrate I did. I mean, I was at the tongue sticking out of side of mouth, eyes squinted and head cocked to the side stage — I was thinking that hard on it. Although I made the circle as one line always leading in the one direction, it was a stop and start job. Not only to keep filling my cup, but also to pause, look at the bigger picture and map out the next bit in my head, before proceeding to pour. As I neared the end of the back-breaking, mind-screaming ordeal of making the circle a horrible thought struck me.

"So tell me Estella, does the circle need to be formed out of one solid, constant stream of salt, or is what I did okay." Dear God don't tell me I need to find a vacuum and start again. Can you use salt again once vacuumed? Did it mean the vacuum was then purified?

"No, it should be fine," she said, looking at the result of my work. "As long as the base circle in beach chalk was a solid line, the salt just needs to be three centimetres wide and thick enough to be a solid line."

"Base line of beach chalk?" I paled. I really felt it happen. Lurching from my prone position I stumbled to the paper holding my instructions. I didn't remember it mentioning chalk, beach or otherwise.

I glared up at Estella and caught the briefest smirk on her face.

"Oops, I was thinking of the circles used to summon and contain demons," she grinned. Did my hand itch from the desire to grab that sword, or just because of all the salt on it?

"Is. It. Okay?" I asked through gritted teeth. "Because if it's not, I may as well chop your head off now before Branwyre turns up, just to be on the safe side." I'd made my point and she knew it, as her smirk disappeared and she looked the circle over again.

"Looks okay to me," she replied lightly, shrugging as much as you can when bound to a chair.

"Fine." I snapped, really already over this whole save my sister from purgatory thing. I slowly finished the last part of the circle, and stepped back to ensure it was as instructed. It looked pretty damned good from where I stood, if I do say so myself. The last task for now was to place the mirrors around the salt circle, link them to the circle by surrounding them with salt circles of their own and then wait for moonrise. When done, it looked like a rather modern art depiction of a daisy . . . with a dead person tied to a chair in the centre. Yep, I shuddered at the thought too.

Thankfully there was still enough space for me to get to and from the bathroom, and so after a quick touch up and removal of salt — the damned stuff had an amazing talent to get everywhere — I wandered over to the information booklet that came with the motel room and sought out a place for dinner. Pizza may not have been my favourite choice, but I had sort of promised Estella, and so phoned a local one and hoped for the best. It was, for some strange reason, very easy to mess up a ham, mushroom, pineapple and olive pizza. Why, maybe I should ask Isis, as God didn't seem to know.

***

The next time I get caught up in something so ridiculous as where I currently found myself, I really must find out when exactly moonrise is, before eating half a pizza after a day as exhausting as I'd found this one.

Thankfully, Branwyre was an excellent timekeeper and just as I was about to nod off for the fourth time, he arose.

I'd been sitting in one of the other motel room's chairs facing Estella across the circle, sword sheathed but in my lap. Suddenly I felt all the hairs on my body stand on end, goosebumps racing to follow. Estella appeared to have fallen asleep herself, and as I sat up in my chair, she stirred too. Until that point I'd never really believed in the whole 'you can feel true evil', but as Estella's head rose and our eyes met, I nearly wet my pants. The whole room seemed to tingle from the nasty, oily presence that was emanating from my recently departed sibling.

She still looked the same; I mean, her eyes didn't turn all black or her face screw up into some monster façade, like those terrible vampire shows tended to indicate. When the nastiest, sleaziest smile I'd ever seen oozed onto her face, there wasn't even a sudden slip of fang poking out from under her top lip. If it wasn't for the complete and utter feeling of dread and evil, I'd have thought she was up to another one of her little games. That was, of course, until she spoke.

"Well hello." The voice was gruff, but cultured. It was also male. Really male, and not just Estella's voice trying to sound like a man talking. It was as if someone else was speaking and she was lip syncing. If my skin hadn't already been crawling from his presence, that would have done the trick.

"A little black dress instead of flowing white robes." The voice purred as Estella eyed me over in a manner that was so obscene, it made my skin continue to crawl. "Don't tell me! You're an assassin of Isis, hence the different outfit?"

I was speechless; even my ever ready sarcastic comments had fled to my hindbrain to avoid him. Thankfully I wasn't to the gaping like an idiot stage.

"Branwyre." I finally managed in a dull voice. "Unpleasant to meet you." Hey, it was all I could manage, okay?

He smirked through my sister. I don't know how, but I could almost imagine the face that went with the voice, and that scared me more than anything else. My imagination wasn't that good so I was pretty sure he was projecting the visual of smooth, cool-looking thirty-something with a typical 'bad guy' black goatee and horrific deep red eyes at me.

"And you are?" the voice said as he took in the room and the set-up on the floor around him.

"Your babysitter." I muttered. Then, forcing myself to look away from the slime infecting my sister, I adjusted the blind to the window outside so that a shaft of moonlight could seep in.

"And what is it you think you're doing?" asked that same, horribly charming and suave voice. "You are an infant in the knowledge of the Other World. Why are you dabbling in it, so far from the shallow end?"

I looked down at the shaft of light. I had a few minutes before it'd reach the closest mirror. Damn.

Trying to ignore him and his questions, I ended up shooting Estella a worried look. The smile on her face widened as she then looked down at herself and flexed beneath the ropes.

"Female," came the voice. "And a weak warrior of Isis at that." The voice sniffed in disgust and then sighed, looking back at me. "But it will do for the time being. Until I find a better model." The leer Branwyre gave me through my sister had me instinctively unsheathing the sword.

"Your sister," the voice purred horribly, "has tried to hide her mind from me, but it's easy pickings. Though, not as easy as yours," he goaded. Damn it! Estella had warned me about putting my emotional shield up. All the weird stuff was just happening too fast for me to remember it all!

"You are Stephanie Muriel Anders. Older sister to my host Estella Claire Anders, Priestess of Isis." sneered the voice, as Estella kept glaring at me. "Closest blood relation to my latest victim, and therefore may possibly have the ability to lay me to my final rest." Why did it sound like there was a silent 'fat chance' in what he just said?

I ground my teeth together to control my emotions and imagined I was dealing with another of Estella's little mind games. My emotional defences leapt up, and instantly the room didn't feel so evil and 'icky'.

Estella blinked a few times in mild confusion, then smirked again.

"Oh very good. What other party tricks do you have to entertain me until my flunkies get here?"

Oh God, was that even a possibility? Nowhere on the note did it mention he'd be able to just summon them to him. Damn you, Roxanna! Still, thankfully my mental shield stayed up, and I knew he'd been unable to sense that fearful thought from the little pout he gave. Very similar to the one Estella gave when she knew her mind games had failed.

"You're not a very entertaining host you know," the voice sounded almost petulant now. Like I cared! I was too busy watching the moon inch its way forward.

"Such low grade surroundings too. Do you really feel this is how you should house a seven hundred year old Lord of Darkness?"

"Oh, I don't know . . ." My sarcasm was back and I said this almost without thinking. "I've been in and around enough retirement villages to know this is pretty high-class compared to what those comparable spring chickens have to deal with."

I caught Branwyre's expression, and gave him my best 'I am so not amused or fazed by you' look.

His laughter was like a thunder crack and it bounced around the room in such a way that it caused me to shiver. Sickeningly some of the shiver was from delight. Ew!

"What spirit and charisma!" grinned Branwyre through my sister. With my mental guard up, I couldn't see his face any more. And that just made it all the worse to watch.

"I can see I won't have to look far for a better suited host." He grinned again. "That is, until I can find one of the correct gender. And then I will show you just what it's like to be taken by a vampire in more ways than one." I gagged; I literally nearly did chuck up my pizza dinner at that thought. Double ew!

His gaze changed to one of cold, pure evil that sobered me up instantly, and thankfully kept my dinner down.

"And then I will lash you down and tear your skin off a piece at a time, while letting my minions have their way with you. To show you no one binds me and lives long to tell the tale!"

Again I felt myself pale and had to look away. Thankfully my eyes drifted to the moonbeam and I saw it was upon the first mirror's surface. About bloody time too!

Trying to ignore the fierce glare and continuing graphically gruesome description of what he'd do to me, I started to angle the mirrors without breaking their salt circles, so that the moon beam was reflected from one to another around the circle.

"You dare to try and double bind me by the light of the moon?" growled Branwyre. I hoped Estella was okay in there, as he was really getting pissy out here.

"Oh more than that, sunshine." I quipped, working on the last mirror. "I'm about to open up a question and answer session you'd be a fool to miss." I angled the last mirror so the moonbeam shone directly into Estella's face.

Branwyre screamed, and I hoped the room was soundproofed enough for no one to come running.

"Remove that from me at once, you daughter of a slave girl's pustule!" Branwyre roared.

"Oh, nice!" I snapped. "I must remember that one for my next Christmas card." I watched as he started writhing around in the light, rocking Estella's body back and forth in the chair to try and avoid the moonlight. I was really quite amazed at exactly how badly he was reacting. That was, until I saw him rock so fiercely Estella and the chair fell over toward the edge of the circle.

Chapter 6

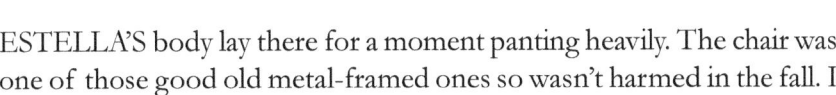

ESTELLA'S body lay there for a moment panting heavily. The chair was one of those good old metal-framed ones so wasn't harmed in the fall. I sort of hoped Estella wasn't either.

"Ah-ha! I have tricked the naïve one and fallen to break your circle!" crowed Branwyre as Estella tried to crane round to confirm it.

"Think again, Lord of Lameness," I snapped, hands on hips and glaring down at them from the other side of the salt. "A novice at all this weirdness I may be, but any moron knows to make the circle big enough to hold the chair and person upright, as well as supine." Yes, the idiot had knocked himself over a good ten centimetres inside the line of salt. There was a reason it had taken me so long to draw!

"Why you slavering whore of a demon's armpit!" he growled at me. My, that had my Easter cards now covered too. "Get me up this instant!"

"And break the circle to do so? Meh! I am not that sort of stupid, buddy." I stepped over to the last mirror and started angling it back into his face. Thankfully it was possible, just.

"Now you nasty virus of a demon's skid mark, have you finished playing? I was hoping to get some sleep tonight."

He howled and had Estella's body writhing on the floor, but to no avail. The metal-framed chair and the way I'd bound her made it near impossible to now move from that spot.

"You will be sliced from your insides out for this, you unholy daughter of a snake's bladder," he spat. Nah, I had no use for that one. Not even for Valentine's.

"You first, blood breath," I muttered, reaching for Roxanna's note again, and hoping I didn't sound as foolish as I would feel reading it aloud.

"Branwyre, eighteenth vampire Lord of the Aegean, I have twice bound you with the aid of Isis, so answer me true." I was thankful my voice was strong and steady; I had expected it to come out all reedy and stilted.

"Your soul shall writhe in the flames of my ire while my servants fornicate with your mother." Oh man, he had an articulate potty-mouth on him, didn't he?

"Oh, just shut up!" I told him. "You're now bound by me and therefore have to do as I say. So quit your bitching, or I'm getting the sword!" Said item was next to me on the chair I had been sitting in.

"You festering bitch of a . . ." I never did find out what it was, as he suddenly shut up, just like I'd ever so nicely asked him to do.

"Right!" I snapped and straightened up. I'd been hunched over the note and wanted to look a little less sloppy now we were getting down to business.

"Where is your crucible kept? Answer me true, you skid mark." I growled the last bit at him, as I could see he was going to use my last command against me and stay quiet. Pillock.

"Die slowly in pain." He spat at me, as I adjusted the mirror so the moon stayed on him.

"Now, is that on the east side of town, as I'm not familiar with that address?" Yes I was getting pissy and so wished I could break the circle and give him a swift kick in the stomach. I had to keep remembering it was Estella's body though, and dead as she was, I probably shouldn't be trying to break her further.

"Just answer the damn question, bat breath. Where is your hideout?" I slowly picked up the sword and toyed with its now unsheathed and razor sharp edge.

"You would truly behead your sister just to kill me?" mocked Branwyre as Estella's body writhed in the moonlight.

"Dude, you so don't know how easy that would be for me to do after all the drama she's put me through. You're just the latest and greatest 'how can I screw up my sister's life' she's done to me." Why the hell was I telling him this? The damned moon would shift again soon and the twice binding would be kaput. I gritted my teeth in frustration, knowing this was why he was doing it.

"Tell me where it is. You are twice bound Branwyre, eighteenth vampire Lord of the Aegean, and you have to tell me." I yelled the last bit; hopefully it hid my own uncertainty in exactly what power I had over him.

"Forty-eight Mannum drive," hissed Branwyre unwillingly. Words had power, or so Roxanna said; perhaps I should keep a note of which worked best on him. "It's south of the river and a warehouse district," he continued before clenching Estella's lips tightly closed, obviously trying to avoid saying more. I quickly grabbed my phone and saved this information into it as a note for later.

"Fine." I growled. "You better be on the money here, toothless wonder, or I'm going to get really angry tomorrow night." He sneered but said no more.

"And," I then added with relief, "as you are still twice bound, I now banish you back to the depths of Estella's subconscious, you rat fink bastard. I mean, Branwyre, eighteenth vampire Lord of the Aegean. You are banished, got it? Gone bye-bye for the rest of the night. Be gone!"

I was hoping this last bit of instructions from Roxanna's note worked, as I really didn't feel like staying up the whole night with him as company, particularly not after the day I'd had.

Branwyre growled something that was obviously foul but also thankfully incoherent. He gnashed Estella's teeth, and her whole body started to shudder. Her eyes then rolled up into her head and all was still.

I sighed, sat back on my own chair and placed the unsheathed sword in my lap. Its cold metal on my thin skirt made me shiver almost as much as the events I had just taken part in did. I couldn't go to bed, not yet. I just didn't trust tonight's little song and dance to be over so easily.

So, lookee there, vampires did really exist. And what utter slimy bastards they were too. Isn't it nice to know that even in your thirties you can still learn something new?

Chapter 7

―――――――§―――――――

"YOU'RE drooling on your sword, and won't get the deposit back if you ruin it." These dulcet words were the first thing I heard on waking the next morning. The room was in gloom from the still closed blinds, but I could tell the sun had risen quite high behind them.

Blinking for a few moments, I realised I was lying on my side on the floor. I had been propped against the bed guarding the circle the last time I checked. Which had been at about three in the morning; it was at least ten now.

My cheek was pressed into the cold steel of the sword as it lay on the floor in front of me, still in my grip. And I had, embarrassingly, drooled on it. Bugger, it'd need purifying again now.

When my mind caught up with my minimal observations, I realised it had been Estella's voice who I'd heard.

"Ella?" I asked, groggily sitting up and wincing. I didn't know if the wince was from the stiffness of my sleeping position, or from using my pet name for my sister when she was young.

"Yes, Ani, it's me again," came her soft reply, using her own pet name for me. Gad damn it, hadn't I gone through enough recently, to now have to put up with us trying to recapture our sisterly love for each other after all we'd been through?

"Don't call me that." I grumped, adjusting my numbingly painful position, and trying to focus on Estella in the gloom.

"You started it," she grinned from her position on the floor. "I didn't think we'd mended that many bridges yet, but it was nice to hear." I ignored her remark and fumbled for the scabbard, sheathing the sword.

"You good?" I asked instead, not wanting any touchy feely stuff right now. It was too early in my morning, after too little decent sleep.

"I appear to be on my side. Still bound to the chair, by the way." I grunted and slowly got to my feet, wincing some more as I made my slow way over to the blinds and opened them enough to shed some light on the room. Then as I was by the door, thought it probably wise to check the 'Do not disturb' and 'No maid' sign was still on the outer handle. It was. After a quick look around and seeing no one, I closed and locked the door again and turned back to my sister.

"I'm still in an unbroken circle too." Estella was saying, now that she could see the room better. "Well done you." I harrumphed. My brain wasn't working nearly so well enough to come up with a decent pithy response.

"But you're good?" I asked again; call it my mantra of the day.

"Yes," came a quiet voice that had me move closer to the circle. "But he scared the absolute crap out of me last night, Steph."

"Not just me then, huh?" I asked as I sat back in my chair, looking down at her. "You remember any of the conversation?"

She shook her head, and had that look on her face that appeared to mean she would now be in tears, if the undead could cry.

"I have no idea what you two discussed. I just felt him inside me. Inside all of me and the way he twisted and turned and consumed my being . . ." She trailed off and her bottom lip quivered.

"Yeah, he was that sort of bastard, wasn't he?" I sympathised, not really knowing what else to do. The sun was up, but was I allowed to release her from the circle? Or did I have to keep her in there until I'd got the crucible, if I could?

"Can I come out now, please?" she asked, still very subdued. I shrugged and grabbed the note from Roxanna, already knowing the answer before I glanced over it. The banishment of Branwyre was the last thing on the bit of paper. Nowhere did it mention the 'to do' list for the morning after. I even flipped it over to the other side, just in case I'd somehow missed it. Nope, still blank.

As I was thinking this over, my phone buzzed on the floor beside me. I leant down and picked it up, not recognising the number at first. Then, after a glance at the paper again, realised it was Roxanna's. She'd sent me a text message.

'What news?' was all it said.

Gee, talk about a sympathetic and concerned High Priestess here. I let my thumbs type away an answer my sarcasm dictated:

'We're as alive and dead as we were yesterday. Met Bran baby, lovely guy, very happy to be killing him soon. Can I let Estella out of the circle now?'

I sighed as I sent it; that breathing motion was becoming a habit with me.

"Roxanna says hi." I muttered to Estella tiredly. "I've asked her if I can let you out now."

"Thank Isis for that!" exclaimed Estella. I could well imagine she was probably uncomfortable in her current position. I mean, just because you're dead and the lack of circulation from being bound isn't an issue, that doesn't mean being tied to a chair on your side all night is a pleasant experience.

My phone buzzed again, it was Roxanna.

'We meet by the sundial in Ruddly Park at noon.' It read. 'Estella is free to join you if not resting. Can be released at sunrise, if Branwyre banished.'

Well, wasn't that just peachy? I was assuming I had just been told to meet her to report on the night, but technophobe or not, surely she could have worded a politer invite? Still, good to know I could at least sit Estella back up.

"You can come out now." I said to her, as I stood up and drew a line through the circle with my bare left foot, before moving into the circle. I really don't know why I felt I needed to break the circle before I could cross it, but it has just felt the right thing to do. "And she wants to meet us in a park at noon. How does one dress for a botanical sojourn with a High Priestess, I wonder?"

I hauled Estella up and listened to her retort about respecting Isis and her Priestess, and the whole Darkness and sarcasm bit again. I was listening, but I was also seeing if I could undo my very sturdy knots without having to cut the rope. If I could use it again tonight, that was less waste than having to buy more. I needed more salt anyway. And probably a little vacuum, as I was fairly certain I'd need to start from a clean slate if planning to bind Estella again. I'd booked the room for three days after all and, unless kicked out by the Manager or chased out by Branwyre goons, was planning on staying the whole time. I wasn't foolishly thinking it'd all be over within three days, but it was as long as I felt safe to stay in one place until it was over.

"You've not listened to a word I've said, have you?" admonished Estella, craning her neck to see what I was up to behind her back.

"Not true!" I protested, back at the tongue out of the corner of my mouth stage of concentration as I manipulated the ropes out of their knots. "Merely skipped every other word. You want me to get you out of this? Or am I expected to cart you to the park tied to a chair?"

She pursed her lips at me, getting the crotchety matron look down pat, but was otherwise silent.

After what seemed like a mind and finger numbing age, I finally started to make progress and could begin actually unwinding the rope that pinned her to the chair. It was rather depressing to realise I had to do the whole bloody thing again tonight, and every night, until I got the crucible done and dusted.

The second coil of rope thudded to the floor on top of the first, and I held out a hand to help Estella to her feet.

"Thank you." She grimaced as she rose up. "That was unpleasant." She walked about a bit and stretched, trying to get life (ha ha) back into her limbs. "Now what, sister of mine?" she asked as I bent and picked up both lots of rope.

"You can help me stash this stuff in the bathroom, scuff the salt around so it doesn't look like we've been up to some sort of Satanic party, and go clothes shopping!" I said, beaming at her in false brightness. I slung the ropes through the bathroom door onto the floor and started gathering the mirrors, being careful in how I handled them. I was actually amazed to see Estella helping. That was definitely not a common trait in her. I'd actually expected her to be sprawled on the bed by then, eating her cold pizza and whingeing about being bored.

"Clothes shopping? Really Steph, I thought you'd be able to prioritise better than that." What was with the admonishing tone again?

"A sword with drool on it can still behead." I warned, "Lay-off the mother-knows-best tone or I'll prove it." She pursed her lips into her matronly expression again, but then sighed and turned to continue picking up mirrors, two at a time, and placing them carefully on the bathroom floor.

"And besides," I continued, feeling I should justify my actions. "I, for one, am not going out in yesterday's knickers and bra, and a sweat stained, salt grimed dress! And have you seen what you're wearing? It's called a death shroud for a reason, you know! And not just because you wouldn't be seen dead in public wearing it. Despite my appearance, you're going to raise a lot more raised eyebrows out there than I am. We'll hit the closest department store, grab some of the essentials, come back for a shower and change, and still have time to make our noon meeting. I promise."

Estella looked back at me with the shadow of a pout on her face and shrugged.

"I see your point," she murmured. "You always were better at playing mother than me." I bit back the bitchy reply that had wanted to leap out. We were playing so nicely again right now, I didn't want to be the one who ruined it. So instead we kept cleaning up in silence.

When done, the main vampire binding equipment was hidden behind a closed bathroom door. There really wasn't a heck of a lot that we could do with the salt. The room didn't have its own dustpan and broom; do any motel rooms? So we just scuffed it into as much of one pile as we could and prayed the maid would take heed to the plastic tag on the door knob and leave the room alone.

After locking up, we headed for the car. I couldn't see a point in hiding Estella on the back seat again, as anyone watching me yesterday would have seen me hauling her lifeless form out of the back seat and across the path to our room. We were also in a part of town I didn't often frequent, so was hoping we wouldn't run into anyone aware of my dear sister's current life status.

It wasn't hard to find a local shopping centre, so we parked and made our way to the first of the many faceless clones of department stores such places always contain.

Despite my sister's new lack of appetite, I made it a requirement to stop at the first takeaway food place open at that hour and get a much needed hot beverage and a cold, sickly-sweet bread-like item. It was my version of the best 'morning after' food after a hard night, cold pizza not being for everybody.

And so, picture it: two women enter a department store. One in a salt grimed, sweaty, little black dress that had seen better days, and the other in a death shroud and no shoes. If anyone was going to turn heads that day, it was going to be us. I was just thankful no one offered to kick us out.

I let Estella have the trolley in the store as I guzzled my oh so unhealthy breakfast and checked items off my mental shopping list. We both needed new clothes and shoes – barefoot being the vogue for funeral shrouds and me in my best black, very high heels – and all those bits and pieces that go with women's clothes. Bras, underpants, socks, jeans, t-shirts, the lot. I thought five days' worth of undergarments was generous, and just hoped I'd find a laundromat if needed. Then gathering the essential toiletries and such, we paid from Roxanna's wodge of cash and got out of there. The looks we were getting from the people we came across were nearly as bad as the ones I'd got at the hardware store the day before.

Damn, that reminded me we needed more salt, so I decided to swing past the same hardware store again on the way back to the motel. Thankfully I had a different cashier that day, and didn't have to explain exactly why I needed so much more salt after the quantity purchased the day before. I also picked up a little bagless vacuum, as the whole salty floor was getting to me. I felt certain I really needed a clean slate, so to speak, before setting up tonight's binding circle. My, my, I had fun nocturnal hobbies now, didn't I?

Back in our motel room, locked away from a hopefully not prying world, I made quick work with the new little vacuum then hit the shower. Despite being dead, or undead as she now kept correcting me, Estella didn't seem to need to wash that often either. I could live with the food part, felt a tad uncomfortable over the no tears bit, but was completely grossed out by the lack of a need to wash bit. It wasn't simply that she wouldn't, but despite my best attempts to not try and smell my sister, it was quite obvious she didn't smell — at all! That was still just a little too far into the new weirdo zone for me. Baby steps to such things, and all.

Once refreshed and in my newly acquired — if slightly too cheap for my liking – jeans, sneakers, t-shirt and needed under garments, I actually felt a heck of a lot better.

Yes, I was still about to go off and meet with the High Priestess of a Temple of Isis — my undead sister tagging along — to discuss permanently ending the undead life of a seven hundred year old vampire. But you know, a hot shower, clean socks, jocks and a slimming new pair of jeans can really make you feel able to take on more of such insanity. Well, it did for me at least.

Despite her protests that it went against being a Priestess of Isis, I had convinced Estella to get kitted out in a similar outfit. It was obvious from the way she had eyed the bed sheets and net curtains at the shop, as to where her real preferences lay. So I had refused to even let her enter the linen area during our purchases.

And so, once more, back into the car we went to meet Roxanna at Ruddly Park. This time, without much protest, I did make Estella hide on the back seat, as we were heading into a more populated part of town. I really didn't want to have to explain my undead sister sitting next to me, singing along to the radio, to anyone I knew. We had discussed this, her lack of argument surprising me, and she also agreed that if Branwyre's bother boys had followed Roxanna, it was best she stay out of sight until we knew all was well in the park. Estella had gone on to say how the Darkness and evil was at its weakest at noon, hence our meeting at that time. But then her lecture on the Light of Isis and controlling the Darkness within ourselves really just became white noise from behind me, as I navigated my way through lunch time traffic. Emotional shields were one thing, but it took true skill to be able to learn to tune her out like that.

We pulled into the Park's parking lot roughly ten minutes before noon, and I had Estella stay in the car until I'd found Roxanna and gotten the all clear. Although I locked her in I did crack the window like the day before, fairly sure that even the undead would start to smell when left in a sealed car in the sun for too long.

Ruddly Park wasn't the only park in town, far from it. But it was one of the oldest and, although well maintained, not one of the most popular of places. Even during lunch hour on a fine, sunny day like today.

Roxanna was in the same style of white robes I'd seen her in the day before. Even her smarter cut version should have looked odd out in the real world, but it didn't. What people there were all smiled a greeting at her, and she received none of the weird looks I'd been getting pre-shower and change.

"Stephanie." she smiled as she warmly greeted me, taking both hands and giving them a warm squeeze. "I see you fared well last night? Where is Estella?" I smiled back. I hadn't really felt like it at first, but there was something in Roxanna's persona that just added a little bit of peace and normality to my life and allowed a true smile to appear.

"She's hiding in the car until we knew it was safe for her to be here." I replied, politely returning the squeeze before gently tugging my hands free. I wasn't really the touchy feely type.

"Our best sources tell us that the followers of Branwyre believe him lost to them. So you are out of danger on that front for the time being. She is safe to come out." By God — erm Isis — that was a relief. Giving her a quick thumbs up, I jogged back to the car and let Estella know.

The two of us returned to the sundial within minutes and I stood uncomfortably to one side as they embraced, and Roxanna fussed over Estella the way a loving mother would a doting child. I did my best to keep a neutral expression on my face as my gall rose over the way Estella acted. I thought of my poor mother, our poor mother, and exactly how badly Estella had treated her. Yet here she was all doe-eyed, polite and loving to a woman who'd only been her surrogate for what, maybe three years?

"Did the double binding work?" Roxanna suddenly asked, breaking away from Estella and turning her attention back towards me.

"She tied me to the chair for sixteen hours!" pouted Estella the snitch from by her side. Roxanna gave her a brief, not too sincere, look of concerned pity before turning back to me. Eyes all sharp and business like.

"I think so." I said with a sigh. I was too new to all this hocus-pocus to truly feel I knew that what I was doing was right. "I tied her to the chair, did the salt circle, did the mirrors and waited."

"Were all the items purified in a solution of sea salted water?" she asked, not unkindly, but intense all the same. This started to make me nervous and I quickly ran through my actions from the night before in my mind.

"Everything I used, even the stakes I didn't need to use, got a thorough soak and wash in the salt solution." I replied as calmly as I could. "I then even gave the area of the carpet we were to use a good scrub with the solution before I started." I added this to try and sound like I wasn't completely dumb.

"Plus she made the circle big enough so that when the chair got knocked over it still fell within the circle, and nothing was broken." added Estella, sounding rather proud of me. Aw shucks!

Roxanna clapped her hands with delight and grabbed mine again for another quick squeeze.

"Oh, well done Stephanie! If you let us, you'd make a fine Priestess of Isis and warrior against the Darkness," she exclaimed happily.

"Pass!" I said, perhaps a little too quickly and a tad ruder than meant. So I added: "Sorry Roxanna. You seem the nicest of people to know, but I've never really been into the same level of crazy as my sister. And this is the penthouse level of crazy, even for her. I like the normal life where this sort of thing is all fiction."

She smiled again and nodded her understanding.

"But were you able to get anything of use out of Branwyre while he was bound?" she asked us both.

Estella paled, even more so than her current undead complexion, and shook her head. "I don't remember anything of last night, except for the feeling of that horrible thing taking me over and being part of me. Of every single little part of me." She shuddered and I felt some true sympathy for her, even if it was Roxanna who put a comforting arm about Estella's shoulders. I'd found the mere presence of Branwyre in the same room unsettling enough. I could well imagine what it must have been like to feel him as upfront and personal as she had.

"I questioned him." I spoke up, eager to break the growing silence. "Learnt some pretty fun curses and swear phrases. Also got an address from him for where the crucible is." As Roxanna smiled happily over this good news, I flicked through my phone to the note I'd made and showed it to her.

"Sadly that address means nothing to me," she said, after studying it for a moment. "Do you have the courage to check it out?"

I shrugged, while putting my phone back into my jean's pocket.

"I guess. It's in a less populated part of town, so explaining my presence to any flunkies I meet might be a tad hard." Actually I would have much rather gone to the dentist for a straight succession of four root canals, but why burden them with the truth when we all knew I was going to do it no matter what. I'd already said I would, and I kept my word. Call it a flaw in my personality.

"Avon lady?" suggested Estella, some of her old cheekiness showing through for a moment. My response was a snort that was a mixture of amusement and total disbelief in anyone falling for such a ruse.

"I could always go buy a dog leash and pretend to be looking for a missing, beloved pooch?" I mused, and we all stood there looking ridiculously thoughtful for a moment.

"Oh! That reminds me." I then said, turning to Roxanna and handing her a handful of receipts. "No idea if you want or need these, but I'm not only an accountant but an honest gal and I think you should know what we've spent your money on." She smiled, nodded and glanced through them all, not even raising an eyebrow at the department store bill.

"Thank you, I too like to keep our finances in order. Do you require any more?" I boggled at the thought. She'd given us around five thousand dollars yesterday, and I'd barely made a dent in it. I was trying to be frugal as well as save the world from Branwyre after all.

"Hell no!" I ended up blurting out. "We're good for now, honest." She smiled again, her intelligent eyes studying me in that way that made me squirm. I'd only known the woman a day and felt she already knew me better than my parents did. So not fair, I wanted that to be my superpower.

"You should leave," Roxanna then announced, "The zenith of pure light has passed, and we have started the slow descent to the darkness of night." I didn't roll my eyes at her sudden switch back to religious mumbo jumbo; at least I tried not to.

"When will we see you again?" Estella asked, suddenly anxious and grabbing at her High Priestess' hands.

"Hopefully tomorrow, my child." Roxanna soothed. "I will be in touch when we have divined the best meeting spot. Go with your sister now, and offer her as much guidance and assistance as you can. You do remember what the crucible looks like, don't you?"

Estella nodded and the pinch of concern that had started to appear in Roxanna's features eased.

"Isis be with you my daughters," she whispered, drawing us each to her for a brief embrace. Then, she simply turned her back to us and walked away through the park.

Chapter 8

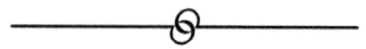

FORTY-eight Mannum Drive ended up being one of those brown brick uglies built in the nineteen seventies, when all the factories and warehouses were moved away from the more popular river and seaside spots and dumped a few kilometres away in what was then a waste land.

Since then the 'in crowd' had spotted them, had closed them down as actual places of work, and were now slowly defacing them by turning them into trendy apartments with hip mod cons on the inside and brown brick ugly still on the outside. Some people just had no taste in architecture, or didn't realise how well stucco can gave a facelift to an external façade.

I wasn't too sure if this building really had been transformed on the inside as, unlike others in the area, it still pretty much looked like the warehouse it was originally built to be. There was no trendy new security door with lists of names and bells to push. Just a locked grille over the only person sized door I could find, and a roller shutter down and firmly locked on the much larger loading bay.

So I stood there, newly bought dog leash in my left hand, and wondered just exactly what I was going to need to do to get inside. Beside me, Estella wasn't looking at her best. As with the day before, she was starting to look less than fresh — all dead jokes aside — and I knew if I wasn't careful I'd be stuck with her in corpse mode if I didn't hurry up and get into the damned place. And I just had to get into there today as the sooner I got the damned crucible, the sooner we could all get on with our lives. Or not, as was the case for Branwyre and Estella. Damn.

I had just finished oh so casually checking all the windows, minimal as they were, on the ground floor when Estella brightened for a moment.

"Do you think we could pick the lock on either door?" she asked, moving back to the person sized door. I shrugged and followed. Out of the two of us, I was certain my undead little sister was the one more likely able to pick a lock. I'd bailed her out for enough 'break and enters' in her earlier days.

I kept watch, trying to look innocent and harmless, as she bent over the padlock on the grille's latch and muttered to herself. Estella then demanded to look through my overly large handbag for the usual bibs and bobs I kept there for my long, unruly, and often tangled hair. With a satisfied look, she removed a couple of bobby pins and a hair clip from said bottomless bag's deep recesses. I went back to my innocent lookout duties while she went back to muttering and fiddling with the lock. Catching snippets of what it was she was actually saying, I suddenly realised she was praying to Isis for forgiveness for going back to her old ways.

"May you forgive your wandering daughter as she uses the Darkness and sins of her past to rid the world of a greater Darkness."

I almost felt tears in my eyes over the words and the regretful tones used to say them. She really did believe in all this stuff. My lost, estranged sister had finally found a way to anchor herself to the world she'd never understood. Found something to help her understand. And she was now going against it and back into her old world of turmoil.

"Oh Ella." I heard myself whisper, hopefully so quietly that she didn't hear. Then, before I could say or do any more, she straightened up, gave me an exhausted look, and said,

"We're in."

***

The inside looked as lair-like as the outside, as in not really at all. We'd managed the grille and door locks and stood in near-darkness now the door was shut behind us. Once my eyes got used to the gloom, I noticed we were in a small foyer type set-up with double doors leading out into, when I looked, the main area of the warehouse. There was also a flight of stairs that led up to another closed door one level up.

Thinking the stairs too obvious, I returned to peeking through the glass and wire mesh windows of the double doors, out at the warehouse. It was basically empty. What little windows it had were all up high, and were all dust and dirt grimed to the point of shedding barely a trickle of light into the cavernous space I was now staring at. The floor was strewn with an assortment of debris I could just make out in the dim light. Crates, scraps of paper, empty drink cans, hopefully just a rat scurrying past — whatever it was, it was big and had moved fast.

"That area is used for raves to call more people into his fold," murmured Estella sleepily from behind me. Her tone caused a small dance of goosebumps up my arms and I slowly turned to eye her warily. She waved a hand to try and dispel my concern.

"I'm just tired," she explained, trying to smile. "And we're close to a source of his energy. The lack of light in here isn't helping me either." Oh boy did I hope there was going to be a big 'But!' coming along any moment now.

"But I'm too weak right now for him to do much through me." Okay, not as good as I'd hoped, but not the worst news either.

"So I'm not about to become a Skid Mark snack?" I asked, trying to subtly sidle back to the door we'd come in by. She smiled again and shook her head with an almost-laugh.

"No, I can feel him trying, but between the two of us, we couldn't fight our way out of a wet paper bag at the moment. Though I can tell you he hates your pet name for him."

"You can hear him? Tell him I say 'hi Skid Mark'." I'd made it to the door, now to sneakily find the handle behind my back.

"Not in so many words, it's not like how we're talking. More like communicating via feelings and stuff. Like, I know what this place is because he knows." She still sounded fairly normal while not making much sense, no artful curses or anything. "And I can see what you're doing, you know," she added in a hurt tone. "The undead have exceptionally good night vision. You can either come upstairs with me now to search for the crucible, or I'm telling the High Priestess!" Oh yeah, that was all my sister in that tone, expression and threat. I was still reluctant to move and only did so when she mounted the steps, dragged herself up a few stairs, and turned on me with a pointed look.

"Steph," she then sighed, "I really don't have that much time before I zonk out again, and would really rather be in the car than in here when it happens. What if you can't get me back out? There's too much impurity ingrained into this place to allow someone of your skill level to bind me." I took another reluctant step, shrugged and climbed up after her.

When we got to the top, it was a relief as well as a concern to find that the door was unlocked.

"Should we knock?" I asked hesitantly, but Estella shrugged and just opened the door and walked in. I mean, she was already dead, right? What else could happen?

The room was a heck of a lot bigger than I'd been expecting and a lot more furnished. It was also, apparently, empty of people. And dear God, what an eyesore! It stretched out before us, taking up at least a corner of the warehouse, all dark red shag carpets, deep red velvet curtains with gold trim and similar tacky and almost laughably movie-prop-like furniture and knick-knacks.

With the old style gold and red velvet covered seats to the brass-bound wooden boxes and badly constructed erotica oil paintings, maybe half of what people thought about vampires was apparently true. All the place needed was a giant heart-shaped bed draped in furs and a mirror on the ceiling above it.

Oh wait, as I moved further into the room I could just see it behind the folding paper screen near the back. And I simply will not go into what the screen depicted. It made the Karma Sutra look wholesome and plain. And then there was the smell. Although it wasn't one of gore, rotting flesh, or anything too foul, the place simply reeked of a heavy musk. I despised my brain for seeking the source, but the place smelt like stale sweat and other human-made liquids. Oh let's face it, it smelt like people had had a lot of sex here and never bothered to crack a window.

"Ick," stated Estella, holding her stomach as if the décor made her feel physically feel ill. Hang on, if she couldn't cry, could she pop her cookies? I hoped I didn't find out. And, knowing some of the people she'd hung out with and the places she'd been arrested at, her finding this place distasteful was saying something.

"Yes, I may have to kill his interior designer, as well as Skid Mark," I commented while looking more closely at figurines and bowls scattered around on the flat surfaces. Some were merely phallic while others were quite simply horrific. I so didn't want to touch any of them without thick gloves on. I don't know why, but gloves seemed a really good idea right about now.

"It's not just that." Estella breathed, looking around the room. "This place is just steeped in evil, and Branwyre's scent and emotions. He's doing near cartwheels inside me, being so close to a source of his power." Okay, so double ick there. She had a right to want to hurl.

"Okay, so can you see the crucible anywhere?" I asked, not wanting to know what Branwyre got up to in here. It was fairly obvious it included things a whole lot nastier than just sex.

"No, but I am being pulled towards that box over there." She pointed to a shoebox sized wooden box ornately carved in dragons and similar oriental designs. Quite pretty really, and almost out of place amongst the other items. Not a nipple or penis in sight on it.

"Is it big enough to hold the crucible?" I asked cautiously, not wanting to open it to find, well, something that wasn't the expected bowl like device. She nodded slowly and approached, tentatively holding out her hand open it.

I felt a moment of panic, suddenly worried it wasn't her making this happen, and found myself squeezing my eyes shut and bracing for whatever evil would happen next, as she pushed the lid slowly back.

"Oh," Estella said dully. When nothing else seemed to happen, I slowly opened my eyes. Look, it had been a long few days, the room was creeping me out and a girl should be allowed to act chicken now and then, okay?

"What?" I asked dumbly.

"It's just the box is empty, except for some grains of rice and what appears to be a Tibetan prayer square." Estella murmured, she really was starting to lag here and I was getting worried. I stepped closer and peered in. Yup, some husked rice and a tattered square of white linen with some writing on it I didn't understand.

"Damn and blast it!" I heard her swear and turned to look at her angry expression. "Branwyre! He must have tricked us as he's feeling very amused right now." She slammed the box shut with a deep frown. "I get the feeling the crucible isn't here at all!"

"Uhhh . . ." I said, catching sight of something out of the corner of my eye. I know; real articulate of me, but sadly it was the best I could come up with at the time. A moment later I realised it wasn't so much a 'something', as a 'someone'. The problem was I didn't really want to face him straight on and acknowledge I'd seen him, but I didn't want to just let him pounce on us either. Reluctantly I slowly turned to face the newcomer. Estella gave me a puzzled expression and followed my gaze.

"Sweet Light of Isis," she whispered. I wouldn't have exactly put it that way myself, but yes. Standing only a few feet away was what appeared to be, of all things, a Buddhist monk of probable Chinese descent. He looked to be in his mid-twenties. Besides the hands on hips and scowling expression, the most unnerving thing was that he had no colour to him, just varied shades of grey. And I don't mean his clothes, I mean all of him. It was like a black and white picture of a Buddhist monk had come to life.

"And what do you whores of an unwed mixed breed think you're doing here?!" he spat. Oh lookee, he had gone to the Branwyre school of English. What a potty-mouth!

"Be silent, shade of the undead, Isis protect you from the stain you leave upon the earth." Estella commanded sternly. The scowl disappeared and the monk blinked dumbly at her for a moment.

"Oh bite my best member! You're one of those fanny flicking Goddess lickers, aren't you?" he said. I was near blushing over the fact nearly every word spoken was filth. Shade, hang on?

"He's a ghost?" I asked Estella, hopefully not too dumbly. "Can you get Buddhist monks as ghosts? I mean, isn't that against their religion or something?"

"I will not repent to you, filth of a scabrous beggar's left nut!" came the ever delightful tones from the monk ghost.

"Not that I can think of." Estella pondered, "But I think any spirit can be bound at the point of death and made to walk the earth as a stain of their former selves."

"Who are you calling a stain you . . ."

I cut the guy off with a look so fierce it apparently even stopped ghosts in their tracks. "Look, you little potty-mouthed holy man!" I growled. "I have enough on my plate right now without having to listen to your filth as well. Either shut it, or be my next experiment in killing supernatural creatures. Got it?" He blinked dumbly at me again, went to say something else, caught the look in my eye and just stood there with a sullen expression. I took a deep breath, then regretted it as it had meant I inhaled in a lot the scents and odours of the place. Gag!

"Okay! So it's time for us to get the hell out of here," I announced. I didn't want to listen to anymore from the grey wonder, and I really didn't feel like thunking Estella's lifeless body down the stairs. I could tell she was almost to that stage. I'd been swapping glances between her and the monk, and she was starting to droop again. We weren't going to find the crucible here today, so it was time to go.

"Estella?" I prompted.

She nodded, and grabbing up the Chinese carved box, held onto it tightly. Without looking back at Ghost Boy, we left the room and trundled down the stairs and out the door.

Once we were back in the car, Estella collapsed almost immediately onto the back seat and played dead, the box clasped tightly to her chest. She passed out so quickly, I had to cover her up with the blankets before jumping into the front and heading off into my much loved, not, afternoon peak hour traffic.

It was over, for now anyway. I could relax as much as the traffic allowed until we got back to the motel and I got to bind Estella all over again. Just a few moments of peace amongst a bunch of morons who needed to learn how to use their indicators, nice.

"So you flea-ridden scabrous female dog, where is this rust bucket piece of half-chewed manure of yours taking me?"

I not only nearly rear-ended the dope in front of me, but side-swiped the parked car next to me when, looking in the rear mirror, I saw the monk glaring back at me.

"No way!" I gasped, ignoring the horns blaring around me. You could see ghosts in mirrors? Since when? Boy was I going to rewrite the book on the undead. And why was that the most important thing I got out of this crazy new part of my life?

"That box." I stammered, trying to calm myself down and edge back into traffic, unconsciously flipping the bird out my window to the git behind me who was using language almost as colourful as my new friend in the back. "You're bound to that box." It was a statement not a question, and I had no idea how I knew it. Why the hell had Estella brought it along? I ground my teeth in frustration and gripped the steering wheel tighter. Branwyre obviously had had enough power over my near zonked sister before we left, to bring this annoying flunky along, but why?

"You mangy cow's ulcerated udder, you just ran a red light. Who taught you to drive? Your syphilitic blind grandma?"

Oh man, as soon as I was out of this car I was ringing Roxanna for a way to get rid of this delight.

"No wonder you're a ghost." I snapped back, my anger fuelled by my hate of traffic. "With that level of crap spilling out of your mouth, you'd never reach enlightenment." I smiled at the expression that crossed his face. Ha! Touched a nerve there!

"Now you keep your lips zipped or that box in my sister's death grip is being burnt the moment I can find a car space." Again, that seemed to do the trick. Perhaps some of the stuff about ghosts was true. You burn what connects them to this plane of existence and they go bye-bye.

The rest of my trip wasn't as peaceful and restful as I'd hoped — idiot drivers around me included — as I kept glancing into the rear-view mirror and getting smug looks and occasional waves from the ghost monk.

"So, potty-mouth, do you have a name?" I asked, growing tired of his mocking silence. "And keep it clean!" I added quickly.

"When bound to this existence, they named me Trishna Duhkha," he murmured, almost sadly. I should have felt some sympathy, I know I should have.

"You're named after a girl and a spice rub?" I snorted my laughter as we pulled into the motel's car park. "Obviously you really pissed someone off to end up with that!"

"Screw you, you septic whore!" he angrily spat. Yeah, I'd give him that one, I had laughed at his name. "It basically translates as a great power brought on by distress and suffering. I'm one of many tools created by the great Branwyre to increase his power." Despite not swearing as he spoke the last sentence, his tone made it all sound like paint peeling filth.

"Lucky, lucky you." I snapped, having stopped the car and began climbing out. I knew I should have felt sorry for him, but I knew nothing about his background. He may have been a monk, but who's to say he had been a nice one in life?

I walked away to my motel room's door, checked for signs of tampering or maid visits and then opened it cautiously before going inside. It all appeared the same as we'd left it. Even the bathroom was untouched. Good-oh.

I turned from the bathroom door to head back out to Estella, and nearly ran into, or through, Trishna.

"Flipping Nora!" I found myself trying to use tamer swear words in his presence. "Don't you need to stick close to your box, or something?" He grinned at being able to scare me and rocked on his heels.

"My bonding to that item allows me to be within a diameter of one hundred metres of it." He managed without a naughty word. "And I wanted to see what sort of a pus-filled cesspit you'd brought me to." I knew he couldn't last a whole sentence.

"Yes, we go all out on living space when it comes to killing vampires and dispelling ghosts." I snapped and walked past him back out to the car. He followed, damn it.

"Oooh, sarcasm." He breathed the words in almost as if smelling something. "So the alpha bitch knows how to play it my way."

Ew, sleazy and a potty-mouth. Gag! And what was it with people and my use of sarcasm? I ignored him and popped open the back door on the same side as Estella's head. I had planned to leave her in the car while I got the room ready, but with the mad monk now with us, I just felt happier if I had her where I could see her while I set it all up. Grabbing her as gently as I could, I hauled her out of the car, past the leering Trishna and into the motel. Removing our newly purchased clothes, vacuum, and salt from the boot, I deposited them just inside the door to our room. Locking the car. I checked for witnesses and, on spying none, locked us into our motel room again. Although my ghosty pal had been by the car when I locked the motel door he was, of course, standing over Estella when I turned around. Man this was going to be fun.

"So, crap for brains. Does this flea pit have room service? I could kill for a cup of tea."

Oh great, the undead sister doesn't eat, but the ghost does? This was just getting better and better.

Chapter 9

ESTELLA awoke to the sound of me vacuuming the area of the carpet I planned on using that night. The items I was planning to use had all gotten a fresh soak in the tub in newly salted water, and I had found a great desire to ensure the carpet was really nice and clean before I gave it another salt wash too. Not that I'm a little OCD or neurotic, honest.

"What in the name of Isis?" she exclaimed, as she sat up from where I'd left her on the floor. But she wasn't complaining about the noise I was making, but about the wooden box she had clasped to her chest. Estella then looked wildly around the room until her eyes settled on Trishna where he sat, hunched over a cup of Lap sang Souchong I'd made for him earlier. Yes, I'd even taken the annoying little so and so out to the closest supermarket and allowed him to choose the teas he wanted. I'd taken Estella too, not just for kicks but because she wouldn't let go of his box. I had refrained from pushing her lifeless corpse around in the trolley, instead leaving her in the car with usual window ajar. Thankfully it was a small shop and the tea was within reach of his box.

Trishna had done his tea shopping in blissful silence and polite sign language motions. We had a deal, if he couldn't keep it polite, he couldn't have tea. It had seemed a fair deal to go to so much effort. Anything to keep what little sanity I had left. Not that he could actually drink the tea, but Trishna could somehow smell it and remember what it was like to drink. Apparently, from the limited and foul-mouthed information he'd given me, he'd been a ghost for a little over a century now and tea sniffing was one of the only pleasures he had left. Ew?

"You cannot be serious!" exclaimed Estella as she scrambled to her feet, kicking the box away from herself as she did so.

"Hey! Watch the box, arse face!" yelled Trishna leaping to his feet in angry defence. I sighed, I switched off the vacuum cleaner and I walked over to stand between them.

"Estella, meet Trishna Duhkha. Trishna, meet my undead sister Estella, current host of your dreadful master come owner. All ground rules you and I have agreed upon for me are also to be followed with her." I gave him the stern look I'd learnt he didn't like. "One false move and your bags of tea are toast!" I warned him. I was amazed at how passionate he was about them, but also sorry in a way that something so small was the only bit of happiness he had after a century of imprisonment as a ghost. It made me worry about what it must be like for other undead forced into the role. Such as Estella. Still, thoughts like that would mean I'd be letting my guard down, and I swear it was the only thing that was stopping me going quite insane right now.

"You brought this stain home with us?" cried Estella in a shocked tone. "He is a slave and tool of Branwyre. You should never have allowed he know where we are located!" Oh, so it was all my fault again? This sounded so much like in the old days between Estella and me.

"I brought him home? Really? This being said by the undead idiot who brought the box he's bound to, back with her in a death grip," I snapped, not willing to be at fault when I was still trying to make the best of the situation. "What was I meant to do? Break your fingers and hands to remove it?" Estella actually looked embarrassed at this, and ashamed. Two totally new emotions for me to see on my sister's face.

"I . . . I'm sorry," she murmured, sitting down on the edge of the bed in a slouch. "I was so very very tired. Branwyre must have got the better of me." She was so downcast she wouldn't even meet my eye. I reached down and grabbed the box and placed it on the table next to Trishna's cup. He looked at me warily, but sank back into a sitting position over his still steaming tea.

"Relax Estella," I said. I wanted to console her, but couldn't bring myself to sit next to her on the bed and offer a comforting arm around her shoulders. We weren't that far into forgiveness yet.

"I rang Roxanna about all this when we were safely back at the motel." I said slowly. "She's explained that Trishna is no more than an object used by Branwyre to increase his power, but not something he should be able to access while bound in the circle. She also said Trishna shouldn't be able to harm us in any way by himself."

There were some darkly muttered words from the grey form at the table that I swear would have peeled my eardrums if I'd heard them clearly. I gave him my look and added:

"She also confirmed that if he really does piss me off I can salt and burn his little box here, and bye-bye Buddhist." I frowned at the floor for a moment. "Sadly that's literally true, as burning his box is as bad as beheading you. I'd have gotten rid of the problem, but his soul would be lost to purgatory. He wouldn't be able to continue his religious journey through life and be reborn or find enlightenment." I was seriously unhappy at being responsible for my sister's undead soul, and now I had another one to deal with. I did not want to make a habit out of collecting the undead and setting their souls free.

"So you gave him tea?" Estella said belligerently, but she at least no longer looked upset over being responsible for him being here.

"Oh trust me, it was the last thing I planned on doing today." I sighed and returned to the vacuum cleaner and cleaning the floor. "But I found it was the only way to keep his damned potty-mouth shut."

Once satisfied with state of the carpet, I switched off my new toy and parked it out of the way over by the bathroom door. I then grabbed yesterday's face washer, wet it in today's salt solution, and set about giving the floor a quick scrub. I wasn't happy to have an audience, but one of them wasn't allowed to help me in case her contact with the items affected the binding, and the other couldn't touch things to help. Even if either of us had wanted him to.

Once the floor was scrubbed to my satisfaction, I brought out the items that had been drying on salted towels laid out on the bathroom floor. Man I was getting sick of salt by now. If it was so damned good and pure, why the hell did it also clog your arteries and cause strokes?

First out came the chair, then the ropes. I then gave Estella a pointed look, hands on hips, and waited for her to get up from the bed and park herself in her night-time spot.

"Seriously?" she whined, very much like the old Estella. "I was in that thing for sixteen hours last night. Can't we just wait a little longer tonight?"

"With the Buddhist bad mouth watching and waiting? Oh hell no!" I exclaimed and motioned for her to come over and sit in the chair. "Roxanna said Branwyre couldn't use Trishna against us if he was bound. I'd much rather have you tucked up safe and sound in the chair, bound in that rope, behind the salt and with the mirrors ready to go, before old Skid Mark gets a chance to show us exactly how much of a tool Trishna is."

"Hey female dog of immoral acts," muttered Trishna from his place by the table. "I know that is an insult you sweaty armpit of a seafarer. And if I have to keep it clean, so do you."

Dog that was what? Sweaty armpit of a what? How could he, I'd had a shower and used nice deodorant afterwards!

"Oh, that is so costing you a tea bag!" I snapped, storming over to the table and snatching at the open packet. "I meant it in the way you are an item to be used against your will. Not in the form of an insult, you . . ." and here I bit my tongue so as not to make matters worse. Then, with him glaring and grinding his ghostly teeth, I finished my little tantrum by setting fire to the tea bag with the lighter I'd also happened to purchase at the shops that afternoon. I then dumped it into the ashtray on the table and we both watched it burn. I could tell he really wanted to let me in on a few more colourful phrases, but also didn't want to lose another bag. Sadly, as much as I realised exactly how childish I was acting, I also realised how good it was to blow off some of my pent-up tension in such a dumb act.

"Keep it zipped," I warned Trishna, a finger pointed as close to his face as I could. "Or the entire packet of Ceylon Orange Pekoe is next!"

I went to turn my attention back to Estella to continue my discussion with her about how she should get in the chair. Which was when I realised she had moved over to the chair and was sitting there, arms crossed, with that matron look on her face again.

"Are you two quite finished with your childish squabbling?" she asked, as if she'd not just now been whingeing about her prolonged time being tied to a chair. I gave Trishna one last glare and walked back over. I really could have given her the extremely sarcastic reply she so very much deserved, but I felt I should save my energy and sarcasm for when Branwyre was here.

"Let me just say, sister dear, that your impression of a saintly matron doesn't fool anyone in this room." I sighed, now able to let the matter drop as I reached for the first rope and tried to remember how exactly I'd tied her the night before.

Estella sighed too, as she watched me.

"So much Darkness in you, Steph, I just wish I knew how the Light of Isis could reach you through it." Oh, here we go! Must I contend with a religious lecture on Isis every single time I had to tie my sister to a chair?

"It's not Isis and her Light that I'm not letting in Estella, and you know it." I muttered, not really wanting to go into the age-old argument now, especially not with Ghost Boy listening in. I suspected that having Trishna around would be like having a recording device stashed in the room, with everything we said being repeated to Branwyre later.

"You still don't forgive me?" it was a bewildered question. Who the hell did she think she had become for me to be able to forgive her for what she had done to me before I finally cut all ties?

"This is not the moment to go into that." I said, making a pointed look at Trishna, who appeared to be finding what we were doing far more entertaining than watching a cup of tea go cold. Heck, binding someone versus entropy in a tea cup wins every time for me too!

Estella followed my gaze and grimaced, realising what I was hinting at.

"Sadly Steph, it is never a good time to try and talk about that. But I do see your point." I may have, accidentally, bound her hands behind the chair too tight at that point. I even heard one of her shoulders click. But besides the slight wince, she said nothing. I found I could no longer talk to her. How dare she bring up that topic again? How could she think I could ever forgive her for what she'd done? Damn it, my jaws now ached from clenching my teeth too tight. I just wanted to get away, walk right out that door, and not look back. This was all too much for me, just too much. After all I'd ever done, all she had put me through

. . .

Purgatory. I really didn't know exactly what it was or if it existed, but deep-down in me something told me how very bad and how very wrong it was to be sent there. To have to spend eternity in its painful grasp. And now I had two souls to save from it. Since when was my life meant to suck so much?

"You! Second grade, small-breasted whore with the rat's nest of a hairdo. My tea has gone cold and I need a new one to smell." Trishna's voice broke through my self-pity party and I realised I'd just been sitting on the floor, rope in hand doing nothing. I also realised that this wasn't the first time he or Estella had tried to break me from my angry reverie.

Blinking back tears, I glared over at him and then up at Estella. Who needed children anyway when I had these two pains to look after?

"I'll give you that one, you annoying little nappy-swaddled pain in the arse." I slowly said, starting to bind Estella once more. "And I'll make you another filthy-smelling cup of your loathsome tea when I'm done binding my sister!"

Actually, I was starting to see the point in all that cursing. It was a really good tension release and you could get really quite creative with it.

***

I straightened up from encircling the last mirror in salt and tried to stretch the crick out of my back. Damn it that it didn't get any easier, trying to get a non-wonky circle and corresponding smaller circles, the more often you did it. But then again, I didn't really want to become an expert in all this either, as it'd mean I'd be spending a lot more of my evenings practising.

"Looks good." encouraged Estella, giving me a weak smile. We'd not spoken much during the process. A small part of me wanted to think that this new enlightened version of my sister had realised how upset she'd made me, and therefore kept quiet. Sadly, the remaining greater part of me felt she'd just had nothing new to complain or lecture me about, hence her silence. Sceptical and sarcastic — my, what a catch!

"Thanks." I replied stiffly, trying to play nice right back at her. Then, ignoring the filthy but silent looks from Trishna, I went over and flipped on the kettle. There was something else I'd like to have flipped him; but if he was willing to keep it to ugly looks, then I'd have to settle for that too.

"Okay, what do we want for dinner?" I asked to the room in general as the kettle started to gurgle, flipping through the piles of takeaway menus in the motel's information folder.

"Estella, fancy anything cold tomorrow? We could do pizza again?" She tried to shrug, but then found she was bound too tight so shook her head.

"No thanks, I didn't really find it that appealing earlier," she said with a resigned expression. "I may just pass on the whole food thing, unless I actually feel hungry."

I cocked my head to one side and gave her a questioning look.

"You can go without food?" I asked, still writing my own 'Dummies guide to the undead' in the back of my mind. "How do you stay animated?"

"My afternoon near-death Nanna naps, I guess," she replied, both of us finding we could at least hold a neutral conversation again. The kettle finished boiling, and it was as if we both remembered Trishna at the same time. Oh God, I mean Isis, should we really be discussing such things in front of him? The look Estella and I shared showed we were thinking the same thing.

"Weather and local news?" I asked her as cryptically as I could.

Another attempted shrug, then nod. "Or fashion and celebrity gossip," she suggested.

"Really?" I allowed myself to wander down this path of inane chatter as I made Trishna another cup of tea. "You never seemed that interested in that sort of thing in the past. That was more my vein, while you were all environment and politics."

"We all can learn to change and think of those around us a little," she replied, trying to avoid her lecturing tone. "Light of Isis or not."

I smirked, I really did. Just the way she'd said it had me almost give a goofy grin. She had made a joke that included her beloved Goddess. The surprises were unending here tonight. Still, I suddenly felt we'd crossed over my wall of keeping her at a distance, and so I turned to Trishna.

"Any preference to what you want to smell for dinner?" I asked, waving the menus at him.

"Anything but that filthy snot-riddled muck you white people call Chinese food," he snapped. I would have penalised him, but actually agreed. If you didn't get the truly authentic stuff from around Chinatown, the rubbish that most people sold out in the 'burbs' was as close to traditional Chinese food as I was.

"What's your view on Mongolian BBQ spare ribs then?" I asked, spotting a menu for a chain of such places I knew was generally good. And you really couldn't have a place smell enough like garlic, when you were expecting a vampire to possess your sister later that night. Right?

"I don't think my dread Lord would appreciate the odour," Trishna said, though he sounded more amused than disapproving to me. Oh hello? Was there little love lost between the soul of a monk trapped on earth for over a hundred years, and the evil slimy bastard that had trapped him here? That could be an interesting thing to know. Tucking that thought away for later, I turned back to Estella.

"Seriously, the garlic thing is true then?" I almost grinned as she tried to shrug again. Maybe I shouldn't have bound her so tightly, or maybe I should stop asking her question she wanted to shrug a reply to. Actually, how could I start wording all my questions like that?

"I don't think it's the deterrent they make it out to be in the movies, but it does still make them uncomfortable," she replied, giving me a sly look, which probably meant she'd just realised what I'd been thinking about the shrugging. Damn. I'd forgotten she could usually tell what I was thinking.

I turned my attention back to Trishna, raising a questioning eyebrow at him as he inhaled a fresh wisp of steam from his tea cup.

"It weakens some of the mental powers and concentration a vampire emits to control those in the room around him," he replied, then looked a little guilty. "But you didn't hear it from me. And I wouldn't go out and buy bundles of the stuff to hang around the place, as all it'd do is make you and your clothes stink worse than the septic pit of a diarrhoeic hospital than they already do."

I gave him my look again and considered toying with the lighter as a warning. But there was something in the look he gave me, that made me wonder if that added swearing wasn't there to cover up him admitting something he shouldn't have. Then again, he may have just been pretending to be covering something up. Damn, who would have thought the shade of a Buddhist monk would be hard to read. Still watching him I tugged out my phone and sent a quick text to Roxanna.

'Garlic, yes or no for Skid Mark?'

I then shuffled through the menus a few more times and decided to just annoy Trishna and order the local poor excuse for Chinese food, just in case he was trying to play me with the garlic issue. The phone in my hand buzzed and I read the reply out loud.

"'Fictional mumbo jumbo, as you would say. Just gives you bad breath but shiny hair – R.'." I glanced at Estella, who genuinely looked interested to know this. But I swear if Roxanna had told her to eat yellow snow, she would have too. I then looked back at Trishna as I put my phone away and gave him an extra good glare.

"Just for that, monk boy, you're not only losing another bag. I'm also getting the sweet and sour pork and the lemon chicken. And then I'm going to sit their chemically reeking congealed sauce riddled containers: Right. Under. Your. Nose." He groaned in dismay before giving me an angry glare.

"Don't annoy me." I warned him again. "And when I ask you something, you either tell the truth or keep your filthy mouth shut." I ran my lighter over his precious box to make a point. "I've only been asked to save my sister's soul after all."

I set fire to another tea bag, boy they stank, and gave him a smug look as I ordered some 'white man's' Chinese. Sure I'd suffer too, but he had to be put in his place, no matter how juvenile my approach was. I felt this was the ghostly equivalent of rubbing a naughty puppy's nose in the puddle it'd left on the floor. Ghost puddles, now that was a nasty thought.

Chapter 10

I WAS more prepared to wait out the moonrise after midnight that night. Not only had I not eaten as much, thanks to what I'd ordered, but I'd also bought coffee at the same time as I'd bought tea. And so was buzzing along nicely, ignoring Trishna's grumbles from the far corner, as I watched the moon's light peek through the slatted blinds.

I glanced over my shoulder to wonder once more at Trishna's reaction to the takeaway containers. He'd moved into a corner as far from them as he could, while still being inside the room. Damn, it wasn't that bad a meal. I was really starting to suspect a lot of what he was doing was just one big act, and was about to ask him as much, when the room took on a nasty feeling again.

My head snapped back to Estella to find her grinning at me, in a rather ugly and slimy manner. Immediately I strengthened my mental guards and tried my best not to grit my teeth.

"Stephanie, what a glory it is to see you again." smirked Branwyre's voice through my sister's mouth. "What, no crucible?" The bastard!

"Evening, Skid Mark," I said bluntly, deliberately not visibly rising to his comment. It just confirmed the he had somehow tricked me the night before. I'd gone over what I'd said with Roxanna on the phone earlier and, as far as she was aware, I'd used the right binding commands. Obviously this leftover stain was a lot slipperier than I'd thought. Ew, that wasn't the best mental image either.

"Well, well, Trishna Duhkha, you rotten little monk with a stained soul. How nice it is to see you again," Branwyre purred in his smooth, charming, and oh-so-irritating voice.

"Master." Trishna spoke softly from his corner of the room and stepped forward a little. "It is a great relief to myself to know your glorious soul still has contact with this realm."

"Oh you big suck-up!" I spat at him. I'd meant to only say it in my mind but really couldn't help myself, as the growling, glaring bullyboy of a ghost turned into a sycophantic, snivelling wretch the moment the blood turned sour in my undead sister's veins. Surely he should save his anger for Branwyre and not take it out on the rest of us. Unless he couldn't, and that's why the rest of us had to suffer his potty-mouth. Then again, Trishna might just be a right grouch and treat people like that naturally.

The ugly sound of Branwyre laughing within my sister's throat brought me back to the bigger problem at hand. I grabbed the sword and unsheathed it.

"Right, buddy." I snapped at him. "If you haven't noticed, I get rather grumpy when kept up past my bedtime and I'd appreciate a straight answer from you this time. Where is the crucible?"

He tut tutted me, with a disgusting depreciating look on Estella's face. "So naïve to the art of binding."

He tsked, pointedly looking at the mirrors around him. Damn! With all the distractions caused by Trishna, I'd not waited for the moon to reach the mirrors to allow the double binding. Nor had I spoken those apparently precious words that gave me the needed control over what Branwyre could say.

I glanced over to the light of the moon slowly creeping across the darkened room. Not quite there yet.

"I do hope you've been treating my monk with the respect he deserves." Branwyre teased me, also noting the position of the moon. If he thought he could rile me while we waited, he had another thing coming.

"Goad me all you like, Skid Mark." I warned, refusing to look at him or Trisha. "I have my happy thought of you writhing in pain from the moon and nothing you can say can remove that." Just a few more minutes now.

"And you really think that is going to actually happen tonight?" Branwyre's quizzical tone made my dinner twist heavily in my stomach. What did he know about tonight that I didn't? Was it going to suddenly be overcast? I refused to bite and just kept watching the light.

"Didn't you check with your beloved High Priestess about my companion here?" purred Branwyre. His voice held an edge to it I didn't really like. It made my skin crawl even more than his presence did.

"She said he couldn't harm us and was of no use to you if you were bound." I snapped, daring him with a look of my own. My heart then sunk from the smug look on his face.

"Yes. But were you listening? Did she say bound? Or did she say double bound? Words are so important you know," smirked Branwyre. He looked over to where Trishna stood waiting. "Come here, boy."

Giving me a look that was almost apologetic, Trishna did as he was told. I suddenly felt so tense I could barely breathe. He was crossing the circle of salt! What would happen when a spirit did this? No one had bothered to mention it to me for my mental book about all this weirdness.

"Oh shit." I gasped as Trishna's ghostly feet somehow stirred the salt from its position as he crossed over it. The salt scattered in a way that should only happen if real, solid feet crossed it. As Trishna came to stand by Estella's side I stopped gawking at the disturbed salt and looked Estella in the face.

"Boo!" teased Branwyre as he stood up, rope ripping and dropping from him like wet toilet paper.

"Oh shit!" I managed again before a fist, a lot bigger and harder than I thought Estella could have, hit me fair in the left temple and I went down amongst twinkling, painful stars.

***

"I said, you festering whore-monger's gangrenous left nipple — Make me some tea!"

These are not the best words to regain consciousness to, but at least it did prove, I hoped, that I was still actually alive. Because, how could I make him tea if I was dead? Unless I was undead, right? And who was it I was making tea for? And why did my head hurt so very much?

I groaned and, on the third attempt, managed to open my eyes blearily and squint around at the darkened room. I was lying sprawled on the floor, by the side of the bed. Before me was the demolished circle. And I mean demolished. All the mirrors had been smashed and ground into the carpet, the ropes were tattered and the metal-framed chair a twisted mess. Still, if it looked like that and I was still breathing — and I did check this — then hopefully I hadn't come off so bad myself.

"There you go, you freckle on a frog's bottom, wakey-wakey." Finally I remembered it was Trishna who spoke like that. And this brought me out of my dazed confusion and fully awake. If he was still here surely that meant that the blood-sucking bastard currently wearing my sister as an outfit was also still here.

I looked about fearfully, waiting for his attack out of the darkness, but nothing happened. I couldn't see anyone, apart from the shimmery grey form of the annoying monk. After a quick look on the floor near me, I also discovered my sword was gone too. Damn.

"Estella?" I managed the word over my thick tongue. Had my tone sounded shaky and concerned, or just confused?

"They're gone. You confused lump on an ass' rectum." If my head hadn't already been ringing from the punch from hell, Trishna's grasp of the fouler side of the English language would have sent it ringing by itself.

"I don't suppose they took my lighter with them too, did they?" I asked him dryly as I hauled my sorry self off the floor with the help of the bed. To this he was silent, and fishing in my jean's pocket I concluded I still had both lighter and phone. That was a start.

"Where did they go?" I asked Trishna as I switched on the lights and made my way slowly over to the table where his box was. I was not happy the little so and so had been able to break my circle. Then again, I wasn't that happy that the supposedly all-knowing Roxanna hadn't warned me about it either, as I swore she'd said bound, not double bound. Now there was a thought. Not caring the hour, I thumbed her number on autodial and put the phone to my ear. After a few rings she answered warily.

"Just an appendix to your book on the undead," I said without returning her greeting. I can't say my tone was that pleasant sounding either. "Don't keep the ghost in the same room as the hell spawn he's controlled by. And it's double bound by the way."

"By Isis, Stephanie, what happened?" Although sleepy to start with, Roxanna's voice was now wide awake and full of concern.

"Branwyre arrived again before the moon was in the right position." I explained as calmly as I could in my current pissed-off mood. "And he was able to get Trishna to cross the circle, which broke it." There was a gasp over the phone and then Roxanna muttering something. Whether it was a prayer to Isis or hurried instructions to someone else in the room with her, I couldn't tell.

"But you are okay?" she asked fearfully. "He didn't hurt you?" In a way that calmed me, knowing she was honestly concerned about me.

"I got the thump of my life after he ripped his way out of the chair and rope." I replied carefully, "But it knocked me out. When I came to they were gone, and so is my sword."

"Leaving me stuck with your filthy, flea-ridden self," added Trishna from his corner. I turned to him and flicked the lighter on with a raised, questioning eye brow. Did he really want to push me right now?

"Oh, Estella!" mourned Roxanna's voice over the line. "You must find her, before Branwyre uses her to return to his followers."

"Well, duh!" I couldn't help my rudeness, just because I was new to all this mumbo jumbo didn't mean I couldn't think through all the consequences and what not.

"I'm sorry Stephanie, I should have realised you would know what to do," soothed Roxanna. Man, she was good at making me feel better, even over the phone. "Do you have any idea where they may have gone?" It was a good question, and not one I could easily answer. I walked to the door that had been left ajar, and looked out into the car park. Well, my car was still there and didn't look like it had undergone Branwyre's wrath at all.

"My car is still here. So either walking distance, or they've somehow hitched a ride." It was all I could tell her. And as she gabbled on in my ear a little longer I found my dazed attention drawn to Trishna. It was almost as if he knew something he wasn't telling me, or was it just another one of his little games?

"Hang on a sec, Roxanna." I cut her off mid-sentence and turned to the scowling grey monk. "Spill, swaddled wonder. Or the tea goes into your box and they both go up." What could I say; the whack on my head was affecting the strength of my threats. He scowled a moment longer and then seemed to relent.

"I will tell you where I think they have gone. But only if that High Priestess you're talking to can remove Branwyre's hold over me." I blinked a few moments. Half from the whack on my head, and half from the fact he'd not sworn or cursed me.

"Did you hear any of that?" I then asked Roxanna over the phone.

"I did," she replied crisply. "Tell the monk we can't release his spirit to its final rest, not until I discuss how with a living Buddhist monk I'm acquainted with. But I think I know how to release him from being Branwyre's slave." She paused and I knew there was going to be a rather unpleasant 'But' about to happen.

"But releasing him from Branwyre can only be done if we shift who controls him to someone else."

I groaned, it was meant to have been one of those silent, inner groans, but it had all been too much for me recently.

"What?" snapped Trishna angrily. "Can it be done, you wretched pustule on a whore's nose?" Ew! Did I really wanted to be in charge of that?

Instead of answering, I flipped the phone to hands-free and let Roxanna explain it all. Apparently, all I needed to do to free him from Branwyre and become master of Trishna myself was to make my own mark on the vessel holding him to this plane of existence with a piece of purified silver. Sure, now that wasn't too hard, was it?

"And what exactly is his vessel?" I asked in a semi sceptic tone. As I don't want to go and think I've done it and then discover I haven't. I've already seen the consequences of that sort of stupidity tonight.

"The box, I think," came Roxanna's now slightly tinny sounding voice.

"Oh come on!" I nearly whinged. "The words 'I think' from the High Priestess who's been guiding me through this insane mess, isn't what I want to hear right now."

"Well, you said he can't be more than one hundred feet away from it." Roxanna said defensively. At this point I glanced up at Trishna and noticed his nervous and hopeful look.

"Would you do it, if you could?" he asked, all anger suddenly gone from his voice. I gave him a look for a moment, and wondered what it was he was hiding from me this time.

"If I'm going to be stuck with you, until I can get your soul released and back on its way to reincarnation or whatever, then I'd much rather be stuck being your boss than having you pull another suck-up job to Branwyre." I told him warily. I still didn't trust the schlep that much. I mean, why had Branwyre left him behind if he'd been so important a tool at releasing him?

"Why did Branwyre leave you behind, Trishna?" I was surprised to find it was actually Roxanna's distant voice asking him this after I'd just thought it myself. He looked shifty and embarrassed again for a moment and then mumbled a reply.

"Because I wouldn't let him take your body. I made him stay in your sister's." Again I found myself blinking a little over this, before remembering Branwyre's threat from the night before, and how he'd said I would have made a better host for him than Estella. I suddenly had a very sick feeling.

"How do I know he hasn't infected me?" I demanded of Trishna. "How do I know that this isn't just a trick to make me your boss to give Branwyre more power over you when he wakes up in me?" I was nearly shaking with the fear of it now.

"Are you breathing?" asked Roxanna, again somehow calming me a little. "If you breathe upon a glassed surface, do you leave a cloud?" What in the hell was she talking about? I glanced to Trishna, who nodded towards the mirror on the wall encouragingly. I moved over to it and huffed at the smooth surface. I fogged the glass.

"Yes to both." I said weakly to Roxanna, hoping this was a good thing. There was a sigh from her end of the phone. Thankfully it sounded like one of relief, not despair.

"Then it means you're still alive and not possessed." I could almost hear the relieved smile in her voice. "Stephanie, this Other World I live in outside of your own, it may seem more complicated, but it isn't. Try not to think up things to scare yourself with, sometimes reality is more than enough." I blinked back the tears I'd caused when scaring myself over thinking Branwyre was slowly stewing inside me.

"So, I'm good? I'm still me?" I had to hear it again from her.

"When one is infected by the vampire virus, it kills you nearly instantly," Roxanna said soothingly. "You wouldn't have woken up again tonight if this was the case. It takes a day or so to grow strong enough to get its undead qualities to kick in." I found myself looking at Trishna and he met my gaze unabashed.

"You saved me?" I asked, confused. "You have been a complete and utter pain in the arse since I've met you, and couldn't kiss up to Branwyre fast enough when he possessed Estella. But you saved me from him?"

Trishna shuffled his feet and looked embarrassed.

"Yes," he finally answered, not seeming to want to give the reason why. "I have been trapped with Branwyre and his followers a very long time. They have used me, abused me and made mockery of me. But not once did those filthy whores make me a cup of tea!" I boggled again, I really did. This was over tea?

"And?" came Roxanna's questioning tone. How could she tell to ask these questions, she couldn't see us, could she? I checked, nope, video phone wasn't on.

"And," Trisha added, even more reluctantly, "Because, rather than just vanquishing me by burning my box, you put up with all my foul-mouthed attitude and took it as given you had to rescue my soul too. For that, I need you alive. No one has ever offered to save my soul before – or bought me tea to be nice to me." Now that made more sense to me.

"How did you protect her?" Roxanna was now questioning him more intensely. Perhaps she was writing her own mental book of 'the undead for dummies'? "You said you stopped Branwyre from taking her, so he took Estella instead." An even more embarrassed and near worried look from Trishna. I was obviously not going to like this answer.

"I stepped into her," he nearly whispered.

"You what?" Roxanna and I asked as the same time, for different reasons.

"I stepped into her," he said it again louder. "It's not as if I fully possessed her, or anything, I simply stood where she was lying. A body already possessed can't be possessed by another."

"You possessed me? You sick son of a bitch!" I nearly threw the phone at him, suddenly having a great need to throw something, and it was already in my hands.

"Only technically!" he snapped back. "So not a single thanks for saving you either, you pus-filled dead tick!"

"Stephanie, peace." came the Roxanna's soothing tones over the phone. "Please remember Trishna just saved your life." I tried to calm myself down. She had a point. Being trodden in by a dead monk's ghost was a far better option than being possessed by the virus of a vampire.

"Okay, I'm fine." I assured them both. "Can we just get back to where the hell that rat bastard has taken Estella so I can get back to trying to save her?"

"Will you take control of my vessel?" asked Trishna earnestly. "I have a feeling I know where they are, but if you go alone you're a dead woman. If you take me as I am, I must obey Branwyre's commands."

"Yes, I will." I said reluctantly. Then thought about what he'd just said. "Hang on, if you have to follow his commands, why didn't he just tell you to get out of me?"

A shrug and a smug look from Trisha. "Because he didn't ask me correctly. The power of a command comes from how it is given. If you don't do it quite right, it won't work." I was starting to think this was how Branwyre had gotten around telling me where the crucible actually was. What did people keep saying? Words were important.

"And Branwyre was in such a hurry to get out of here he didn't stick around to find the right combination to make me move." Somehow this almost seemed believable.

"Roxanna, your views?" I asked the black box in my hand.

"Chinese ghosts are reputed for being able to twist words so they only need to respond to their literal meanings," mused Roxanna, "It's one of the reasons they're some of the hardest stains to remove from this earth."

"I'll take that as a compliment, no matter how bad it sounds," muttered Trishna, I could tell he was trying to not swear or curse Roxanna. What a suck-up!

I found myself gently touching the egg-sized lump on the side of my head as I tried to think this all through.

"So, you stood in me, saved me, he couldn't find the right magic words to get you out of me to possess me himself, so he left and ran away in my sister's body. You think you know where they are, but won't tell me unless I become owner of you. And I don't think it's as simple as just writing my name on that wooden box because it's full of rice and bits of cloth, any of which could be the vessel binding you to this existence. Are we all on the same page here?" So I was into inner monologuing out loud, what else was new?

"That sounds about right, and fair point on to what exactly is his vessel." came Roxanna's voice. Did she actually sound proud I'd thought of something she hadn't?

"Yes, but you will not own me. The ritual will simply bind me to your will, ensuring I can only be faithful to you," Trishna warned.

That had me stop for a moment as it sounded rather more serious than I had originally thought. Besides my sister, I had a hard enough time just looking after myself. I didn't even own a pet. Now I was meant to bind a ghost to my will? What a horrendous thought. Still, it was obviously what had to be done to get Estella back, so I focused on the task at hand.

"Do you know which item within the box actually has trapped you here?" I asked Trishna. "I mean, the box is so obvious, but I have no idea what a vessel to capture a soul looks like at the best of times."

Trishna shrugged and waved a vague hand at the box and its contents.

"A ghost can be bound to any item of its making, meaning a vessel can be anything I made when alive. I carved that box, I wrote the prayers on the flag and I threshed the rice. I wasn't exactly paying attention to which was used when Branwyre and his thugs pegged me out on the side of a mountain and bled me dry until my spirit was easy enough to be captured." I was starting to understand the source of Trishna's anger. I would be pissed-off too if that was how I'd died, then found I had to serve those who'd done it for over a century. I was also very impressed he could actually string such large sentences together without swearing once.

"But what you degraded ulcers of a fallen virgin's tongue need to realise, is I've been around Branwyre long enough to pick up a few ideas of how to work around such tricks." Oh, and he had been so close there to being a reformed ghost too.

"Trishna." I warned, waving my lighter at him. "If we're going to actually agree to this I expect you to keep your language a heck of a lot cleaner. So any time you see me wave my lighter, or a tea bag, at you just shut up. Got it?" He actually grinned at me, proving he'd deliberately sworn just to see if I'd been paying full attention. If he knew I didn't like such language, why keep doing it? Some people were just destined to be annoying I guess.

"High Priestess," he said, addressing the phone in my hand. "Correct me if I'm wrong. But if we could get Miss Messy Hair here to inscribe all items within a circle of the moon upon the box and bind it with her name, that should do the trick. Right?"

I was so annoyed at them talking shop around me I let the quip about my hair slide. He'd not used a rude word and I'd seen it in the mirror, he had a point. I'd given up on my hair years ago as there was just no taming it.

"Yes . . ." Roxanna replied slowly, obviously thinking it through as she replied. "The box itself has been either the vessel, or the vessel of the vessel. And so inscribing the ward upon it should do the trick."

Why did I start thinking of old Danny Kaye movies as they chatted along that vein and I stood, piggy in the middle, trying to keep up? When they both stopped talking and Trishna gave me a questioning look I knew it was time for me to show I'd been listening.

"Okay, so you're saying, keep everything that's in the box in the box. Using purified silver, draw a picture of the rice, prayer flag and box on the box in a circle of the moon, initial it and you're all mine?" I hoped I had sounded smarter and more confident than I felt.

"Precisely!" replied Roxanna and I could almost see her proud smile at my knowing what to do. She had an amazing way to make me feel better than I really was.

"Brilliant" I sighed. "Now I just need to know exactly what a circle of the moon is and whether one of my Stirling silver earrings dipped in salty water is a good enough inscribing implement." Trishna actually stifled a laugh at that comment. Great, that was all I needed, him now laughing at my complete lack of experience in all this freaky stuff.

"Stephanie, do not doubt yourself, it is amazing how quickly you grasp this new information." soothed Roxanna over the phone. Trishna snorted again. He was so losing his ginger green tea for that. "As long as the earring is purified the way you did the other objects, it will be perfect. A circle of the moon is just that. Draw a circle and place the eight phases of the moon around it. The full moon is the apex, the new moon the base. I will send you a picture if I can figure out how."

I grimaced, was I really doing this? I couldn't see any other reason not to bind Trishna to me and that was just depressing in itself. I just wanted to find Estella, and make sure she wasn't being harmed too badly by Branwyre. She had been good at self-harming herself for years, but I had the feeling that that bastard now inside her could really do some damage to her, both mentally and physically, and not bat an eye.

"I'm putting the phone down while you try that Roxanna, and am off to purify my earrings." I laid the phone down on the table, gave Trishna a warning look, and made my way over to the bathroom. I filled the basin with water, mixed in some salt until it dissolved, then removed both my small, thick hoops of Stirling silver and plopped them into the solution. They'd have to sit there for a few moments before they'd be truly purified. As much as I wanted to find Estella, I wasn't going to rush any of this as I'd rather not find out the hard way that it hadn't been successful. And, in this situation, I was only ever learning I'd done something wrong the hard way. This was quite obvious as I looked at my bedraggled reflection in the mirror above the basin. My hair wasn't alone in looking terrible. My eyes had joined in by getting horrendously dark rings under them and the whack I'd got on the side of the head wasn't helping pretty me up much either.

"I think the High Priestess managed to send the picture!" came Trishna's voice from the main room. "Proving you can teach mangy, flea-ridden old dogs new tricks."

I sighed and clutched the basin tightly, as if seeking strength from its cold, hard surface. Why was I binding that horrible shadow of a person to me again? Oh, that's right, so I didn't end up dead and possessed when Branwyre came back and had figured out the right words to control him. Bugger.

I re-entered the main part of the motel room to hear Roxanna giving Trishna a stern lecture on his choice of words. What was more surprising was that he looked cowed, rather than defiant. He stood over the phone, hands cupped in front of him, solemn looking and nodding his head with an occasional "Yes My Lady," thrown in, to show he was listening. I was really starting to like Roxanna. The power she had was amazing. The purity of that power just made her even more awesome.

"Stephanie is one of the kindest, most tolerant people I have met," Roxanna said. She'd only known me a day or so, so I decided not to correct her just yet.

"And so I expect to hear you respect her, and speak only in a plain and polite voice once you are bound to her. Spectres have the right to be laid to rest and I can assure you the quickest way for you to reach enlightenment is to not piss her off!"

"Amen to that Roxanna," I smirked, letting her know I was back and listening. I glanced at Trishna who had the decency to look embarrassed while still surly. It was quite a feat.

"Did you get the picture I just took?" she asked, totally unembarrassed I'd heard her sing my praises. I thumbed through my phone and opened the new attachment. It was a photo taken of a picture of the circle from a rather old looking book. The circle looked pretty much the way I thought it would from her earlier description, but it was good to have a legitimate version to work from as I'd never realised each phase had a name.

"Sure did. Want to hang around while I do it up? Or am I keeping you from your beauty sleep?" I tried to sound casual. Our phone conversation had started with me in such a foul mood and she'd been nothing but patience and kindness. I was fairly sure I could do the rest alone, and it was late. I didn't know exactly how much sleep one needed to be High Priestess.

"I trust in your instincts, Stephanie." came Roxanna's calm tones. "If you feel you can handle it from here, I will go. Isis be with you, my child." And then it was just me, and the ghost I was planning to bind to myself. How nice.

Chapter 11

"THERE, so that's seventeen grains of rice and one prayer flag." I mumbled. I was sitting at the table, Trishna's wooden box in one hand and one of my earrings, now purified, in the other. I can't say I was the world's best artist, but I'd like to think all those little oval shaped things and a few squares and lines would be universally recognised as rice, flag, and box.

"Crude, but a good depiction," muttered Trishna. He'd been watching over my shoulder since I'd begun. But had thankfully been silent since our argument over why exactly I felt I needed to count out everything in his box, and then draw every single one. My logic had been that if I didn't draw the exact amount, it just wouldn't work. He'd already proven there were loopholes in all this mumbo jumbo stuff and it was time to be anal about my precision. He'd called me something a lot worse, something along the lines of a pedantic pus-riddled part of a cat. I'd just seen red and grabbed the nearest tea bag and the lighter. I had then decided on a new rule. He was to keep it clean or else. If I felt he was straying off the G rating, I'd hold up a tea bag as a warning. If he continued, the lighter would come out and bye-bye tea bag. It all seemed so stupid, but would hopefully to do the trick and curb his foul tongue. I really didn't have time for all this, and was stressing over exactly what would have happened to Estella. Surely Branwyre would have reached his thugs by now, and who's to say they wouldn't come back and beat me up, or worse. It was time to move.

"Focus on the here and now, not the 'what might be's'," warned Trishna, "As it's making your circle wonky." Damn, he was right too. I still hadn't mastered drawing a perfect circle free hand so I slowed down and concentrated on scratching marks around the images I'd already done. I was drawing it on the smooth, uncarved base of the box itself. I'd wanted to draw it over the lid and base to encircle both parts of the box, but Trishna had pointed out that if someone opened the box the circle could be broken and who's to say my 'ownership' over him wouldn't then also be broken.

My concern was what if the lid was taken off, who's to say I would be in control then. His oh so reassuring reply was if the lid was broken off, it meant all hell was breaking loose and the last thing I'd have to worry about was no longer having him bound to me. We'd compromised by doing the carving on the base of the box. Still, at least he hadn't sworn during this particular little discussion.

I was still a little grumpy at Trishna over not telling me where he thought Branwyre would have taken Estella until after we were bound together. Surely sitting here watching me start the carving would assure him I was being true to my word, but no. He had obviously been tricked, teased, and manipulated for a hundred years, and was determined not to share until I'd completely fulfilled my promise. I could sort of see where he was coming from, but still felt he could trust me a little more. You know, 'bringer and maker of his tea' and all. Ignoring the 'burning and destroyer of his tea' part mind you.

I looked down at the circle I'd scratched in a single line, around the depictions of rice and prayer flag and box. I'd of course stooped to having to have my tongue out of the side of my mouth in fierce concentration, so popped it back in while I looked my work over.

"Would you say it's a complete circle?" I asked the shadow at my shoulder. Being dead did mean, thankfully, that he at least wasn't breathing in my ear. And I had a feeling he'd have been one of those annoying mouth breathers too. Ew!

Trishna cocked his head to one side and studied the box and new carving a little longer.

"It feels solid." He finally replied, and I really didn't want to know how he could feel my circle. Still, I guess it meant the binding was starting to work. I gave him another of my sceptical sideways glances, always keeping in mind he'd already said he could twist words so he didn't have to answer them correctly. But still, that was when dealing with the one he was bound to, right? Not the one he wanted to be bound to. Unfortunately, that didn't make me feel any better.

"Okay, time for the moon phases." I sighed, bringing my phone forward and looking down at the picture of the circle Roxanna had sent me. Tongue popping back out in concentration, I started to carve them all. Starting at the full and ending at the waxing gibbous. I then counted them all, ensured there were indeed eight and sat back in relief. So now I had the box and all its contents captured in a circle of the moon. Yay me? Now to put my mark to it, how did I do that again?

"The quarters of the moon take up most of the space around the circle." I commented to Trishna, he knew what I was meant to be doing, so he should have the answer without me needing to ring Roxanna again. That is, if he was going to answer me truthfully. "So how do I put my mark to it? And more to the point, what is my mark? My initials?"

"Not your initials, as many people can have the same initials." Trishna murmured, while giving my circle close scrutiny. He then nodded and seemed satisfied with my work. "Your mark is something special to you, like a special symbol or way of writing your name. And it has to fit into the centre of the full moon as the apex. The circle was sealed by the moon phases; your mark will bind it to you."

He almost sounded weird when not swearing as he spoke. I then looked down at the full moon. It was maybe as big as a five cent piece, if I was that lucky. Damn, I wish someone had mentioned that to me before I'd drawn it all. What was special to me that would fit in there? Certainly not Stephanie Muriel Anders. I then leaned forward, tongue at the ready and slowly carved 'ANI' into the wood's surface. It was how I used to sign my pictures as a child, a long-lost pet name given by the sister I had once loved when she was too small to be able to say my whole name. For some reason, I let all these old thoughts of love, pride and identity pour out of me as I carved it in. I then sat back and looked to Trishna as he sucked in a deep breath and straightened up behind me. I turned to watch him more closely as he seemed to shimmer for a moment and his shades of grey appearance moved into more calming shades of blue.

"What the hell?" I questioned, while grabbing for my phone as if having Roxanna on the other end would protect me.

"It's okay you rat tail haired idiot," Trishna grinned, releasing his breath in a deep sigh. He was genuinely smiling at me, which made me even more uneasy than I'd been before.

"You've changed colour." I pointed out, wondering if stating the obvious would make the situation any better.

"My shadow form comes from a reflection of the aura of who I'm bound to," he replied calmly. I was waiting for the ending curse, but none came.

"And you're now bound to . . .?" Okay, so I was taking the dumb approach, I wanted to make sure I was getting this right.

"To you, you pointless creation of the Divine Buddha's will," he replied, still grinning. And that hadn't been such a bad insult either.

"My aura is blue?" I couldn't help it; I was at dumb question central now. And did I really want to know what it meant?

"Yes, and that's actually a comforting thing for me to know," Trishna replied watching me expectantly, waiting for the next dumb question no doubt. But I instead shut my gaping mouth and tried to ease my thoughts. So, I now had a ghost bound to me, I had a blue aura and that was a good thing for said ghost to know. It was also now three in the morning, and I still wanted to find my sister. And I was hoping to find her before dawn as Isis knew where she would end up if Branwyre's flunkies found her before I did.

"Okay, so I kept my side of the bargain, you're bound to me. I still don't know if that's a really good thing or not, but hey! So where's my damned sister?" I wasn't in the mood for small talk and I hoped I'd worded it precise enough to get the right answer.

"I don't know where your sister is," smiled Trishna and I was about ready to flame the entire collection of tea bags. He must have realised this as he suddenly looked worried.

"You're not asking me correctly!" he bleated as I got up and stacked the cardboard boxes of tea in the motel room's small kitchenette sink and rummaged in my pocket for my lighter.

"I'm too tired for your 'riddle me this' routine Trishna." I warned him, giving him my best pissed-off look. "You either pretend like I asked it right, or your new master is chargrilling the Darjeeling!"

He sighed and gave me his best disgruntled look. It didn't look any better in blue than it had in grey.

"I don't know where your sister is," he muttered. "But if I had been asked where I believe Branwyre would have taken his host body to contact his people, I would have answered there is a nightclub three blocks from here, called by its regulars the Tormented Whore. It wasn't his regular place to go for new victims, but he often used it to hire thugs." He then looked at me and the pointedly at the sink. I took one of the boxes of tea out, put my hands on my hips and waited.

"Why would he need to hire thugs? Why not just call his own personal ones to come and get him?" I felt it was a valid enough question.

I was also still trying to get the name of the club out of my mind. I mean, ew!

"Not being a mind reader, I can't say for sure that he has gone there to hire thugs." Trishna grumpily replied. "But it is a neutral place to go. Despite him being an ancient piece of devil's doo doo, he isn't the King of Nasty out there. I know an imbecile like you has no grasp on what the real world is like, but Branwyre has other enemies — besides the Priestesses of Isis — and he isn't about to take a deficient body like your sister's out into the night without protection."

I took one of the bags of tea out of the rescued box and put it back into the sink.

"Hey!" he yelled at me. "I just gave you some free bloody information, you demented two legged cow!" Another bag went back into the sink.

"The first one was for calling me an imbecile," I warned him, "And I think we both know why the second one was dumped in there." He growled at me under his breath, but said no more. Merely crossed his arms and looked angrily around the room.

"So, Branwyre is a bad guy, but not king bad guy?" I asked, picking up one of the bags from out of the sink and waving it at him.

"Yes. There are far nastier things that walk in the Darkness out there. He may have once been near the top of the food chain in this city, but the Priestesses of Isis were doing some of the out of town nastier guys a favour by nearly destroying him the other week."

The bag landed safely on the counter and I picked up another one and gave him a pointed look.

"And were you there when his little possession ceremony was interrupted?" I asked, it was actually kind of irrelevant, but I was curious to know all the same.

"Of course I was you fes . . ." Trishna paused a moment before continuing. "Yes. I am, or was, a source of his power. I was present at all such times to channel his raw power and refine it into a more usable force. That's my purpose." For that amount of information, as it sounded quite believable, he got the entire box of ginger and green tea back on the counter next to the Darjeeling.

"Okay so we head to the Torm . . . to that club you mentioned and we find them there. Then what? I can't expect him to come quietly, hired thugs and neutral ground or not!" As much as I had been enjoying learning more about the 'guys who walked in Darkness' who I was helping save my sister from, it was not actually saving her. It was time to stop with the tea games and just get going.

"Are you asking this as my new master? Or as the evil bitch threatening to burn all my tea?" Trishna asked warily.

"Which one gets me the correct answer?" I replied with a not too pleasant grin. Hey, I was a multitasker and could wear more than one hat. Again Trishna's expression grew dark and angry, but he kept his cussing to himself.

"If you can douse him in purified water and get out his full name and banish him before he caves your head in, there's a chance you can get rid of him for the rest of the night. It'll then be up to you as to whether you can get your sister to a safe place before the thugs, hired or personal, catch up with you and . . . as mentioned, cave your head in." My, without that cursing, didn't he just have the nicest turn of phrase about him? Not.

"Fine!" I then snapped, coming to a decision. I scooped up all the tea in and out of the sink, raced over to the duffle bag I'd been storing all our stuff in and crammed them inside. Moving about the room like a whirlwind, I grabbed anything that was ours or could be traced to us that hadn't been destroyed, and also threw it in the bag. I didn't have the time to clean up the ruined circle on the floor, so left a fifty dollar note amongst it as a form of apology to the maid. I was fairly certain the money wouldn't be mentioned to Management when she complained of what she had to clean up.

The last few items I grabbed were the empty scabbard, my ginormous handbag, the bottle of salt water I'd made earlier, and Trishna's box. These last two items were crammed into said bag. One last check to ensure nothing was left behind, then I threw the key onto the bed and walked out, closing the door behind me. It was time to load up and get the hell out of there before Management could ask me too many questions.

Once in the car I checked to see Trishna was sitting in the back; he was and proved it by flipping me the bird. Damn, and I was now bound to that? Still, he'd given me an idea of where Estella might be, it was time to go.

"Now listen you blue freak." I warned him via the rear-view mirror as I drove out into the night. "You're going to tell me how to get, by using this car, to that nightclub you mentioned earlier. To the . . ." here I suppressed a shudder, "Tormented Whore. Got it? Any false move and I will see what it's like to send a soul to purgatory."

I gave him my best threatening look and awaited an answer. He glared at me a while longer as we motored along and then cheekily sneered,

"Well, if you want it that way. You should have turned right out of the motel car park, not left, and we should be heading east right now. You directionally challenged hippo's nipple."

As I slammed on the brakes and did an impromptu — and rather illegal — U-turn, the box of ginger green tea scattered into the gutter as I hooned off. Isis knew what I'd do, once I'd run out of tea to threaten him with.

Chapter 12

---⊘---

DESPITE my urge to keep the car idling out the front for a quick getaway, I had the feeling that might just get it stolen. So instead I parked it in the shadows out the back of the nightclub amongst the other nondescript cars in the parking lot, and locked it up tight. I had Trishna's box still in my bag, now slung over my shoulder, as I approached the neon glaring entrance to the club.

I really didn't know whether he'd just been making the name up, or whether it was some Other World name for it, but the sign beside the door proclaimed the place was known as the Angry Pickle. I seriously couldn't decide which name was worse. The pickle or the whore? Either way, there wasn't a queue to get in and, once I'd paid my entrance fee, I strolled on in as if it was something I did every day at three in the morning.

Despite the lack of a queue, it was fairly heaving inside. Through the bone rattlingly loud music and seizure-inducing strobe lighting, there were at least fifty people writhing on the small dance floor come bar. Though barely able to make it out, I couldn't help but notice it was rather smaller on the inside than the out. Did that mean I'd be able to find Estella easier? No. I unwillingly squinted into all the darkened booths, to see if I could spot her. When I copped an earful from some of the preoccupied couples nestled in them, I instead decided to approach the bar to ask if they'd seen her.

The barman — a piece of testosteroned meat with an IQ less than the number of fingers on one hand — just gave me a surly, dumb look when questioned about whether he'd seen Estella or not.

"Buy a drink, dance or get out," was all I got. I was about to turn my pent-up rage on Trishna, barely visible in the mixture of strobing white light and sheer darkness, when he put his mouth to my ear and shouted.

"This is the normal part of the bar, you half-witted female! You want the area out the back!" He pointed to a doorway barely visible as an entrance next to the bar. It was well hidden amongst the fake potted plants and a beaded curtain.

As I approached it, another mountain of meat shaped like a man moved to stop me.

"Password," he grunted, making the word sound like an innuendo.

"Twisted are they who enjoy entering the Tormented Whore." answered Trishna before I could even come up with something. I digested what he'd said and cringed. Ew! Still, it had worked; the mountain grunted and stepped aside. The fact a ghost had just given him the password didn't seem to faze him at all. That couldn't be good.

Still, I wasn't stopping to discuss this with him and slipped through the beads and into a darkened corridor before Mr Mountain could change his mind. It ended at a thick velvet curtain, which lifted as I approached it, opening out into a far larger area.

Although the music was still loud in here, it wasn't at the 'shake your teeth out' level it had been in the other room. The lighting was calmer too, not all flashes and strobes, just a consistent dim orange glow. There were more seats, couches and tables here too, than out the front. And not a dance floor in sight. Obviously, if you wanted to dance, you mingled with the 'normal' in the other room.

"May I take your order?" came a voice from my elbow. I looked down into the eyes of a disturbing small man. I mean, he looked normal enough — bordering on slime ball — with his slicked-back hair and smarmy expression, other than his eyes. They weren't completely black, there was white where it should be, but his irises and pupils were a solid, unchanging black. And from that blackness oozed the most heinous feeling of nasty I could think of. He had some sort of word tattooed on his forehead in an orange that almost glowed. It just looked out of place amongst his overall greasy, sleazy look, and for some reason irritated the shit out of me. He must have sensed me staring at it as he raised a hand to touch it.

"Haven't you ever seen an Earthbound demon before, darling? I can assure you we're much more fun to play with than some wisp of a ghost," he added giving Trishna a look of disgust. Trishna was rather restrained in return and just flipped him off. "Newly admitted to the funner side of the world are you honey?" he addressed me again, I really wished he wouldn't. "Let me be your host for the night, I can assure you once you've gone black magic, you'll never go back." I suppressed the shudder his vile words caused, surprised to find I could reply in a stable and calm voice.

"Thanks, but no. I'm just here to see a man about a sword and get my sister back from a prick of a vampire."

"Sword? So not a White Witch come to teach us the merits of pure thought and harmony with nature?" quizzed the short man. I really didn't like the way he was questioning me, as I didn't like these people knowing more about me than I felt they should. Knowledge, like words, contained power here, and all that.

"Look, just go hump that bar stool or something." I'd lost my 'playing nice with others' tone as he was really giving me the creeps. "I'm not interested in you showing me anything. I'm just here to find my sister and get home before dawn." He snorted in disgust at me and turned on his heel.

"They let any little wannabe know the password these days!" was the last thing I heard him sniff, before he moved off into the gloom.

"Ignore the filthy little snot nose," mumbled Trishna behind me. "He's not even a real demon. He looks more like a dark Djinn some idiot trapped here to wait tables. The day he gets loose, his captor better already be dead, or he soon will be. He's a slimy little pus ball, and they love to play with sharp things." My skin still hadn't stopped crawling from our run in with the little 'demon', and so to have that load of information added — well, as if I needed an excuse to not sleep at night.

"Let's keep this to a need to know basis, Trishna." I murmured, while scanning the duskily lit area. "If it doesn't affect my life right here and now, I really don't want to know." I then sighed, realising I probably shouldn't have said that as I was sure it had just set-up some lovely loopholes for him to squeeze through later.

"Can you see Branwyre anywhere?" I asked, then stopped myself and added, "Or my sister Estella being possessed by Branwyre?" Must remember to be as pedantically specific with him as possible, right?

"Oh, them," he murmured, also looking about the room. "Yeah, he's over in the far left corner. I smelt him as soon as we came in." I sighed, and would have banged my head against a wall if one had been handy.

"That was a need to know." I growled at him. He gave me a deliberate look of doe-eyed innocence.

"But it doesn't affect your life right now," he protested. "Yes, admittedly, once they spot you're here or you go over there, it will. Right now, I'd be more worried about who the little Djinn turd has gone to speak to."

"And why should I be concerned about that?" I asked, looking around wildly, trying to see where the little slime ball had gone.

Trishna shrugged and pointed towards the bar where the little man was nearly jumping up and down as he spoke into something's ear. And I will call it a 'something' as it was large, hairy, orange, and had no discernible head and body. Just one big mass of hairy orangeness. It was squatting on the floor by the bar, too big to fit on a bar stool, and as I watched, it turned to follow where the Djinn was pointing.

"Oh shit," I breathed heavily as two bright red sparks of eyes gleamed out at me from amongst the masses of orange hair. It was like a giant, nasty version of Cousin It. And I didn't like the way it looked at me, despite there being no discernible face or expressions.

"Just to prove I am keeping up my end of the bargain." Trishna murmured in my ear. "That is the owner of the Tormented Whore and the shitty little Djinn who's been Earthbound by him just pointed you out as being unaffiliated with anyone and new to the area."

"How do you know that?" I asked, feeling panicky now as he was only meant to tell me something that affected me right now. Oh. Shit!

"Because, you flat breasted virgin to the Other World, that's what we flunkies do when an obvious newcomer with no clue about our world walks through the door," he sneered.

"But I'm affiliated with the Temple of Isis, with Roxanna, right?" I tried to insist. Hairy red eyes was still watching me so I tried to turn my back on him to hide the fear in my expression.

"Technically . . . No." grinned Trishna, obviously enjoying seeing me so worried. "You're just helping them out with something. And without the sword that was given to you by the High Priestess to show you're working with them, you're as unattached as a head next to a guillotine."

"Aw crap!" I muttered, looking over my shoulder. My remark was as much aimed as a reply to him as it was an exclamation to the fact the hairy orange monolith was on the move, towards me.

"That the best you got when the shit has just hit the fan?" sneered Trishna, for someone who was bound to me in the hopes I may release his soul rather than condemn it, he sure didn't show his gratitude.

The smell of old orange and hairy hit me metres before he himself did. Musk gone bad was the most simplest way to describe the myriad of odours and heavy scent drifting before him in a great big cloud of ick. If I'd known socialising in the Other World would expose me to such nasties, I would have brought along a gas mask. Though, that might be seen as pretty insulting, right?

"Any advice on what I do next?" I almost squeaked out of the corner of my mouth to Trishna, "I mean, I'm not going to be able to save you from purgatory if I'm an ugly brown smear on his paisley carpet!"

But before Trishna could come up with an ear blistering retort, Estella was there. Or at least Branwyre wearing my sister like some sort of sleek outfit was. I hadn't even recognised her at first, as Branwyre had obviously stopped for a quick wardrobe change on his way here after knocking me out. Estella was wearing a long, sequinned, slinky dark blue dress that was split up one side to almost her navel. Sadly it showed she wasn't wearing any underpants. Or bra, if her flat chest beneath the upper part of the dress was anything to go by. Yes, we Anders women have never been blessed with much in the way of breasts, something I'm sure Branwyre had regretted as soon as he'd had the chance to do a stocktake on Estella's body. Her lank blonde hair had been piled artistically atop her head and the make-up that had been applied, badly, gave her the look of expensive prostitute gone to seed. The overall look of power and money it appeared Branwyre had been going for just didn't quite hit the mark when he wore it through my sister. Aw, what a shame.

"Mandra," crooned Estella in a voice not quite hers, but definitely not Branwyre's either, as she stopped between me and old orange and hairy. Now that I was closer to her, I knew it was Branwyre in control. I could feel his sick dominating presence oozing towards me. I doubled my efforts to maintain my emotional wall, but could still feel him brushing against my mind.

"Mandra," the faux Estella crooned again, this time making the great lump of orange come to a grinding halt. "Don't fuss yourself over such a skinny green stick of nothing like her. She's with me." Branwyre come Estella flicked a dismissive look over me, then made urging motions for the nightclub owner to go back to his spot by the bar. "Stupid little slip forgot to mention me when she came in. That's what happens when you let Jamal greet the customers." The sneering tone then turned on the slimy little man standing beside his boss.

"She has no affiliation with you," rumbled the heap of hair. "No markings and no scent. House rules clearly state that makes her mine."

"No markings?" exclaimed the Estella encased Branwyre. "She has come with my favourite ghost! She is his lackey. Look in her bag, she carries his vessel. And you remember Trishna don't you? We used him just the other month to help oust the Crimps from taking over this part of town." The red eyed lump of hair switched his intense stare from me to Trishna at my side and studied him carefully.

"Why yes!" wheezed Mandra. "Your foul-mouthed little religious chap. You have some newb carrying his vessel around? Such favouritism for a mere tool."

"But what else would she be good for?" sneered Trishna, getting in on the act. "And just think of whom you're calling a tool, you drain-clogged mass of orangutan pubes!" I found myself having to stifle a grin. That had been a good one.

"Trishna!" warned Estella, more of Branwyre's real voice coming through on the harsh tone. Trishna took a step back and bowed his head, taking up a cowed pose.

"Now, as you were, Mandra." Estella was dismissing the great hulk, waving him away. "She's with us, not something for you to amuse yourself with for the rest of the night. Off you go." Even speaking through my sister and trying to act more feminine, Branwyre truly was such a wanker.

"She's not just a tool carrier, she was asking for a sword and her sister," bleated the little Djinn, but his boss just grunted and continued to seep his way back to his place at the bar.

"You need to be careful," Trishna warned the little slime ball. "One day you might say the wrong thing, and find out exactly how painful it is to have that mark removed from your forehead."

Mandra turned back briefly. "The binding mark is forever. Boxes can, however, be burnt." He exchanged a piercing red look with Estella/Branwyre then headed back to his spot at the bar. Branwyre turned his full attention to me, twisting my undead sister's face into an ugly parody of a smile.

"Stephanie, about time you turned up, and you brought Trishna along for me too. Such fun!" Branwyre's real voice made Estella's expression all the more ugly. I almost felt sorry for her.

"Please! Come over to our little booth and join us for a drink or two." From the fumes curling my hair as Branwyre came too close for comfort, I was fairly certain he/ she was already way past two drinks.

Damn, how would that affect Estella if I banished Branwyre? Would I need to roll her home drunk?

"Thanks, but I'm just here for my sister and sword." I said in my best pseudo-sweet voice and tried to find the weapon. I really don't know why it was so important to me, but I just had to have the sword back as much as Estella. Was it to ensure I could chop her head off at will to send her to purgatory? I didn't think I still hated her that much.

"Oh, did you really think it would be so easy?" teased Branwyre's voice as he caused Estella's face to make a little moue. Her eyes glanced behind me and I realised the stale smell of sweat and garlic had increased, as two rather large thugs came to stand just behind me. Oh screw that! No one said I had to contend with thugs too! I glanced at Trishna and, in his expression I saw that yeah, he had mentioned thugs. Bugger.

And so I shortly found myself squished into a semicircular booth with a thug either side of me and Branwyre breathing heavy alcohol fumes all over me via my sister from the other side of the seat. Why in the hell would an undead person need to do that? Breathe on me I mean. Just to be rude and annoying no doubt. On the brighter side, lying across the back of the seats where Estella/Branwyre sat, was my sword. Seriously, leaving it out in the open like that in public? Show of power no doubt. And probably the only one he had without having a dick to whack out and size up against the others in the room. My I did get catty when feeling near to death like this!

"Don't look so worried, Stephanie my dear," oozed Branwyre's sleazy voice, now sounding slightly slurred, from Estella's dolled up face. "Chip and Don here are just the hired help until my real posse comes to play." He paused as he made Estella take another shot of some sticky bright yellow liquid. "I'd say you'd like them, but then again I really do doubt that. What with what we plan on doing to someone who dared double bind us and banish us like a mere sprite."

"Oh have a cry, Skid Mark." I growled back, my teeth grinding together to stop them from chattering with fear. "If I was so scared about your pathetic threats, would I really come here alone just to get back what is mine?"

"What is yours?" grinned Branwyre, he seemed to find my bravado a lot funnier than it should have been. "Once I am inside a body, it is mine until I decide otherwise. You should try it sometime." I really didn't like the drunken leer I was now receiving from Estella as I could almost see Branwyre in it too. Damn, I really should have thought this whole 'rescue my sister' thing through better, shouldn't I? I squirmed in my seat slightly, not just from the pressure of the two thugs either side of me, or from the way Branwyre had Estella look at me. I was starting to feel a numb tingling in my right shoulder and wondered what the hell trick was causing that. It wasn't the nicest feeling in the world and I really hoped it wasn't an indicator that Branwyre was finding cracks in my closed mind.

Then suddenly, as if forgetting he was in the middle of threatening me, Estella was turned around and made to order more drinks. This time the order included tea. Damn, I'd nearly forgotten Trishna there for a moment. Where the hell was he? I then looked at my shoulder and realised it had a blue shimmering hand laid on it. I followed the hand up the arm to find Trish was standing behind me in the booth chair. I turned my attention back to Branwyre and the ugly drunken sneer he was making on Estella's face.

"Forgot about my little power booster there did you?" grinned Branwyre. "He's just making sure you don't do anything too rash with say, that bottle of purified water in the top of your bag."

Oh screw that! If everything I was trying to do was so damned obvious, why string me along? Following a nod from Estella, Chip or Don or whoever the testoseroned idiot on my right was suddenly reached into my bag and dragged the cleansed and refilled water bottle out. I had purified it in one lot of water, and then filled it with a new batch. You can never be too purified, right?

"This it?" grunted the thug. "Purified huh? Must taste good." And then the idiot opened the bottle and drank it down in near to one gulp. Branwyre had been about to protest, but the drinks had obviously dulled his reflexes. I did my best to move as far from the man who had just slugged down the bottle of salt water as I could. Thankfully he'd been the thug on the end of the booth.

Shortly thereafter, what normally happens when you drink salt water quickly did indeed happen. At least he had the decency to stagger to his feet and empty his stomach in the plants on top of another booth a few metres away. It wasn't the nicest sound or smell, what had he been eating? But at least it meant I was one thug down. That meant just one thug, a vampire possessing my drunk, undead sister to go. Damn, make that 'and a rather short Earthed demon or Djinn' too as the little slimy man came hustling over to see what all the noise was about.

"Must have been something he drank," grinned Estella/Branwyre drunkenly resting her head on one of her hands now propped on the table by an elbow. She had turned her back on the scene, dismissing the stupid man and his extremely stupid action.

"What can I say?" continued Branwyre to me, eyeing the other thug over, "They know little enough of the world in general, let alone the Other World. But they're cheap and will do anything for the right price. Won't you?" she added, winking at the man. He had looked a little unnerved over what had just happened to his friend, but focused his small-minded attention back on Branwyre and nodded. He then smiled at the rather grotesquely lewd gestures Branwyre was making Estella do with her hands and mouth at him. I was so not letting him make my sister do that sort of thing for real. There was no doubt in my mind she had done it many times in her past, but I would like to have thought it had been done of her own free, while stupid, will.

"Don't even think about it, Skid Mark." I growled again. The tingling in my shoulder increased slightly. Was Trishna trying to tell me something or hold me down better? I was still a little sceptical as to whose side he was really on.

"What is the meaning of this?!" squawked the little demon, summoning some type of cleaning lackey out of the shadows to deal with the now dishevelled and still heaving, thug hunched over the potted plants. He had advanced on our table and was addressing Branwyre in a manner that reminded me of a miniature poodle yapping at a Clydesdale. One false move and he'd be squished.

Branwyre caused Estella to laugh until she almost slid out of the booth; it went on so long and hard. Her hand was then waved in my general direction.

"Blame her!" he leered at me while settling more firmly into the cushions. "She's the one who brought in what he drank."

"No outside substances to be drunk on the premises!" the little demon with the annoying orange mark on his forehead then squawked at me. "You might be a newb, but surely you know some of the basic house rules?"

"Listen graffiti head!" I snapped, finding it easier to take my anger out on a supposed Djinn than a drunk vampire possessing my undead sister. "I didn't ask the numb nuts to drink it! It was for external use only! And for my sister here too!" I knew I must look as flustered as I sounded. "I was hoping to use it to banish Branwyre the unbearable from my sister."

"You think you can banish an ancient vampire from its current host?" gawped the Djinn, making me feel even dumber than I had five minutes ago. "I knew you were new. I hadn't realised you were mentally retarded too."

Estella giggled and almost fell off her part of the booth again. How much had she had to drink? And exactly how well could a vampire, who could only partially possess her at the best of times, handle large amounts of alcohol in his host?

"Call me what you like, Oil Slick, but I had him double bound by the moon last night and it was my first day on the damned job!" I growled back. "And I banished him then too!" I was not about to have my abilities questioned by some idiot stupid enough to get himself Earthed, AKA bound by another. Uh-oh, isn't that what I'd let Trishna do to me? Damn!

"Oh really, double bound, you say?" the little man asked me sceptically. Then why couldn't you manage it again tonight?" Instead of answering I glared up at the ghost above me, getting annoyed at the intensity of his hand on, or was it now in, my shoulder. The little Djinn suddenly burst into laughter, causing Estella to do the same as if it was contagious.

"Rookie mistake to let the ghost bound to the person you've put in a circle be in the same room as it." He then grinned at me. "But I like your style."

"You should," Trishna said, speaking for the first time. There was almost a note of warning in his voice. "She has a blue aura."

Branwyre made stupid oohing and ahhing noises as if this meant something, but not something he took seriously. The little man however, Jamal was it, gave me a studying look.

"Blue you say?" he mused just as another lackey approached from the bar with Branwyre's latest order of drinks. The little oily man broke into a wide grin and threw his arms open in a warm welcome. "That is always something useful to know," he announced warmly. "And due to that, this round is on the house. Enjoy!" He helped the lackey set the drinks down on our table, paying careful attention to the remaining thug's soda water, then giving me a wink left. Why didn't any of that make me feel any better?

Branwyre promptly had Estella down three more of the sticky yellow shots in short succession, she'd ordered half-a-dozen, then sighed loudly.

"Bah, this weak-willed sister just can't hold her liquor," Branwyre said, his tone considerably more unsteady now. "I would have thought with her shadowed past, she'd have stood up to it better than this." He carefully pushed the cup of tea in front of me.

"Oh Trishna, cup of tea for you!" he crooned in a nasty and teasing tone. "Do let the silly bitch go. I need a better host than this one, before it passes out on me." There was a pregnant pause by everyone at the table as we each waited for something to happen.

"Why don't you go stick that floor sweeping excuse for tea fair up your arse, you decrepit fart of a flea?" Trishna said, in the nicest tone I had ever heard him use. And then used his free hand to flip off Branwyre.

Estella's drunken features clouded with confusion for a moment and then grew ugly as rage took over.

"You unbound my best ghost from me? You interfering waste of space!" roared Branwyre. He tried to swipe at me over the table, but he'd gotten Estella too drunk and she was barely able to move her arm to bat at the air between us.

"Grab her!" he snarled at the remaining thug who had just been sitting there sipping his soda. The thug gave Branwyre a bleary look, me a crooked smile, and then toppled over sideways away from me. What had the little Djinn put in his drink?

"You should have listened to the monk when he said she had a blue aura, Branwyre," tsked said Djinn, suddenly standing by our table again, a tall clear glass of something on a tray in his hand.

Branwyre was trying to get Estella to her feet, but she was scrabbling drunkenly and unable to put both feet under herself at the one time.

"Traitor!" growled Branwyre, now sounding really angry. "A blue aura means nothing, just that she knows her place in the world."

"Actually, when dealing with someone who can bind themselves to a ghost first try, it means they are a rescuer of the damned," corrected the little Djinn, an evil little glint in his eyes. "Purified water, madam?" he asked, holding the tray out to me. As I went to grab it, he held it out of reach.

"If I may suggest a deal first?" he grinned in his oily like manner, "You're going to need a way out of here shortly. Rescue me too and I'll ensure you all get out safe and as alive, or dead, as you were when you arrived. Deal?"

This was all happening too fast and I suddenly realised Branwyre's slurred curses and flailing movements were drawing a lot of attention to us. Most of which seemed to be coming from Mandra. I leapt to my feet, not too sure what to do and found myself turning to Trishna, as he stepped through the chair, for advice.

"Sounds fair to me," he shrugged, "Just make the fetid droppings from a greater demon promise to never come after you to harm you, once released. A free Djinn is going to make a mess and it's best you're never a part of it." I turned a questioning look back to the oily little man.

"Well? I asked him. "If I free you, you've got to promise to never harm myself, my family or those I love. Deal?" he looked angry for a moment, feeling this shouldn't be part of the deal, but then saw Mandra approaching and nodded.

"Deal." He answered, handing me the glass. "But free me first."

Branwyre was now howling swear words more colourful than any I'd heard from Trishna and screeching for assistance from anyone willing to get paid the right price. He had stupidly got my sister's body so drunk that he couldn't get it to do what he wanted it to do. Idiot.

"How?" I asked both the little Djinn and Trishna. Both looked perplexed for a moment.

"That is something you should know how to do," the oily little man hissed. "Don't tell me I've made a deal with a complete idiot?!"

I glared at him, so sick of him, this place and the whole damned Other World situation I'd gotten myself into. No, that Estella had gotten me into. And that damned glowing orange hieroglyph on his forehead was annoying the absolute bejesus out of me.

Then, before I even realised what I was really doing, I dipped my thumb into the purified water and was rubbing it across the mark on his forehead. I just wanted to get the whole stupid situation over and done with. To free him so I could get free of here myself. There came a bellow of protest from the approaching monolith that was Mandra and the great orange haired beast came to a stop.

"What have you done?" Mandra yelled at me. "Releasing a demon like that?"

Oh shit, what had I just done? Wasn't he just some little Djinn? Nothing so bad as a real demon, right?

The little man was suddenly not so little any more, as he used the back of one of his hands to wipe away the moisture I'd left on his forehead.

"Thank you!" he hissed happily, and as he grew he became a whole lot scarier looking. What had I done?

"Well, would you look at that, he really was a demon after all." clucked Trisha with astonished amusement from beside me. I so had to stop thinking he was an expert in any of this, even if he had been exposed to it for over a century.

Great, so I'd just freed an Earthed demon. A real demon and not just a little Djinn. Would Roxanna return my calls when she heard about this?

The newly released — and now considerably bigger and uglier — demon turned from me and approached the one who had obviously Earthed him. This wasn't going to be pretty, and so it was time to leave.

"You stupid afterbirth of a pox-riddled whore!" screamed Branwyre, still trying to get Estella to stand. "You bind yourself to a ghost and then release a demon? What sort of suicide ride are you on?" Oh that didn't sound good, but neither did the sudden screams of panic and nasty crunching sounds that were happening about me. My head hurt, I was sick of this Other World malarkey, and I just wanted to go to bed.

Looking at the glass of salty water in my hand I then threw it into Estella's face.

"Branwyre, eighteenth vampire Lord of the Aegean and complete and utter jerk face, I banish you to my sister's subconscious. Piss off you annoying little turd!" And then I snatched back my sword.

With a howl of rage he was gone, and Estella was sitting there bleary eyed. She tried to focus on me, failed, and as her eyes rolled up into her head, she finally succeeded in falling out of the booth and under the table. Great, this next bit was going to be just so easy! Hauling her dead body about was one thing, having to drag it through the carnage that was happening in the Tormented Whore — and no doubt the Angry Pickle — out to my car was going to be Such. Fun.

Chapter 13

---⊗---

I AWOKE the next day to the sounds of my undead sister being violently ill, repetitively, into the motel bathroom's toilet. Yes, the wonderful sounds, sights and odours I got to wake up to these days. Rather than rush to her aid like any caring person who has never dealt with a friend the morning after a drinking binge, I instead rolled over in bed onto my stomach and groaned angrily at the world in general. She couldn't cry, she didn't need to eat and only slept when she passed out midafternoon, so why the heck could she ralph so loudly at, what was it? Nine in the morning? When I'd only found us this motel, checked in and collapsed into the bed three hours before. Is this what life as a rescuer of souls was like? If so, where did I need to go to resign?

"You're not going to help her, you bedraggled semblance of a drowned rat?" Oh look, Trishna was out of his box and adding to my inability to sleep.

"Trust me." I muttered into my pillow. "The human body knows all the best ways to get rid of too much alcohol without needing me there as a witness. It's like giving birth, it all just finds its own way out and the person doing it is just along for the ride." In my earlier, more caring years, I'd tried to be there for Estella the morning after such nights. All I'd ever gotten was blame, abuse and someone else's vomit on my clothes, shoes and hair. Pass!

"If that is the case and you are now awake, get your bony backside out of that flea-riddled bed and make me some tea." I could tell from his tone it was more wishful thinking than an actual rude request. I angled my arm out from under the blanket and pillow and flipped him the bird in response. Yes he'd been some sort of help the night before, but afterwards I'd made him a cup of tea just before collapsing into bed, as a form of thanks. He'd have to wait a while longer before he was getting a refill.

There was a pause in the gut wrenching sounds coming from the small ensuite bathroom, and I heard it replaced with a sob. This woke me up more than I really wanted to be, and with a sigh, I hauled my sorry arse out of bed and stumbled over to the door.

It was ajar and I could just make out one of Estella's bare feet poking out from beneath the tangled leftovers of last night's dress. Heck, I'd had to drag her dead weight, in said sequiny dress, across two nightclubs, through what remained of the patrons who hadn't fled the demon in time, across the dimly lit car park, into the car, then into this motel room at the other end of the drive. The dress wasn't looking that sleek and shiny anymore and I was guessing neither was the person wearing it.

The smell of all the sticky yellow alcohol Branwyre had had her drink, now regurgitated, kept me from opening the door further.

"Estella, you okay?" I asked warily, waiting for either her usual line of abuse or another outburst of hurling.

"Steph?" I heard her pant warily, and then purge herself a little more. "Am I with you? Or did Branwyre escape the circle and snatch us both?" she sounded concerned, tired, unwell and unhappy. Not the usual bitchy 'blame anyone else for the state I'm in' tones I was used to. It set me back a moment.

"You're safe with me," I said reassuringly. "Yes he got out of the circle, got you drunk and was a complete arse hat. But I banished him when I finally caught up with you, and got you out before the shit really started to hit the fan." Let's just not think about the intestines and other internal body parts I'd had to slip and slide through to get out. I was fairly certain I was in big trouble for releasing a demon, but now was not the time to dwell on that boo boo.

"Where are we?" she managed to gulp between barfs.

"Right across the other side of town from where we were. Hopefully we weren't followed either." I'd driven around a good hour to try and lose anyone I thought may have been following us. Yes I was a rookie at all this, but I was doing my best. Sadly the motel I'd found us in the end wasn't as nice as the last. But it was just meant to be a bolthole for a few hours.

"You okay?" I asked, surprising myself at asking such a dumb thing of her.

She groaned a little before replying:

"Yes and no. I'm still undead, I seem to be expelling half my body weight in some horrid drink, but I'm with you and you've made us safe."

She sighed. "And now, if you'll excuse me, I want to be alone in this private hell induced by Branwyre. Please tell me you're going to kill the bastard." She nudged the door closed with the foot I'd been staring at and I heard the purging continue. I was so shocked at how well she was handling the whole situation, that I almost felt sorry for her. Almost.

***

I was on my second cup of cheap and nasty free hotel coffee when Roxanna called. I had been dreading it and just stared dully at my phone as it wriggled on the floor. As our new motel was nowhere near as nice as the first, there was no little kitchenette or table and chairs to be settled into. Instead I was sitting on the unpleasant old carpet, leaning against the bed staring at the now buzzing phone. Trishna sat cross legged next to me, hunched over his morning cup of Darjeeling, happy in just sitting quietly amongst its steam.

"Don't be a lily-livered, yellow-bellied chicken's bottom," he mumbled in a tone that wasn't quite as harsh as usual. "So you released a demon without the usual banishment after retribution deal. Rookie mistake. It's not as if she can haul your skinny little arse over the coals for it after all the other dumb luck things you got right."

I squinted angrily at him through the steam for a moment. I was fairly certain he'd just given me some sort of compliment. I was going to pretend he had anyway. Before he could disprove me, I snatched the phone up and answered it.

"Roxanna," I started cautiously.

"What news? Are you safe? Is Estella with you? What about our ghost friend, did he behave himself?" she blurted, her normal calm and stately demeanour completely missing.

It took a moment for my sleep deprived brain to absorb her quick fire questions and reply.

"I'm fine, we're fine. Well, as fine as can be expected. We've changed motels, Estella is recovering after Branwyre's possession and abduction, and Trishna has successfully been unbound from him too." There, not a mention of the released demon or carnage it then caused within two nightclubs.

There was a sigh of obvious relief and Roxanna's voice became more its normal self.

"Good. Bless Isis for that miracle. It was a dark night to be out there last night and I'm glad you found her in time."

"Um, yeah, sure." Yes I was floundering. I'd had maybe three hours' sleep in a small, dusty room, and my guilty conscious was almost suffocating me.

"Stephanie, you didn't come across any problems last night, did you?" There was a wary edge now showing in Roxanna's voice. "Trishna was able to take you to where Branwyre had Estella and you were able to get away without trouble, before he was able to make contact with his people. Correct?"

"As far as I'm aware, Branwyre didn't get a chance to meet his people." I replied, on firmer ground as I could speak the truth without having to mention Jamal. "Though I do have the feeling he was waiting for them. It was difficult to tell."

"How so?" she was still sounding wary, as if waiting for me to confess.

"Well, basically he got Estella so blind drunk that the only reason I think I was able to banish him was because she was pretty much legless and passed out from it all soon afterwards. I literally had to carry her to safety."

"Yeah, and we won't mention the bloodthirsty piece of hell on earth in the form of a demon you released to clear the path you walked out on while carrying her," muttered Trishna, inhaling his tea deeply.

"That can be thrown down the sink!" I hissed at him, my hand over the receiver part of the phone. "Just. Don't!" I glared at him a moment longer and then tried to catch up on what Roxanna had been trying to tell me.

"But Estella is okay? She's conscious now?" Roxanna was saying.

"Yes, well as far as I know. She asked to be left alone while hurling up all of last night's cocktails," I replied nervously. Should I sound more concerned than I was about her?

"That will be because she doesn't know how to make her body digest things," Roxanna mused, as if it was an everyday topic. "She hasn't eaten or drunk anything while with you has she?" I thought this over and no, Estella had bypassed all offers of food or drink when not possessed.

"Nothing." I replied, starting to relax a little now we were nowhere near discussing the nightclub.

"Good." Roxanna seemed pleased and I felt I was missing something important. "The newly undead need to learn how to make their bodies do simple tasks like breathe, blink, digest and so on. Her body will simply reject the attempt and, when it comes to eating or drinking, expel the attempt." Oh, that was so nice to know.

"Only a long undead has learnt those tricks of the trade," she went on. "How to eat to maintain their undead body takes a little bit longer, as they need to be able to do that to heal their injuries. If she's started to eat and drink but otherwise remain herself, I would see that as a warning Branwyre's virus was growing stronger in her and was able to control her on subconscious level needs." Well that was just dandy to know now. And what if she'd been fine wolfing down the cold pizza yesterday? Why hadn't this little tip been shared earlier?

"And I'm only being told this now?" I tried to sound polite while asking. Roxanna sighed and sounded as tired as I felt.

"Because I only just learnt it myself last night from someone in the know," she replied wearily. "Look Stephanie, you're doing okay. If Estella is resting and comfortable right now, you should try and catch some sleep too. Trishna can keep watch." I ignored the belligerent monk's scoffing sound. I also ignored the 'Estella resting and comfortable' bit. She'd shut the door on me, I was taking that as a good sign to leave her to it. Whether that meant she was sprawled out on the cold bathroom tiles or half in, half out of the toilet, her choice.

"I will try my best." I answered, my own voice sounding weary in my ears.

"Good." There was the smile sound back in Roxanna's voice. "We will meet at Hale Park at noon today." I took a mental note of the name of the new destination.

"We can then discuss what is to be done about the demon you released last night," she added before hanging up and leaving me gawping at the room in general. How did she do that?

Chapter 14

"MY TEA is cold, make me some more you idle whore. My tea is cold, make me some more you idle whore. My tea is cold, make me some more you idle whore." It was an insistent droning right by the bed and it took me a while to realise it wasn't the clock radio, but Trishna chanting that same charming line over and over again.

I cracked an eyelid, too tired to flip him the bird. When he noticed I was awake, he straightened up from where he'd been bent over the bed.

"You wanted to be woken at eleven in the morning," he remarked grumpily. "It is now eleven oh five. Get your skinny little bag of bones self out of that fungus-filled bed and make me some damned tea!" Urgh, and I had bound myself to him why? At least his choice of words had improved a little.

So I'd maybe gotten a few more hours' sleep, I still didn't feel either happy or refreshed. All the same, I hauled myself out of the bed, managed to flip him the bird on the way to the kettle and flicked it on. I frowned at myself, surely if I treated him better; he might learn to do the same? This whole rude, crude and finger flipping was getting too childish, even for sarcastic old me.

"Did you check on Estella for me, like I asked?" I questioned, moving tentatively towards the bathroom door. All was quiet on the other side.

"I stuck my head through the door," replied Trishna in a frustratingly annoying noncommittal way. "She's still undead and remarkably unattractive for a naked woman sitting on the floor staring at nothing."

I was about to tentatively knock when what he'd said sank in.

"Naked? Trishna, she is my sister and such remarks will get another tea bag burnt." I tried giving him a stern look, but he just shrugged and turned to watch the kettle boil.

I turned back to the door, braced myself for Isis knew what came next, and knocked while entering. It's an art form I'd perfected in the years of having walked in on Estella, in my own home, getting up to all sorts of nasties. The memories of which were burnt into the back of my brain.

"Estella?" I called, trying to hold my breath in case the place still smelt of vomit. Thankfully it didn't. If she'd made much of a mess, Estella had already cleaned it up.

I found her, as Trishna had described, sitting naked on the floor, back against the wall between the toilet and bath come shower. At some point she had cleaned herself up too. All traces of the night before were removed or scrubbed away. She had been staring dully at nothing and now stared sadly up at me.

"I had to get out of that horrendous dress, but I didn't want to go get some new clothes with that ghost out there." She sighed, looking rather sad and pathetic. Again I could have almost felt sorry for her. "I mean, the leer he gave me when sticking his head in here every five minutes was bad enough." There was a shadow of her old spoilt brat pout now showing. But she had a point about Trishna.

"You want me to burn his Lap sang Souchong?" I asked her sympathetically.

"No. That little game he and you play is kind of perverted. What I want are some new clothes please. I may be undead, but sitting on a cold tiled floor naked still isn't the nicest thing to do." Again she had a point, so I made a quick exit and rummaged through the duffle bag until I had a new change of clothes for her. We'd have to stop for new shoes though, as yesterday's sneakers were gone, and I had lost one of the six-inch stilettos Branwyre had gotten her when I'd dragged her out of the nightclubs.

Once dressed, Estella still looked sad and bedraggled, just not so piteous. She sat quietly on the end of the bed as I filled her in on the night before, occasionally glancing towards Trishna who was seated on the carpet hunched over a polystyrene cup of steaming tea. I'd put in a takeaway cup as we were leaving and I couldn't cope with the verbal abuse I'd get for making him leave it behind. What the hell was wrong with me? He was a foul-mouthed, annoying and rarely helpful ghost, and yet I thought of his feelings and made sure I didn't upset him? Damn!

"And he is now blue because he is bound to you?" Estella asked again as I gathered up our gear and shoved it away into the various bags. I'd left Branwyre's dress behind in its gore stained heap in the corner where Estella had thrown it. This time the maid was left a fiver.

"We are bound to each other." Trishna seemed to need to correct her every time she asked the question. She'd done so four times already. I was starting to get worried about what the difference was.

"And you released an Earthed demon?" that was the sixth time for that particular question. I shoved Trishna's tea bags and box into my handbag and started shooing them both towards the door, we would be late otherwise.

"In my defence someone, not too far from us with a tea fetish, kept assuring me he was a more harmless Djinn. And I had him promise to never come after me or anyone I loved." I scooped Trishna's cup of tea off the floor and walked out the door, just expecting them to both follow me to the car as they'd ignored the shooing.

"So you're still a target, undead wonder," teased Trishna as he and Estella did indeed follow me. I tried to ignore the remark, as it made me feel bad about the Estella and me situation. And then I felt bad about feeling bad and got myself into a nasty mood. By the time I'd stashed the luggage in the boot and slammed down its lid to try and vent some of my anger, they were both in the car.

Estella was in her usual spot under the blankets and Trishna, unfortunately, was in the front passenger seat next to where I'd popped his cup into the cup holders. I cursed my car for not having cup holders in the back and then got in. We were going to be late.

***

Hale Park was a little busier than the park we'd met in the day before. Again it had a sundial in the centre of it, and this was again where we found Roxanna. As the day was overcast and had a humid feel of oncoming bad weather, I really didn't see her point in staring at the sundial to tell the time, but she was a High Priestess and I was fairly certain it was one of the less weird things she did.

"Estella!" again it was like long-lost mother and daughter reunited. And, if my undead sibling could still cry, she would have been sobbing as she poured out all the horribleness she'd just endured, including a number of lesser accusations that apparently I had been responsible for.

"And she's released a demon!" she finally gasped, tearing herself away from Roxanna's motherly hug to point at me with a look of accusation. I found it very hard to suppress my sigh and the roll of my eyes.

"You forgot to blame me for the time I told you Santa wasn't real on your sixteenth birthday and that our budgie didn't really turn from blue to green but was eaten by the cat." I said. I couldn't help it. Yes I was feeling dreadful over the demon thing and fully ready for any and all retributions from Roxanna. But Estella's tattling mood just annoyed me.

"Crispin ate Beaky?" Estella squeaked, before hiding her head back on her High Priestess' shoulder.

"And I'm making her walk around barefoot too as we would have been really late if I'd stopped for shoes." I went on to say dryly. "I felt being a bit Dickensian this morning would lighten my mood."

Roxanna gave me a look over my sister's head. I had been expecting disproval or anger, not the tightly held humour I swear I saw.

Once she'd calmed Estella down enough, and they'd shared a small prayer, Roxanna made her sit down on the park bench nearby and meditate in the sun. I was amazed at the mild tone and lack of condescension in her voice. Roxanna then turned her attention to me briefly, before flicking it to Trisha, who I swear was only visible as the sun was hidden by clouds.

"Namaste, Trishna," she greeted him, including the hands clasped in prayer before her, bow. I was surprised, but not as much as when he returned the greeting and motion very politely. And I'd just been about to warn her not to talk to him as I'd expected something rather offensive about me to be added to Estella's tale of woe.

"Thank you for your assistance with the binding and then the rescue of our precious Estella last night," she went on calmly. "I have been in touch with the Lama of a Buddhist temple I know of. He is looking into your plight and hopes to provide a helpful solution to allowing you to move on in peace." Trishna bowed to her again and smiled.

"Thank you, High Priestess. Knowing that you are trying means a great deal to me." Oh God! Where the hell was the usual pain in the arse, peel your ears with expletive words monk I was stuck with?

"Why don't you ever speak so nicely to me?" I demanded, unable to help myself. He blinked a few times in confusion.

"Because you're not the High Priestess of the Temple of Isis," Trishna replied finally, as if stating the obvious. I gave him the squinty eye for the moment, expecting the cuss words that usually followed. But the damned rat fink gave me his best sweet and innocent look. Oh to keep Roxanna with me at all times, to keep these two pains in my arse on their best behaviour.

I realised Roxanna was giving us both a half-amused look and decided to let Trishna's fall into good graces slide for the moment.

As she turned her full attention to me, I held out my wrists to her as if handing myself in.

"Do what you will, I freed a demon and can tell no lie." I said sadly. What else could I say; we both knew I'd done it? I was hoping to at least get some brownie points by offering myself in as the guilty party.

"Yes, I do indeed find that a rather interesting thing," Roxanna remarked calmly, giving both my hands a squeeze before allowing me to drop them to my side. "And you say you've never worked in the occult before?"

It took me a moment to realise she didn't seem at all angry with me. It was a demon, and her lot spent their lives killing such creatures. I'd released one and wasn't in trouble?

"Oh, trust me, you are indeed in trouble," she smiled at me, once more amazing me at how she could read me like a book. "But what my Temple is finding more curious is that you were able to free an Earthed demon in the first place. You should not have been able to do that." She looked me over again and urged me to the park bench next to Estella's. "How exactly did you do it?"

I sat tentatively, thought for a moment, then shrugged. "I don't really know. I mean, he had this orange symbol emblazoned on his forehead, it was lit up like some sort of orange flame." I tried to explain. "It was annoying me each time I saw the little slime ball. Like really annoying me. And so, when he gave me the glass of purified water and demanded I release him as part of our deal, I just wiped the stupid thing off his head. I felt if I got rid of it, I would get rid of him too."

Roxanna sat back in a stunned silence and watched me some more. Personally, at that point, I'd have much rather she'd been angry at me and ranting over the horrific nature of what I had released into the world.

"You saw the mark that held the demon to its master, and you rubbed it out." Roxanna murmured, trying to voice what I'd told her in ways she obviously understood. "You were able to see the mark that made it an Earthed demon . . . and you just wiped it away with purified water?"

I nodded. I wasn't feeling any more comfortable no matter how she reworded it.

"Right, well that is a new one to me, and something we will have to take in our stride." And that was it; she just brushed it aside to deal with later. I, on the other hand, wasn't feeling like ignoring it, as much as I had when I'd first arrived at the park. The way Roxanna worded it was as if I'd done something the average person wasn't meant to be able to do.

"And then there is her blue aura." Trishna decided to add. If I didn't already feel childish enough in front of the High Priestess, I would have burned another tea bag. Why did he need to bring that up?

"And then there is your blue aura . . ." she repeated, musingly.

"But let's not forget my dead sister and how I got stuck in this madness in the first place." I replied, trying to stick to one level of insanity at a time.

"Undead," corrected Estella with a pout, "And yes, it would be nice if people could remember we're trying to help save me right now." Her tone held so much of her old selfish self I could have easily just gotten up and walked away. I had forgotten the pettiness her voice took on when she was talking as if the world revolved around her. Instead, after a look at Roxanna, I just gritted my teeth and tried to stay focused on what the High Priestess was saying instead.

"You are correct, both of you," she said, sharing a kindly look with both Estella and I. "Time is of the imperative here so we must try and focus on one thing at this stage. Are we any closer to finding the crucible?"

I shrugged and looked at Estella, she was the one possessed by Branwyre after all, and surely she had a better idea as to how close we'd gotten to it yesterday. Roxanna turned to her too, giving one of her hands a comforting squeeze after seeing the hunted look in her eyes.

"Last night was terrible." Estella finally said in a small voice. "What little I can really remember of it. But I don't think he did it because we'd gotten too close to finding the crucible. I think he just did it to be in possession of my body." She looked at us both to see if we understood what she was trying to say.

"He wasn't abducting you to stop you from finding it where you were yesterday, he was just taking possession of what he thought was his to use as he willed?" asked Roxanna, obviously getting the gist of it all far better than I did. Estella nodded, looking relieved.

"That's right. I really don't think he cared one way or the other what we did yesterday. Not after we retrieved Trishna and his box from his hide out." She shot the Buddhist ghost a dirty look, still not fully trusting him. "Which is why I don't think the crucible was actually there. He wanted us to go there for Trishna, he encouraged it. I could feel him as we explored the place." She then shuddered and I remembered how she'd spoken about it yesterday and nearly felt sorry for her.

"So he knew it wasn't there, or he wouldn't have been so encouraging for us to be there." I finally felt I had something useful to add to the conversation. "He did say last night it hadn't been there, but I was taking everything he said with a pinch of salt. No pun intended." Estella looked at me with mildly less disgust than she had Trishna. What now?

"That's right. I feel the crucible is held elsewhere. In a place he doesn't want me to know about so is keeping still within me so as not to draw my thoughts or attention to it." Estella agreed. In the level of crazy I had been working on in recent days, this actually made some sense.

"Which is why it is good to now have Trishna on our side." Roxanna announced, smiling towards the shimmering blue shadow still in his place by the sundial. "As I am sure he is aware of far more places the crucible is likely to be held. Am I right, Trishna?"

I braced myself for an onslaught of swearing and obscenities. Instead, we were met with silence.

"I knew he couldn't be trusted," muttered Estella, taking his silence as a personal slight.

"That or he's following the lesson of staying silent if there is nothing nice to be said," I muttered, not impressed by his silence. I'd freed him from Branwyre upon the agreement he would help me. It then sunk in. I had freed him on the agreement of him helping me find my sister last night. I don't think I'd ever stated the help was to continue beyond that.

"What would I have to offer you to help us now with the answer?" I asked him, standing up from the bench and approaching Trishna. "He won't help us without a bargaining chip," I explained to the others.

"But you freed him from Branwyre!" Estella protested. "He is bound to you, he has to help."

"No," I sighed, hoping I was wrong. "I mean, yes he is bound to me and I can use his life force to increase my own, but I seriously don't think that means he has to help me with finding the crucible. I have a funny feeling we only bargained for him to help me find you last night."

At this point Trishna proved me right by giving me a sly wink and looking rather smug. So help me there would be no tea left within one hundred metres of him when we finished our meeting with Roxanna.

"Yes," agreed Roxanna also rising and coming over to us. "As we know, Chinese ghosts can be some of the trickiest to wrangle information out of." She gave Trishna an assessing look. "But they can also play dumb to look as if they know something while they really don't." As we watched him, Trishna's smug look faltered and he shot Roxanna an angry look. I really do feel he would have let her have an earful of disgusting phrases if it wasn't for her religious standing. Yes, I knew who I would put money on in a battle of wills between the two. With a satisfied nod, Roxanna glanced to the sundial, then turned to me.

"Stephanie, if he is willing to help, Trishna is obliged to answer you more truthfully than anyone else. So I strongly suggest you try asking him plain and basic, 'yes' or 'no' questions about the location of the crucible. It is my hope he will answer truthfully what he can. Especially if he wants me to keep talking to the Lama for him." She was starting to sound hurried now. "But as the apex of the sun has been reached, and we are now descending into the Darkness of the day, I must leave you. Contact me when you have found new lodgings. I strongly suggest somewhere to the south this time. Keep a low profile where you can." I took this all in with a nod and another glance at my two wards. Roxanna embraced me quickly before going to say a longer goodbye to the still bedraggled looking Estella.

As we made our separate ways out of the park, the rainclouds above grew thicker and there was a distant rumble of thunder. So, not only did I have to find a new place to hide out in, but I also had to purchase all the binding items destroyed the night before and pray the storm cleared enough to allow the moon to do the double bond tonight so I could get the real location of the crucible out of Branwyre. Yeah, sure, no problems.

Chapter 15

———————⑨———————

NAVIGATING the lunch time traffic, I headed south as directed and started looking for what would hopefully be another one of those nice motel chain places and not the rat hole we'd ended up in in the wee hours of that morning. I also needed a hardware store to replenish my goods. Estella was silent the whole time, staring out dully from under the blankets on the back seat. I couldn't blame her for the silence, as I was fairly certain that even someone who is undead would feel dreadful after what she'd been put through the night before. I didn't even know all of what she'd been through, but what I'd seen was enough for me to let her work through it silently. Heck, it was a wonderful change to not have her filling the silence with inane jabber. Today, sadly, that was going to be my job as I played pedantic twenty questions with Trishna. He, unfortunately, was seated once more in the front passenger's seat. His tea was cold, but he still seemed to enjoy being able to sit up front. He was almost like a dog allowed to stick its head out the window and let its face play in the wind. Thinking on it, despite his attitude toward me, I was fairly certain Trishna had been treated worse than a dog by the last person he was bound to.

"Ever get the opportunity to get out much before we met?" it wasn't the essential and urgent questions I had been lining up in my head, but it was still the dumb one that popped out first. Trishna turned from his study of the building we passed and gave me a quick look of uncertainty.

"Out of what exactly?" he asked puzzled. Oh, I hadn't thought of that. I'd meant out and about in the world, especially during the day. Could he have been kept in his box when not needed?

"Out in the world! Out to see the sights and delights of modern man and how we're screwing up the world." I replied lightly, trying to not think of keeping a sentient life trapped in a wooden box for the better half of a hundred years, it was just such a nasty thought. He looked at me again and shrugged.

"I am a tool used to enhance the powers and ability of the person I'm bound to," he said dully. "Do you take a hammer or saw out of the toolbox and take it sightseeing?" At this I felt really angry. Yes Trishna was a foul-mouthed pain in the arse, but I probably would have been too if used and abused in such a way for so long. And, I might add, if he kept this nicer attitude up I may even try and swing past a Buddhist temple or something and see if he'd like a little time off.

"Look, just cut the crap, you useless handler of the undead. The High Priestess of Isis expects you to grill me so save your putrid breath smelling of a sow's pus-riddled ears, and just get it over with." Or maybe I wouldn't.

"Fine." I said stiffy, trying to ignore the grunt of amusement from the backseat as I casually flicked a tea bag out the window as I drove along. "Answer me truthfully yes or no: were you present when the crucible was used last."

"Of course I was you fetid daughter of . . ."

"Ah!" I warned him, steering with one hand for the minute needed to drag another tea bag from the crumpled box of tea sticking out of my handbag and dangle it out the window. "I said answer me yes or no." I gave him the look I knew he didn't like and waited.

"Yes." He finally muttered. My hand went back on the wheel and the tea dropped through him and onto the seat he was using.

"Did Branwyre's followers believe him to be lost when the ceremony was interrupted?" I continued, working my way through the questions I'd slowly been making up in my head.

"Yes," he muttered again.

"Were you and the crucible always kept together? Being tools of Skid Mark and all?"

"No." Trishna had a slightly pained expression and I wondered whether it was from trying to answer things less than truthfully, trying to answer them with just a yes or a no, or trying to answer them without peeling my ears with profanity.

"Was the crucible taken to the same location we found your box when you were taken there last?" I steamed ahead, wanting to finish the questions before I forgot them.

"No." he replied again, giving me a scowl this time.

"Would you know the crucible if you saw it?" It was a valid, if a little dumb, question.

"Yes," another scowl.

"Would you know if the crucible was stored near you, even if you couldn't see it? Can you like, sense it?" he gave me a look that, in the politest sense, would be saying 'you idiot'.

"No and no." was all he actually said though.

"Do you know the current location of the crucible?" I was nearly at an end and had just spotted the sort of motel I had been seeking.

"No." he sighed and looked out the window away from me. It had started to rain, great, just when I was about to get out of the car too.

"Fine." I ended my questioning as I pulled up in front of the motel office. "Thank you Trishna, I do hope you were being truthful." He looked at me with a startled expression. Was it from me thanking him, or me asking if he spoke the truth? Damn, I realised I hadn't asked him to truthfully answer me yes or no the second time I'd demanded he do it. Damn, would I have to start all over again?

"You're most welcome." He surprised me with that response, that's for sure. "And, yes." I gave him the squinty eye a moment longer and then clambered out of the car.

"Stay here both of you. The last thing I need when trying to check into a motel room unnoticed is a ghost and an undead sister tagging along." I slammed the door and scurried to the office through the rain.

***

Once checked in and the less questionable things unloaded from the car — I still had a bag and a half of salt and the wooden stakes — we set off again. Estella hadn't really wanted to come, but I didn't want her out of my sight. Yes she was going to be playing dead for a few hours soon, but we didn't know for sure if Branwyre had given her description to his flunkies, nor did I feel happy leaving her in one place while I was out and about collecting the things needed to tie her to a chair for the night. Bind her, I meant bind her. If I described it the first way, it didn't make me want to groan when I thought of all the salt and circles ahead of me.

Still, when we found a convenient shopping square of various shops, including a hardware, she decided to stay in the car under her blankets. So I cracked a window, and Trishna and I were off. Heck, he didn't have a choice, as his box was in my bag. Plus I wanted to ask his Other

World advice on item choices. What did I care if I was seen walking around some shops followed by a blue ghost. It was still raining heavily and so he was near invisible in the shadowy verandahs and awnings we passed under. Besides, I'd seen people walk ferrets on a leash in this area and no one batted an eyelid. Different was normal here.

The good thing about the southern suburbs of my city is it had a lovely ethnic blending of cultures. It meant the little shopping complex we had stopped at not only had your usual newsagent's, hardware, independent supermarket, beauty salon and corner deli. It also had, to my hopeful then happy relief, an Asian grocery store tucked away at one end. I swear I could sense when Trishna spotted it too, as his reluctant slouch behind me stiffened a little and the distance between us lessened.

I stopped outside and turned to him, successfully hiding my smile at seeing his usual surly look replaced with a slight look of hope.

"Ready for some more truthful yes or no questions?" I asked, looking over at the entrance of the little store.

"Yes," he said quite neutrally. Nice start, I hoped.

"Good, now I didn't want to ask this in front of Estella, but do you think Branwyre made contact with his people last night."

"Yes," he said uneasily. It wasn't the answer I had really wanted, but it had been the one I'd expected.

"Right, so have you seen any of them following us around today? Recognise any 'Other World' goons tailing us?"

"No and no." he added with more confidence. Well, that was a small relief, right?

"You will tell me if you spot anyone who fits that category, right?"

"Yes." Did he really have to look so bored? I was worried about being lynched here. I still had vivid memories of what Branwyre said his flunkies would do to me if I was caught. My last ditch attempt came next.

"Do you have any possible, even just the slightest, idea of where the crucible is?"

He sighed and looked sadly over at the store as if bidding its contents farewell before even meeting them.

"No." he replied. Meeting my eye he seemed to wait for something. I sighed and let my disappointment show. It wasn't disappointment at him, just at not being able to figure out where the damned crucible was without having to talk to Branwyre, double bound.

"Fine," I then announced to the world in general. "So Skid Mark double binding it is then. I don't suppose there's an 'Other World' shop I can go to where my shopping list won't look so odd and out of place?" Trishna almost smirked at this one, and I could actually see the humour in my stupid question.

"No," he replied, cheering a little after not getting the bawling out he seemed to have been expecting. I mean, I know I could be a bitch, but I hope he was basing the expected ear bashing from his previous 'owner's' behaviour and not just from what I'd shown him so far.

The rain got heavier and a wind started blowing it onto me under the shops eves. I sighed again and headed in.

"Come on then, let's see what they have in the way of tea." I called as I went. He didn't follow and I turned to see why, was there a curse or demon or something I had missed.

"You're still going to give me a reward for that sack of useless horse droppings of answers I just gave you?" he asked bewildered. I shrugged,

"You answered me truthfully, didn't you?" I gave Trishna a suspicious look at this point. I mean, hadn't I just asked in the plainest and most simple manner for him to give me truthful answers? Had he found loopholes I was just too tired and stupid to see?

"I did." He replied, then on seeing my expression added, "Honestly I did. To my absolute best knowledge I have no idea where the cursed thing is. But as I was of no help, why am I being rewarded?" This caused yet another sigh from me; I was really good at them now too.

"Trishna, I may be an utter cow and stroppy at times, but I also like to be nice. You played nicely, barely swore, and answered my questions truthfully. So I'm shit out of luck on finding the crucible without facing Branwyre, welcome to my crappy life! You obviously need some cheering up in this world and if I'm going to be bound to you, I want you in a nicer mood than that paint peeling vocabulary you used on me yesterday." We then stood there staring at each other for a few moments, as if assessing each other.

"Now get your damned nappy-clad butt into this store and choose some tea! You've got five minutes, mister." That shifted him out of his bewildered state and he broke into a half smile, flipped me the bird and pushed past me, almost through me, into the store.

I gave the driving rain one last annoyed look and followed him in. If this rain didn't clear by moonrise I was fairly certain I wouldn't be able to bind Branwyre. And then what? Beheading undead sister time? Quite a large part of me actually hoped not.

***

I looked out at the heavy downpour with an even heavier heart, only half listening as Estella carried on to Roxanna on my phone, on loudspeaker, about the calamity we faced that night.

"And you're sure the weather isn't going to let up before tomorrow's dawn?" asked Roxanna's normally calm voice, though it now held a sharp edge of concern. I looked back over at Trishna and gave him a questioning look.

He sat back from within his cloud of white tea's steam — what can I say, I'm a sucker for the underdog — and sighed.

"As I said before, you with the rat's nest hair and face like a horse's arse, I am not a weather station. But I feel it in my chi that it isn't letting up before tomorrow." I winced, sadly knowing that was as polite as he would get, despite the horrendously expensive tea I could now threaten to burn.

"Then you must come back and we will try and bind you within the Light of Isis," insisted Roxanna again. This is what she and Estella had been arguing about for the last ten minutes or so.

"As I have said, High Priestess, that is unacceptable." This was Estella's second attempt to explain, "The demon stain grows stronger in me every night and I will not risk my beloved Temple in such a way."

"I could always behead you." I stated dully, really seeing no true fix to our situation. Yes I could bind Branwyre, but unless I double bound him with the light of Isis, I wouldn't be able to control the situation or find the damned crucible.

"Also an unacceptable option," came Roxanna's voice sternly over the phone. It matched the cross look Estella was giving me. What? I hadn't been that serious, honest!

"Fine," I said more reluctantly than I actually felt. "So, is there another source of the Light of Isis that I can use? I mean, does she have a wet weather cousin that can help us out?" That comment didn't go down so well amongst the women in white robes either. Oops. I then spent the next ten minutes copping an earful from Estella about my total disrespect for the sanctity of Isis — like she could talk — while

Roxanna's patient undertone tried to explain things to me on a dumber level.

"Okay!" I finally shouted at them both, I couldn't help it; they were giving me major systems overload here. "Just tell me this then, what exactly is it in this Light that binds him. Your Goddess and the purity of the moon aside. Why does the light affect him so much?"

There was a puzzled silence. "Vampires can't stand in the light of day," Roxanne explained patiently. "Not just because of the theological Light it shines into their Darkness, but because the virus is light sensitive. It cannot cope with being exposed to UV light for long periods of time."

And that, my friends, was when a little light of my own dinged on in my head and even Trishna looked worried by the sudden smile it caused on my face.

Chapter 16

———————— ⊙ ————————

IT HADN'T been easy, for many reasons, but hours later I found myself staring nervously at my latest attempt at a purified circle of salt. The reason it hadn't been easy was because it had taken a lot of time to convince Estella and Trishna as to what we needed to do. Even Roxanna had sounded incredulous over the phone, but quite frankly she wouldn't have been able to stop me unless she decided to get in her Goddess mobile and come and find me.

And so within hours of moonrise, currently still hidden by the torrential downpour, I had driven us back to the now closed and thankfully deserted shopping centre. Where, working in unison on lock and security devices, Estella and Trishna had broken into the beauty salon. You see, despite current laws saying to get rid of them, I had remembered seeing a sign on our last visit mentioning a sunbed.

Call me crazy — I mean hello, of course I was to be in this stupid mess in the first place — but a sunbed was just something that gave you massive doses of UV, right? Roxanna had said that this wasn't something old Skid Mark was going to be best pleased with, thanks to the virus that he was being sensitive to it.

Look, it was worth a shot, okay? I wasn't going to be able to double bind him anyhow. And Estella looked like she could use a bit of colour to her skin.

As luck would have it, the power cord for the device hung down from the ceiling and would therefore technically not cross the circle on the floor. As neither Estella nor Trishna could tell me if it really did mean it would classify as an unbroken circle, I just ignored them, cleared a space and got to work.

By then, as I quite frankly didn't feel this was going to be the best binding ceremony in the world, I didn't bother with purifying the floor. It smelled enough of bleach and other chemicals in here as it was. I had, however, purified the rope with which I then spent a lot of time and muttered swear words figuring out how to tie Estella to the sunbed. It had also been given a quick wipe down with purified water, which I was now afraid might have shorted it out. Look, if I was going to die tonight, I may as well go out with originality and style, right?

Trishna found the whole situation highly amusing, and kept telling me so in his usual not so polite grasp of the English language, as I got Estella ready. She was totally unimpressed with the idea, however, and when her mouth wasn't pursed in her best matron mode, it was flapping about how irresponsible I was being and how I should stop treating the situation like a big game on how to embarrass her further than she already was. I had, however, made a great show of setting up my newly purified sword nearby, and kept commenting on how the sunbed was almost the perfect height for a chopping block. Sadly, it actually was, and we both knew if this really didn't work, beheading Estella would be the last thing I tried. Probably ever.

I soured Trishna's jubilant mood when I informed him he was being left in the circle to operate the sunbed. I wasn't about to tie the already tightly bound Estella to it, switch it on, make my circle and let her slowly crispy fry until Branwyre turned up. Despite my major dislike for my sister, I didn't hate her that much. Plus, think of the smell. And so instead Trishna was commanded, as my bound ghost and tool, to stay in the circle and flip the switch just as Branwyre turned up. He hadn't been happy about it, but could see my point. Especially when I made it while holding his newly purchased white tea in one hand and my lighter in the other.

So, undead sister bound tightly from head to foot had been laid upon the sunbed. I had then done my best to tie her into place, wondering if I could use purified ocky straps next time, if I ever got a chance to try it a second time. Once satisfied Estella was secured, I made my circle of salt, leaving the two of them complaining on the inside as I sealed it with me on the other side.

I had then found a convenient chair, made myself as comfortable as I could with my sword on my lap and rehearsed what I hoped I was going to get to say that night. In a way, I sort of wish I'd gotten a chance to call my folks to say goodbye, just in case. But a part of me had refused to let it happen, saying such a defeatist attitude would mean I would definitely fail. By not calling them, I was giving myself a fighting chance? Yeah right!

It was with my heart beating wildly that I stood slowly to my feet at the first feel of Branwyre's slimy presence. As I did so, I gave a nod to Trishna. I was fairly certain the binding wasn't going to hold, but I was really hoping the UV light would at least slow Branwyre down. There was a purified bucket of salt water at my feet too; it was banishment or death time. Oh joy.

I don't know exactly how he did it, but Trishna reached his hand into the sunbed and it soon started. Ghost powers? He was a tool to extend my own power after all. Wasn't that a stomach churning thought?

As the sunbed flickered into life, the body of my sister within it went from testing the ropes and peeking out at me in mild confusion and amusement to a stiffened form gritting back a scream of pain. Oh good, maybe this was going to work after all. I cleared my throat, time to see if the next bit worked.

"Branwyre, eighteenth vampire Lord of the Aegean, I have twice bound you with the aid of Isis, so answer me true." My voice held steady and you could barely hear in my tone that I was telling a bit of a porky.

"No you haven't you filthy, septic, pustule of a hell's spawn's leftovers!" screamed Branwyre as he writhed in my sister's body in the light blue glow of the bed. "Release me from this torturous device before I . . ." he had to stop at the point, in obviously too much pain to continue. Part of me hoped Estella wasn't in as much pain as he was right now.

"Just shut up, you filthy little Skid Mark and listen!" I thought I had growled this, I had wanted to, but was surprised when I met Trishna's eye to see it was him who had said it. He actually seemed to be enjoying the show too.

"You double crossing shadow of my creation," Branwyre hissed at him through the pain. "Release me now if you ever want to see the afterlife."

"Fornicate with your demon maker until Judgement Day, you scum from a pox ridden whore." Yup, Trishna was enjoying it, possibly getting some of his own back at last. "I am no longer bound to you, so you can just writhe in pain, you pustule of a leper's dried nut sack." Ew. I think that was enough from the bound help for now.

"Branwyre, eighteenth vampire Lord of the Aegean, I have bound you in a purified circle to a sunbed and it obviously stings like a bitch —

and I assure you it was done with the aid of Isis — so answer me true or I'm turning you into a crispy fried Lord of the fricking Aegean." Man I had been hanging around with the wrong crowd to find it so easy to talk like that. It would have been depressing if it wasn't for the zing of adrenaline keeping me going at that point.

"I will pry your eyes out with my teeth and defecate in the empty sockets," growled Branwyre, trying to hold back the obvious scream of pain he so badly wanted to release. Trishna started saying something, but I'd had enough. It really wasn't pretty seeing Estella in so much pain, no matter how much pain she had caused me.

"Just. Shut. Up!" I snarled through gritted teeth. And they both did. Hopefully it meant Branwyre was bound all the same. Hopefully.

"Branwyre, you virus dwelling waste of space, what is the current location of your ceremonial crucible?" I demanded, trying for a slightly nicer tone. I had tried to word it in the plainest English as I could. "Answer me true now, or spend the rest of the night slow cooking."

"You shall burn in the pit of torment while my legions of the damned rape your parents and destroy your home," growled Branwyre, obviously not as bound to answer me as I'd hoped.

"That's nice." I said in a really not so nice tone. "The clock is ticking, Branwyre. I can let you slowly burn, I could break the circle and cut your head off, or you can tell me where this damned crucible is so I can at least kill my sister in a nice way. Your call, Skid Mark."

All was then silent, but for the muted whimpers from my sister's body and the steady buzz of the sunbed itself. As I watched, Branwyre turned Estella's face back towards me and stared balefully out at me from under the lid of the bed. Just stared, nothing else. What, he was going to have a waiting game?

Fine! I sat myself back down, sword across my lap again and just stared neutrally back. At least Estella was going to get a bit of colour.

This went on for maybe another ten minutes, before Branwyre cracked. About time too.

"You are wasted working for Isis," he growled through the obvious pain. "You would make the perfect torturer for my group. If I was going to let you live for this injustice."

"What is the address of where your crucible is currently located?" I said in as calm a tone as I could. Ignoring the rest.

"I don't know." Branwyre grunted in obvious pain. "Banish me so we can play again tomorrow night you putrid breath of a plagued beggar." Really? That was all he could come up with? Hopefully that meant the pain was getting to him.

"Fine. If that is true — and I'm not saying I fully believe you — what is the address of where the crucible is usually kept? Remembering you are bound by me and must answer true."

He muttered something rather rude about where I could stick my commands and whimpered in pain once more. I could keep waiting if I had to. I leaned back in my chair as if to prove this point.

"Banish me you half-witted whore!" he screamed. "I cannot think straight to give you the desired answer." Or, my cynical mind silently added, think enough to give me some made-up answer for another wild goose chase.

"I wonder how you treat the undead for sunburn?" I mused out loud instead, pretending to check my nails. Then winced from the shriek of pain that ripped through the beauty salon. As it seemed to be a mixture of Estella and Branwyre's voices, I started to really wonder how much pain I was also putting Estella through right now. From my expression, Trishna could tell I was starting to waver.

"Don't weaken now," he said. "The cesspit-scented bum wipe is almost at breaking point." And, hey twenty minutes in a sunbed would have me wanting to get out and scream, so I could see his point.

"You shade of a wasted life!" hissed Branwyre at hearing this. He really looked in a lot of pain right now and I was starting to feel very uncomfortable about being the person who was inflicting it. I mean, yes he was some horrendously putrid life sucking, evil bastard. But what was I if I was causing him so much pain? Did it make me just the same? Worse?

"Answer me true." I demanded again. "Where do you think the crucible is currently kept?" I was going to have to end this soon, one way or another.

"The Fallen Church of the Unforgiven," Branwyre finally hissed through my sister's gritted teeth. "All crucibles of lost Lords are taken there in remembrance of our glory-filled days."

I quickly took a mental note of this location, still not trusting the information completely, but hey. He really did seem broken from that lack of originality in his last insult. I mean, it was so lame I could have made it up. I sighed and glanced to Trishna, who gave me the briefest of nods.

"Right then." I announced, clearing my throat and really hoping the next thing I said would work, "Branwyre, eighteenth vampire Lord of the Aegean, I banish you back to the depths of Estella's subconscious. So just go away and don't come back tonight as I need my beauty sleep."

I watched as he writhed within my sister for a few moments longer and was about to reach down for the purified bucket and try again when her whole body shook and shuddered, and was still. A minute later it started writhing again, but as it was Estella's petulant voice that whimpered:

"Turn it off! Turn it off! Turn it off!" and I could no longer feel Branwyre's sickly presence, so I gave a sigh of relief, and nodded to Trishna to do just that. Wow, I'd made it through alive, now what?

***

It was some hours later when we stepped out of the beauty salon and the door snicked shut, locked, behind us.

Yes it had been me who decided to break in and use their facilities uninvited. But that didn't mean I wanted to leave it in a mess. I'd released the rather tender-to-touch Estella and sat her down to one side while I'd swept the floor, rearranged the salon back to how I thought it had been and ensured there was no visible trace that we had ever been there. It had taken me a while as all my dearly undead sister could do was wince and whimper, she was barely pink — I swear. And all Trishna could do was point out spots I missed. Tool to extend my own powers or not, he was useless with wielding solid objects and we both knew it.

Still, it had stopped raining and the late night suburban air had that freshly cleansed smell to it you often got after a decent amount of rain, even in the centre of big cities. And so I set out, sword sheathed at my side, coils of rope over one shoulder and bag containing Trishna's box and tea over the other and the leftover half a bag of salt in my left hand. To one side — my dishevelled, and slightly burnt, undead sister with the banished soul of a vampire stewing in her subconscious. To my other side — the blue shade of a Buddhist monk I had bound to myself. Was there ever an odder group of people to be walking down a deserted back alley, still dripping with rain, at four in the morning? If there was, I couldn't think of one.

And despite the horrendous ordeal I had just put us all through, I actually felt quite chipper at that moment. To the point I glanced at both my companions and gave a brief smile. More surprising, they both returned it. We had a new address for the crucible we could try tomorrow, erm I meant later today. After I caught up on some much needed sleep that was. Things in this crazy life I was currently in were actually starting to look better. Yay me!

It was then I discovered my car had been stolen, skid marks on the damp ground showing where it had been until recently.

"Oh come on!" I yelled in frustration. I had been saving the world after all, so why the heck did some sick bugger have to steal my car?

While Estella groaned at this, Trishna stepped forward and sniffed at where my car had been.

"Fond of the car, were you?" he then asked, straightening up and quizzical.

"Not particularly." I muttered darkly, what did he care? "I can't say I am that fond of any cars or the whole driving experience at all." I then turned my dark look on Estella. "Not any more." I added as a stab at her. She had the decency to look ashamed as we both remembered why. But I was so not stepping any further down into that deep and dark memory right now. Instead, as it was only a few kilometres to our motel, I decided we would just have to hoof it.

"Curious," was all Trishna said, as if Estella's and my sibling exchange had been invisible to him. He was annoying me now and as we set off, I glanced at him and knew from his smug grin he knew it and was enjoying this new way of tormenting me. And he expected to reach enlightenment at the end of all this? Fat chance.

***

We found my car. Though I sort of wished we hadn't. It appeared someone had driven it at speed into our motel room. We were now watching from within a crowd, as the fire department tried to get under control the ensuing fireball it had caused. It had consumed my room completely, but I really did hope they could save most of the rest of the motel. What in the hell?

I found myself in the tension filled situation, to be holding Estella's hand tightly in my own. It wasn't for comfort, more really to ensure she stayed with me in the crowd and wasn't whisked away by whoever had driven my car into my motel room. Yes, I was taking it personally, wouldn't you?

I didn't really like the idea of being so close to Estella, or Branwyre for that matter, but was finding comfort, small as it was, in the tingling sensation I felt down my other arm from where Trishna had stepped into me to protect me. Whether he was doing this out of duty or just in case Estella suddenly grew fangs and bit me, I have no idea.

"You can't say you exactly loved that motel room, or anything in it, could you?" asked Trishna lightly as we watched the drama unfold. I was so on edge I failed to try and spot the cutest firefighter. How tragic!

"Um, should I have?" I found myself answering his dumb question with one of my own; it was the best way to not be swearing right now.

"Trishna, don't tease. She can't see it, okay!" this was from Estella, who gave my hand a tight squeeze. "Let's not rub it in."

This brought me out of my miserable but mesmerised stare at the flaming motel. What were they not saying right now? I gave them each a quizzical, grumpy, look. Trishna was mildly suppressing a grin while Estella was trying to look sympathetic, without succeeding.

"The good thing is I can assure you it wasn't one of Branwyre's people who did this," she said in her version of a soothing tone. It wasn't that helpful. What did they know that I didn't? What had she said about me not being able to see something?

"Who then?" I asked, now getting more angry than bewildered.

"There is spirit writing here." Estella went on to say. "Something only visible to the dead, undead and major creatures of Darkness." How comforting, not!

"And?" I demanded, possibly squeezing her hand too tight. I was about ready to cancel my membership to the freaking 'Other World' and leave these two to their own fate. I think they sensed this too, as even Trishna relented.

"'With my deepest thanks, Jamal'" Trishna intoned, as if reading something written right in front of us. The demon I'd released had done this? That rat fink bastard had promised to leave me alone and this is how he repaid me? I groaned loudly as all the hints Trishna had been giving me sank in. When I had released Jamal, I had made him promise to never harm myself, my family or those I love. Nowhere had I mentioned cars, motel rooms or newly acquired vacuum cleaners.

"Damn your fricking loopholes all to hell and the Darkness beyond it!" I found myself yelling to the world in general. I felt mild relief from it, but the looks I was now getting from the crowd around us filled in the void my emotional release had created rather quickly.

"Forgive us, she is not feeling herself." apologised Estella, in her best Priestess' tones, to those closest to us before manoeuvring me to the outskirts of the crowd, away from the fire.

"That rat fink stinking bastard of hell's most unwanted," I swore as we moved away.

"That's my girl, better out than in I always say." Trishna smirked, enjoying seeing me down at his level of use of the English language. I was too angry to respond with tea burning retaliation, and too embarrassed at my already foul-mouth to dare say any more too. Instead I dropped the bag of salt I had still been carrying and gave it a darn good kick.

"I may not have loved it, but that was my car! He had no crapping right!" I fumed, as my undead sister hustled me, now hobbling slightly, away further.

"Was he just asking to be added to my 'to do' list of Other World things to tidy up? As he is so on there now!" I couldn't help it. This had been the last straw after being forced into this crazy paranormal world only a few days before. This just wasn't fair. I'd spent the last few hours not only fighting off a right evil sod of a vampire, but got the location of his crucible and even cleaned up afterwards to ensure I wasn't getting into the bad books of the innocent people I happened to be involving. And some demon filth I had freed had to go and repay me by trashing my car and destroying an innocent motel? The bastard! I had had enough!

"I quit!" I screamed, drawing more attention from the crowd. Wrenching my hand free of Estella's I stormed off. The end! That was it, all over and done with.

Chapter 17

———————⊗———————

THE things you forget about in your moments of complete and utter anger and resignation of the situation you find yourself in. Like the fact I may have left Estella standing bewildered and alone outside a blazing motel, but I'd still not only had my sword and a large coil of rope with me, but my bag and therefore Trishna's box. Bugger.

Still, it took me a while to realise all this. In the mean time I had found a crappy fast food joint that was still open and who were prepared to serve me their doubly crappy coffee, sword and all.

It was as I was cooling off, along with the coffee, sometime later that I caught the flicker of him out of the corner of my eye. How Trishna had managed to stay so quiet and unnoticeable until then I'd had no clue. Still, he had the decency to look repentant when I shot a glare at him. So after I had convinced the fast food attendant to sell me a cup of plain hot water, I put some of his tea into it to show he was allowed to join me at the counter I was sulking at.

He did, still repentant and blissfully silent, and so I continued my glum stare out at the world on the other side of the plate glass frontage of the shop.

If I hadn't felt it would draw even further odd looks towards myself that night, I would have started banging my head against the counter top when I spotted Estella and Roxanna approach the doors into the place. I so didn't need this right now; couldn't they at least have let me have a good old sulk until morning? Dawn was nearly here as it was.

I felt the sudden tingle of Trishna touching my arm and looked down at it and then up to his face. What in the —? He was comforting me? Or warning me?

"You are worth the effort you know, you pain in the bottom of a broken backed old woman."

Despite my miserable, overtired, and over emotional mood, he made me smile. Damn him.

"Here she is, High Priestess!" Estella said, sounding more eager and relieved than the shrill and accusing I had expected her to be. I turned away from Trishna and shot them both a wary look. As if the minimal staff in this place didn't think I was weird enough as it was, Roxanna in full High Priestess garb would definitely give them something to whisper about in the freezer room.

"My dear child, are you all right?" came Roxanna's soothing question as she approached. I turned away from her, not allowing her to give me the usual loving embrace I knew she'd use on me to make me feel better. I was sulking and didn't want to feel better just yet.

"Your Pagan network must be broken," I announced to the world in general. "Didn't you hear I quit your stinking job?"

"I see," Roxanna replied slowly, easing herself gracefully up onto a stool next to me. "And is that really the best response to all the mayhem and mess you've caused me? To just up and quit, when things are getting interesting?" her tone was still light, but held the judgemental tone of a cherished school teacher. Damn.

"The mess I've caused you?" I gaped at her, turning once more to look her right in the eye. "If you bunch of white robed crazies hadn't gotten my sister into beheading bad guys in the first place, none of this mess of mine would have happened!" I was surprised I hadn't sworn, but Roxanna had that effect on people. I had, however, been overly loud and was sure the fast food attendants would enjoy adding that to their gossip about early morning freaks after we left.

"White robed crazies, of all the irreverent, uneducated and ..." Estella was still standing at Roxanna's side and this was her contribution to the conversation. It was cut off by a politely raised hand and look from Roxanna. On my right, Trishna seemed to be ignoring us all while immersed in his white tea's steamed bliss. Let the guy have it, I wasn't the only one who'd had a rough night. Why was I thinking like that? Why did I care if the ghost of a complete stranger, and total pain in the bum from what I could gather, felt? For that matter, why did I care so much as to not swear out loud in front of some so-called High Priestess of a phoney baloney Temple of Isis? While all this skittered through my, in desperate need of sleep, mind Roxanna just watched me in her patient cat and mouse way.

"Sorry." I suddenly found myself saying to her. And I meant it too, even if I wasn't too sure as to which recent thing I was apologising for.

"That is perfectly all right," Roxanna soothed with a smile. "You have been put through a lot recently Stephanie and I can understand your need to blow off steam and have a minute to yourself." She then took a moment to look around at our little group. "But you need to be proud of everything you have accomplished in these last few days too. Promising to help save your sister from purgatory, releasing a ghost bound to a vampire Lord, and finding the location of the crucible . . ."

"Binding a foul-mouthed ghost to myself, releasing an Earthed demon and allowing him to destroy two nightclubs and I don't know how many people, getting my car and a motel burnt to the ground . . ." I added.

"Don't forget giving your undead sister a pretty bad case of sunburn," the still rather pink Estella said, with a smile in her voice. I stopped staring at Roxanna for a moment and shifted my attention to Estella. She wasn't upset I'd gotten her burnt? What the?

"Bad things happen sis, but if you do them while striving to make the world a Lighter place, it's not always as bad as it seems. It's what I've been trying to explain to you." Oh God, I mean Isis, if Estella was being this nice to me it meant she really needed my help. What right did I have to be sitting here at now five in the morning having a pity party? Yes I so deserved it, but I had made a promise to her and Roxanna. Trishna and I also had a similar sort of deal going. So some horrible little demon destroyed my car, and a motel with it? I had just double bound and banished a goddamned vampire Lord with a fricking sunbed! So what if I now had no transport or a place to sleep, I couldn't let the bad guys win when I was so close to ending all this rubbish. Once it was all over would be the time to curl into a ball and continue the pity party and have a bit of a cry. Just add it to the misery of laying my sister to her final rest, again, and allow myself to spend the week in bed with several kilos of chocolate and a few bottles of red wine. Right?

"I can't let the Darkness win, can I?" was what I actually whispered, facing Roxanna once more. She gave me a sympathetic look and shook her head.

"No my dear Stephanie, you have too big a heart to let something as silly as that happen." She smiled a little, in sympathy, as tears pricked my eyes. Sometimes I just wish I hadn't been the one born all heart, as it was probably why my sister had had none until she'd met Roxanna and her blessed Isis.

"Fine!" I then announced, swinging off my stool and going and grabbing two take away lids for Trishna and my drinks. "Find me a safe place to get a few hours' sleep, get me some transport in the morning and point me at the closest department store for a change of clothes and I will recant my resignation." I sighed, not as much from the delight in Estella's face, or the hug Roxanna was finally able to give me, but from the whole damned stupid mess I was stepping back into.

"Oh, and someone find me the 'How to kill demons for dummies' book as I'm starting a new hobby." I must have been feeling better, my sarcasm was back!

***

I awoke some hours later, stretched out in the super soft bed, and for a moment just let myself lie there in the quiet, dimly lit room, listening to the bird song from its high window blend nicely with the distant chanting song of the Priestesses of Isis.

Yes, after much protesting and a near temper tantrum that would have put me on par with the old Estella, I had finally given in to Roxanna's suggestion of going to the Temple to rest. As I had already banished Branwyre for the night, and Trishna hadn't spotted any of his flunkies following us, Roxanna felt it was the safest place to be for the moment. I, on the other hand, thought it went totally against everything she had originally told me when I had been forced to find a motel, but by then I was really too tired to put up much of a fight and just wanted to sleep. Hell, I'd have taken a bench at the central bus station if she'd suggested it, how much of a difference could her Temple have been in comparison?

Quite a bit actually, as I had been hustled to cloisters — previously unknown to me — at the back, given a fresh nightie and tucked into a remarkably warm and comfortable bed. Weren't religious types meant to sleep on hard boards in draughty dormitories?

It was with these thoughts I had quickly drifted off to sleep, knowing Estella was safely laid out under the Light of Isis in their very deep basement and Trishna was wherever I'd left my bag in the confusion of being prepared for bed by a lot of well-meaning, and overly hands-on, white robed ladies the previous night. Or should I have said, just a few hours ago. I sat up slightly in bed and grimaced at the nightie I found myself in, as it damn well made me a white robed lady right now too, being one of those full length frilly Victorian replicas.

"The abysmal lank haired walking curtains don't know how to make a decent cup of tea if their lives depended on it," came a grumpy tone from the corner of my darkened room, proving some well-meaning soul had brought my bag into me as I slept. And Trishna's damn box along with it.

"And a delightful good morning to you too, oh shade of happiness and sunshine," I replied in an overly light, and possibly too sarcastic for the hour, tone. Although I could barely make him out in the dim light, I was fairly certain he flipped me the bird. The fact he stayed quiet other than that was nice though. Maybe he was mellowing at last?

"What time is it?" I then asked, deciding I couldn't stay in the uber comfy bed all day.

"Do I looking like a walking clock you hairy legged, tatty haired ex-cuse for a female?" came the grunt from the shadows. Or maybe he wasn't mellowing as much as I'd thought.

"No, but you don't look like someone deserving a decent cup of tea either." I said bluntly, now out of bed. I looked about the small stone walled room, wondering where the hell my clothes were. Yes my sneakers and handbag were over in the corner where Trishna sat, but the only other items in the room was the bed, an empty wardrobe and the rickety chair said ghost was perched on.

"Where the hell are my clothes?" I complained, slamming the wardrobe door. "I am so not going to be seen wandering around in a white frilly robe all day. What if someone mistook me for one of the damned curtain wearers?"

"Oh Isis forbid that ever happens." It was Estella's half-amused voice as she opened the room's door unannounced and came in, dressed in white robes herself, carrying a pile of my freshly laundered clothes. Of course they would have cleaned them for me while I slept. The good guys always did considerate things like that. I gave Estella the once over, deciding it wasn't worth the energy to go all Trishna on her. Was it the light in this room, or did she look less sunburnt this morning?

"The Light of Isis holds healing properties, even for the undead," she remarked, as if reading my thoughts. "Here are your clothes." She dumped them on the bed and grabbed Trishna's box. "Come, shade of a foul-mouthed monk, let's allow my dear sister to get dressed in private." She'd said the last bit rather tersely, and you could tell she didn't like having to touch his wooden box, but I appreciated the thought. Especially after the look of mild disappointment Trishna shot me as he left. Oh he was so not reaching enlightenment with that attitude.

***

Dressed and with my horrible hair mildly tamer and bag on my shoulder, I left the room and wandered out into the long hall that connected all the rooms within the cloister. Estella and Trishna stood at the other end of the hall, which had thankfully been over one hundred metres away from where I had been changing. Taking the box back from Estella, and shoving it back in my bag, I asked what our next move was, and seriously hoping it included a hugely unhealthy and very greasy breakfast.

"Roxanna is waiting for us in our refectory," Estella replied, obviously happy to be relieved of the box and its attendant ghost.

The refectory wasn't the bare stoned hall of long wooden tables and benches my mind had stupidly suggested to me. It looked more like the little dining room of an old style hotel, consisting of brightly painted walls, carpet and a scattering of tables and chairs. There was even a row of cereals, juices and bain-maries steaming in one corner. It was also thankfully empty but for the High Priestess. Obviously my idea of them living an ascetic and bare lifestyle could now completely go out the window. Comfy warm beds, decent smelling food, I was starting to see why the life as a Priestess of Isis at this temple was so tempting to those lost in the world. As we approached Roxanna's table, one that was slightly more ornate and grander than the others, she rose from another one of those wonderfully carved throne-like chairs, and ushered me over to the food. Man, she was good to me. With my plate liberally loaded with bacon, eggs and various hardy breakfast staples, we headed back to her table. Before sitting down, I did have the forethought to go back and pour some of the available hot water into an empty mug. Returning to the table I served Trishna his tea before starting on my meal.

I looked up at the silence that followed, as I'd fully expected Roxanna to start talking as soon as I started eating. Estella sat there cross armed and disgruntled, whether at not being able to eat, or me for making a pig of myself, I don't know. Trishna sat enveloped in steam with a grateful and happy look on his face and Roxanna just sat there, one elbow on the table, chin cradled in her hand, giving me a look of mixed emotions. Amusement, bewilderment and admiration being the ones I recognised in the blend.

"What?" I asked, having the decency and manners to swallow my mouthful first.

"You serve your tool of a ghost before you serve yourself is 'what'," Estella said, jumping in before Roxanna could reply. "After all you've been through surely he could have waited until you'd looked after yourself."

There was so much of the old Estella tones in her words I had to bite back my original response with a sigh. "A bit of the pot calling the kettle black there," was all I muttered, focusing on cutting up my bacon and sausages. When I'd finished I looked up at Roxanna with a frustration.

"Seriously? I am being judged on making him a quick cup of tea before sitting down to eat. If I hadn't I would just have to sit here listening to both of them bitch, instead of just the one."

Roxanna's face chose a more neutral expression and she leaned back in her chair. "That was a little uncalled for," she said. "Yes Estella could have worded it better, but she was just voicing her concern for where your priorities are." I shot Trishna a look at this, wondering how he was enjoying getting me in trouble over something as basic as adding tea leaves to damned hot water. Yes it was tea that cost over forty dollars a kilo, but it kept him quiet okay? He had the decency to look a little uncomfortable over it all. I just turned back to Estella and Roxanna.

"Look, from what I can tell, his last hundred years or so haven't been the nicest they could be. So I spoil him with the tea. But it really does allow me to enjoy a meal, without phrases that would peel paint off the walls." I refused to meet Trishna's eye over this. I wasn't feeling sorry for him, honest. He was just someone else I was trying to save, like Estella. "How is it any different from offering you cold pizza, it used to be your favourite." I asked Estella.

"It is more the fact you unthinkingly put them before yourself that had me interested." smiled Roxanna, "I simply find it bewildering that someone with such a big heart is so defensive about her actions." I supressed another sigh, I really had been doing that too much lately. All this talk was doing was making my eggs and fried foods congeal in an ugly way on my plate.

"I'm a big sister; it's built into me to put those I'm looking after first." I said dismissively and started eating once more. Hopefully they'd realise it meant I was done with the subject.

"It's not something that a lot of big sisters do, and is something that should be seen as a gift to those it is bestowed upon." I looked up at Roxanna after she said this, to find her attention focused on Estella. And surprise, surprise my dearly undead sister actually had the decency to look repentant. I could live with that look on her face.

I turned back to my breakfast, feeling I really wanted something in my stomach before the day got any worse. I mean, I'd been criticised for serving a ghost, before meeting my own needs and now used as the poster pin up of how a person should really behave. If anything more deep and meaningful was to happen, I wanted to clear my plate of its delicious breakfast and at least be on my fourth coffee.

"Trishna tells me you have what you hope is the address to the crucible's location?" Roxanna announced, after a few minutes silence. I glanced up again, the last piece of sausage poised on my fork; she had that amused look in her eyes again, uh-oh.

"Information gained through a, um, rather unconventional way," she added. I shrugged and kept eating. I was new to all this mumbo jumbo after all; of course I was going to go about it like an idiot.

"She could have gotten herself killed or worse, possessed, if he'd gotten out of it," Estella protested, but after Roxanna's earlier pointed look, she appeared to be trying to play nice.

"I had the sword and a bucket of salty water ready. If he had got out I'd have gone down swinging," I muttered grumpily. I really didn't want to be reminded about exactly how stupid I had been the night before. Yes, the whole interview with a vampire on a sunbed had actually worked, but how much of that was down to pure dumb luck and how much was down to me really thinking it through?

"It was a very ingenious way of solving a nasty problem," was all Roxanna said, although her eyes were glinting. "You really have a natural skill for this line of work, Stephanie. It is a job that would suit you." I pushed my plate away, suddenly having no appetite for the rest of my meal. Watching Roxanna again I really couldn't tell if she had been in jest or serious. Either way, that was my breakfast done for the day.

"So anyway, this lost church of the fallen . . ." I began, trying to ignore her remark and change the subject.

"Fallen Church of the Unforgiven," corrected Trishna, from within his tea dreams. "Seriously, you naïve piece of fluff on legs, haven't you cottoned on to the importance of words yet?"

"You're back on the generic hotel tea bags for that." I mumbled, trying to hide my embarrassment in forgetting the name of the church. Words and names were very important, I was getting that.

"Oh, perish the thought!" snickered Trishna, giving me a cheeky grin. Great, so I had a foul-mouthed ghost who thought he had me wrapped around his little finger. I shouldn't have bought him the white tea, that much was now obvious. Ignoring him and trying to ignore the looks from the other two, I cleared my throat and tried to start again.

"Right, words are important. Have I mentioned how much I love this church and all its buildings and deeply care for all who inhabit them?" I tried to make it sound serious, but it didn't help when both Trishna and Estella burst into a fit of giggles. Roxanna smiled too and leant forward to touch my arm in a gentle manner.

"It's okay Stephanie, the Temple of Isis is already protected against demons by the guarding Light of Isis herself. But we appreciate the thought."

Damn, would I ever stop looking like an idiot way out of my depth? As I actually felt like an idiot way out of my depth, I seriously doubted it.

"Aw, crap." Was all I managed, not knowing what to say next in case I just embarrassed myself further.

Roxanna gave Estella a pointed look and, without a grumble or pout, my undead sibling rose to her feet and started clearing the table for me. Wow, I wish I could've pulled that off with a look when we were growing up!

"The Fallen Church of the Unforgiven is a rather interesting place," Roxanna went onto say. "It is a building in the central business district built on the site of an old church that burnt down under what you might describe as 'mysterious circumstance'."

"Demon?" I asked, trying to redeem myself from dumbness.

"No, humans." Roxanna shrugged, "But they were worshippers of the Darkness and so could very well have been doing it to get in favour with a demon. People of the Darkness do some rather strange things."

We both chose to ignore Trishna's snort of humour. I hadn't been too sure if it was his way of agreeing with her, or him making a point that the people of Light, such as herself, weren't any less strange.

"So, what is it now?" I asked, opening a new chapter in my mental book.

"An auction house. One that specialises in rare pieces that the general public sees more as tat, as they don't know the item's true worth." Roxanna said. "It is of course a front, and a way for them to pay the bills. There are some items that once there, never leave. They are put on public display as homage to their former owners."

"Such as the crucible?" Yeah, I was still keeping up.

"Precisely," Roxanna smiled. She looked rather relieved I had taken it all in so easily. Oh boy was she in for a doozy.

"And so, you're telling me, I have to find my way into an auction house, slash museum, owned by followers of Darkness which will be either heavily guarded or have a massively complicated security system to bypass. Then all I have to do is find one particular item out of who knows how many, and just waltz out of there unnoticed by the bad guys? Oh sure, they're so going to let that happen." I was beginning to really like Roxanna, so I had kept my tone polite. My sarcasm had a tone all of its own though.

"I knew I got myself bound to you for a reason," chuckled Trishna. Floor sweeping quality tea bags it was then! I ignored him, switching glances between my sister and the High Priestess.

"Oh!" I added, shifting sarcasm gears. "And wait. The Priestesses from the Temple of Isis just happen to be unable to enter such a place without alarm bells going off and a Darkness versus Light war breaking out."

We exchanged further looks, Estella not appearing too happy with my attitude, so what else was new? Roxanna, on the other hand, went from mild agitation to a thoughtfulness I wasn't too happy to see.

"Actually, we can go there without too much of a fuss," she mused, thinking out loud. "I mean, yes there are some areas within the building we would not be welcome. But the main auction room is a neutral meeting area, as items sold there can often be beneficial to both sides."

"Oh. Joy." I said through gritted teeth, as I really didn't like the sound of where this was now going. I usually liked to be proven right, but not this time.

Chapter 18

I HAD had to command Trishna to get back in his box. Part of me really hated myself for doing it after my thoughts the previous day of how long he might have been trapped in there by Branwyre. However, it had either been that or leave him behind with Estella to avoid having to hear his constant laughter.

I can tell you, I was not happy with the turn of events that now had me decked out as one of the white sheeted, lacy curtained acolytes of Isis. But Roxanna had had a point; it would get me into the auction room without people paying much attention. Who paid attention to the dopey faced lesser Priestesses, especially when they were following in the wake of their eye grabbing High Priestess?

Yes, Estella hadn't been that happy to be left behind either, but had accepted it a lot more easily than I had about getting into the horrendous get-up I now wore. The risk of her being at a place of great Darkness, with who knew what, or who, recognising her was just too great. So instead, she got to bask in the Light of Isis down in the deep cellar while I, as usual, did all the hard work.

And so, now in the heart of the city, I found myself following Roxanna into the auction house within the Fallen Church of the Unforgiven. We weren't alone; she had ordered half-a-dozen of her real Priestesses to come along too, to make up the numbers. Thankfully none of them appeared to be as wool-blinded by their love of Isis as Jasmine had been — the first Priestess I had met all those days ago. And, despite their best impressions of being exactly the same as Jasmine, I got the strong feeling they were as sharp as Roxanna. Her private guard, maybe? Still, I felt the total fool wandering among them, decked from neck to floor in some of the more curtain-like robes of a Priestess. We had so better find the crucible here, and not bump into anyone I knew. At that point, I really didn't know what would be worse, discovering the crucible had already been moved on, or having someone spot me in this get-up and share it amongst my friends. I still had some Estella hadn't estranged from me completely.

The pretence of our being there was to sell a box, currently hidden underneath a sheath of white cloth. Yes, it was Trishna's box, but I wasn't carrying it. One of the other Priestess was. They all knew what it was too, and despite showing their obvious dislike for it while at the Temple of Isis, they now strode forth holding it proudly as if it was some sort of treasured possession of Isis herself. I was really starting to like a religion that freely let you lie and make things up, as long as you did it for the sake of the Light. They just needed a better uniform.

I had considered trying a theory of gathering all items in the box and hiding them on my person, just to see if it was the box or one of the items that held Trishna to our world. The two problems with that were: one, the binding I had done on him apparently would only work if all the items stayed together, the box included. And two, the only real place I had to conceal some rice and a prayer flag was down my cleavage, and there was just oh so many reasons I wasn't putting them there. Besides, that spot was already taken by a vial of purified water that apparently all the Priestesses carried there, just in case. In case of what, I hadn't wanted to ask.

So, instead of hiding Trishna on me, the plan was to crack the lid of his box when it was time for me to spilt from the group and have ghost boy follow me into the rooms that made-up the Darker side of the Fallen Church of the Unforgiven. Main reason for doing that was that he knew what the damned crucible actually looked like. For all I knew, in this weird and wacky Other World, it could be a Tupperware container.

The auction room we entered appeared pretty typical, from the limited amount of time I had spent in them. We entered through a foyer, where our party registered its name and were assigned a number, under the pretence of being there to buy as well as sell. Ushered into the main area, we were asked to await an appraiser who would assess what we had to sell. While we waited, we were informed we were free to browse the items on display in this room alone. And, for a largish reception room, it was full of some of the strangest things I would have thought to see in an Other World auction room. I mean, it looked just like a normal auction room filled with furniture and other household bric-a-brac, paintings and prints, and simply shelves upon shelves of items of ceramic, silver, brass, glass and plastic. The only thing that put it apart from the other auction houses I'd ever been in was that our outrageous apparel blended in quite well and was honestly not the weirdest kit there. I mean, there was a group of men and women dressed in feathers. Just. Feathers. I did my damnedest not to stare, but man it was amazing what you could make out of just sewing feathers together. Fascinating, but I didn't feel the urge to take a closer look as they gave me that uncomfortable feeling I was starting to recognise as the Other World vibe I got from some of the nastier people who walked under that banner.

Trying to ignore the other patrons, while keeping up with my curtain clothed party; I instead tried focusing on the various items. It would have been helpful if someone could explain to me exactly how a ratty old bookshelf was so important and Other Worldly. I mean, it wasn't even some old wooden edifice carved in spooky runes. It was a waist high laminate escape from a flat pack shop. Weird.

And yet, as we moved through the shelves of smaller items, I got goosebumps. There were things here of great power, and it annoyed me that I could sense them so easily. I was a normal person, not some Other World wonder, and it felt so wrong I could sense all this stuff. Moving in the middle of the group of Priestesses, I was suddenly drawn to the shelves on our left, and a small, white porcelain bowl that caught my attention. It seemed to stand out while still being amongst a clutter of other items. Could it really have been that simple to find the crucible? Was I being drawn towards it as part of my new destiny?

"It is a bowl of trickery," whispered one of the Priestesses of Isis next to me. "It has been cursed by the Fae of Northern Ireland to be attractive to those seeking something. But to touch it would rob you of the memory of what you really seek, and instead encourage you down a different path." I blinked at her kindly face, taking this all in and wondering if she was about to snicker and add 'Tricked you!' She was, sadly, deadly serious.

"Isn't that a bit callous of them to leave it out amongst the other things?" I asked as we moved slowly away.

"Not really, anyone who touches it with their bare skin to examine it will forget their true cause for coming to the auction, and will only want that bowl. They usually sell for an outrageous amount of money as there are always a few schmucks who'll touch them, causing a huge bidding war."

"Which is why I suggest we all just look with our eyes and not our hands," smiled Roxanna, looking back over her little group with a matronly demeanour. "Such items are what the auction house owners use to make most of their money, and why they have this room open to the general public."

The whole room suddenly took on a rather menacing feel for me. I had thought this was meant to be a neutral area, but I guess that all depended on whether you believed in Isis, vampires and ghosts. Oh my, what had I gotten myself into? This whole place was just a nasty honey trap to capture the unsuspecting and rip from them everything they held dear.

Our group was just rounding a corner of the shelving area and passing a side door, when one of the Priestesses to Roxanna's right suddenly decided to make a scene.

"High Priestess, I protest! We simply cannot go through with this!" she exclaimed, and all colour drained from my face. Um, uh-oh?

"Peace Hilda. You knew all along this day would come." Roxanna soothed, turning her attention to the Priestess and trying to lay a hand on her.

"But this box! Please not this box. It is the sacred container of our rescuer." Oh hang on, it was diversion time. Not as bad as I thought, as I'd thought good old Hilda there was about to blow our whole mission. Yes, I was still the dumb one of this party.

While Roxanna continued to make soothing sounds and motions, Hilda tried to make a grab for the covered box being held by one of the other Priestesses, and they literally tussled with it, trying to wrestle it out of each other's hands.

"Please stop this nonsense!" Roxanna tried her best to sound the concerned, and mildly embarrassed head of our group. However, she didn't appear to have that great a control over her Priestesses and more of them started to scrabble for the box too, joining in either their agreement or disagreement with Hilda. And look at that, we were drawing a crowd. Oh, how nice.

Wanting to blend in, I decided to be anti-Hilda and tried to get myself on the team trying to keep the box off her. Man you couldn't see elbows coming that quickly beneath the sheets and curtains. I copped one in the stomach that took my breath away and when doubled over from that, copped another in the nose that had me seeing stars, before I fell on my arse. Unfortunately it meant I ended up on the bottom of a pile of squirming Priestesses of Isis as more joined me on the floor.

"Ladies, ladies please!" came a flustered voice from above. I couldn't see who through the limbs in white atop me, but whoever they were, they were male. "Being a neutral place, this also means no infighting within your own sect is allowed. Can we please show some decorum in front of the other patrons?"

"Get up all of you; you are an embarrassment to the Temple." This was Roxanna's voice, almost in tears above the screaming and groaning from the pile of Priestesses, and not all those sounds were coming from me either.

People started to calm, become silent and slowly the weight of many robes, knees and dumpy middle-aged bodies was lifted from me.

"Oh no, she's bleeding!" came the cry from one of the other Priestesses as all eyes were on me, the last person still on the floor. I didn't know her name, not having been actually introduced to them all. And, yes, she was right. I was indeed bleeding from my nose, probably thanks to the second elbow that had floored me. Still, it could hardly have been said to have really ruined my outfit at all.

Kindly arms hauled me to my feet and as the room spun around me a bit, I took in the crowd we'd gathered. And look at that, another Earthed demon. These buggers were everywhere.

"Mr Vontant, I am so very sorry for the most intolerable behaviour you have had the sad luck to witness." It was Roxanna; looking less like her normal controlled self and more like a simpering old dear. My, she was a good actor. "It appears that not all of my Priestesses feel today is the right time to be selling."

I looked at the small man in front of me. He was well dressed, and nowhere near as slimy and sleazy looking as Jamal. In fact, if it hadn't been for the bright green emblem on his forehead — and general sensation of chained evil — I wouldn't have even guessed at his origin.

"Tut tut, this will not do," he said, shushing Roxanna's explanation. I flinched away as he reached for me, not wanting to be touched by a demon, Earthed or otherwise, but he grabbed again and started pulling me away from the group and through the crowd to the nearby exit.

"We cannot have blood split in the neutral area. Even you lily-white Isis goons should realise how dangerous that is. I will return your Priestess to you, once she has been appropriately cleaned up."

And before I could even yelp a protest, I was hauled through the side door. I turned wild eyes back to the white sheeted group, but none moved to stop him. Roxanna, however, had a rather pleased gleam in her eye. Damn her and her plans, I wouldn't have put it past her to have been the one who had elbowed me.

***

I was hustled to a small, darkened room some corridors down and deposited in a seat with the strict instructions to stay where I was while Mr Vontant hurried off muttering to himself about how the pious should know how to behave better.

I took a few moments to just catch my breath before taking in the situation. My nose had stopped bleeding, though my robes were now completely streaked in blood. What surprised me more though was that I was clutching the white sheathed box of Trishna to my chest. When had I gotten hold of that?

Probing my fingers beneath the cloth, I cracked the lid, knowing he could come out if this was done, whether commanded to or not. He, of course, started laughing almost straight away.

"What sort of dumb little crumb brain lets the Temple of Isis dress them?" he snickered, looking around the room. Not one mention of the great stain of blood down my front, gee ta!

"Thanks for your concern, you can shut up now." It was honestly the nicest thing I could say.

Trishna gave me one of his annoyingly cheeky grins and kept on looking around the room. I joined him in his perusal. It wasn't much. Just a smallish side room that looked set out for private business deals. Simply furnished with some paintings on the wall, old rugs on the timber floors, a set of chairs by a table against one wall, an old style fire place, and a sideboard displaying some rather ugly little figures.

It was these figures that Trishna was studying and, from the look on his face, it wasn't something he found very appealing.

"You were escorted to this room by another bloody demon weren't you?" he said. "My, my. You do have a way of attracting their attention." He pointed to the figures. "Little caricatures carved from the bones of his victims. Demon scrimshaws if you will." Um, ew!

"I wouldn't have thought an Earthed demon would be allowed to do that," I protested. He snorted in response, though I suppose there were worst things he could have done.

"It all depends on exactly what the person who Earthed him lets him do. I mean, some of the numpties who go for Earthing a demon — rather than just summoning it for a job and banishing it when done — feel their demon won't be as angry at them if it's ever released. That is, if they're given a little demon freedom now and then. They so don't know demons."

He turned to the door, as if hearing someone. "Hide my box under your chair. He may not notice," Trishna hissed, before then stepping into the darkest corner of the dimly lit room and basically vanishing.

I had just managed to slip his dark wooden box into the shadows under my chair when Mr Vontant returned. He looked me over, clucked his tongue and handed me a wet, warm face washer.

"Clean yourself up my dear, you look a fright." His tone wasn't cruel, but it wasn't nice either. "Blood spilled in a room filled with Other Worlders. It not only leaves a terrible stain in the carpet, but has the tendency to set some of the nastier fellows off. How is one supposed to run an auction with all hell breaking loose, literally?" He clucked and fussed over my robes as I wiped my face clean. When I'd finished to his satisfaction, he took the cloth between two fingers with disgust, and turned to leave again. "Tea?" he asked before he went. I found I only had the ability to nod dumbly, so did so. He was then gone again and I was bemused. How on earth could that be the same sort of slime that Jamal was?

"Well, isn't he just some anal little bloated tick short of a mangy dog?" Trishna said, stepping out of the shadows as he said it, and I was in a way glad it wasn't just me who felt there was something not quite right about Mr Vontant.

"I did wonder why he wasn't as smarmy and oily as Jamal," I agreed, starting to feel uncomfortable at the whole situation. I didn't want to sit around all day drinking tea with an Earthed demon, no matter how polite he appeared. I just wanted to find the damned crucible, get back out to Roxanna and the rest of the white robed wonders and get the hell back to the Temple of Isis. My God, I mean Isis! I never would have thought I'd have been happy and willing to actually want to go back to that place. Still, the sooner I handed the crucible over, the better right?

Let's just not start thinking over what having the crucible actually meant, and what they'd then do to Estella.

"You do realise you go all lemon-sucking shrew-faced when you start on an obvious inner monologue about your sister," muttered Trishna, now examining the paintings on the walls. I made a different face at his back and he flipped me the bird without turning around. Yes, nothing wrong with the relationship I had with the ghost I'd bound to me.

"Yeah, but at least I'm not a grown man in a nappy." I shouldn't have bitten back, it was childish, but I was feeling stressed worrying what all this was about.

Trishna gave me a glancing frown and then stepped back into the shadows as Mr Vontant returned with a tea tray in his hands and some sort of clothing draped over one shoulder.

"Here we go," he fussed, putting the tray down on the table next to me and started unloading all the contents onto the table. "I have brought a third cup for your ghost; I am assuming you've brought him. I was fairly certain it was his box you brought in."

I tried my best bland and innocent look, but my eyes strayed to Trishna as, scowling, he stalked out of the shadows. Mr Vontant turned to see what I was looking at and smiled.

"Ah, here he is, and as charming as I had been told," he tutted. Dismissing Trishna with a glance he turned back to me. "Here, it is the best I could do," he said handing over the garment he had had over his shoulder. "It's a dust coat, but should fit you and cover the areas most women of your sort like to keep hidden."

When I just stared at it he shook it at me impatiently. I really didn't know what to think. He was a demon; he was acting overly nice and polite, despite obviously knowing more about me than my get-up should have told him.

"What's the catch? What is it you want?" I asked, refusing to take the coat in case it meant I was agreeing to something before I knew what it was. The little man in front of me with a green symbol emblazoned on his forehead, just sighed and shook his head.

"Up, up, let's get this blood soaked curtain ensemble off you and put your new little costume on," he insisted briskly and pulled me to my feet. When he started pawing at my robes I at least had the sense to slap him away.

"Will you just stop that?" I hissed, snatching the dull grey dust coat from him and throwing it over the back of my chair. Trishna moved to my side and I suddenly felt we were getting into a battle stance for whatever came next.

"You simply cannot go walking around this place with blood all over you!" insisted Mr Vontant irritably, the mark on his forehead starting to glow brighter. "Especially now we're out of the neutral parts of the building. You're simply asking for trouble. It's all I'm saying. You want to stay safe don't you?"

"It's obvious you want her to stay safe, you little wart on the backside of a hippo." snapped Trishna. "What's the deal with that then?"

Despite it being one of his lesser colourful insults, I was severely tempted to pour him a cup of tea just to shut him up. I could fight my own battles after all.

"You know who I am, don't you?" I demanded. "Possibly not exactly who I am, but you've heard about me. Right?"

"Oh, I know exactly who you are, Stephanie Muriel Anders," hissed Mr Vontant, his prissy little neat freak shell cracking for a moment to show me the true level of evil that lay underneath. I shuddered and took an involuntary step back, feeling the tingle of Trishna as he placed a hand on my shoulder for what little protection he gave.

"And now I want you to take that sweet, sweet smelling dress off before I break my dry spell and add more blood to it as I rip you from it in bite-sized pieces." He was actually growling by the time he'd finished that little speech, which had him looking more like the oily little Jamal with every word. His Earthed mark was now a green fire sizzling so bright it hurt my eyes. Okay, he had sort of been trying to warn me about the whole blood thing, I got that now.

Feeling a lot less self-conscious than I thought I should, I found myself pulling the robes off over my head and dumping them on the floor before me. I'd been wearing a plain, white t-shirt over my bra and knickers, and thankfully there was no blood on any of them, as I definitely didn't want to go the full Monty. Before I could grab the dust coat off the back of my chair, Mr Vontant had snatched my discarded robes from the floor and flung them into the little fireplace. Upon impact they burst into flames and were rapidly consumed and turned to ash.

"Ah, that is much better." sighed the little man, straightening his suit and sitting down at the table to pour out the tea. As he did his mark subsided to just a dull glow. "Milk and sugar, is it?"

Yes, the dumb stare was still on my face. I had just been threatened at becoming a demon snack and now he wanted to know how I took my tea?

"I take mine straight, none of your white man frilly frou-frou." commented Trishna, removing his grip from my shoulder and taking a seat next to mine. In autopilot I slipped the dust coat on and blindly did up the buttons, taking the whole scene in as if in a dream. This Other World place was just getting freakier and freakier.

"Sit, Stephanie, there is much to discuss," Mr Vontant said, once again the calm, neat, and polite little man; giving me a smile that scared me more than his offer to, um, eat me.

I did sit, however, wishing the dust coat had been a little longer as it rode up and I suddenly became self-conscious of the amount of naked thigh I was showing. Trishna's casual ogle didn't help either, but it did snap me out of my shock.

"Cut that out!" I snapped at him, before turning my attention on the demon and deciding I would try to play along as if we were all sane, human and alive. "Milk and two sugars, please." I smiled at him, wishing I could kick Trishna under the table for his muttered comment over my tea blaspheme.

The tea was prepared and politely handed over. I just as politely took it, thanked Mr Vontant, and placed it gently on the table.

"So, what the hell do you want from me?" I asked, and suddenly remembering Trishna's box, bent to scoop it and its sheath up off the floor, before placing it in my lap possessively.

"I am aware of what you did at the Tormented Whore two nights ago," Mr Vontant replied calmly, ignoring my rude tone. It had annoyed him though; I could tell by the way the mark on his forehead briefly glowed.

"I'm pretty sure the majority of the Other World heard about that by now," snickered Trishna, head amongst the steam from his tea. "Mmmm, Darjeeling!"

I didn't want to show the wince I dearly wanted to have, so turned it into a scowl at Trishna instead.

"And I suppose you want me to do the same for you?" I asked, knowing I may be from the dull end of the tool shelf when it came to

Other World things, but still could see where this conversation was going.

"In a sense," Mr Vontant said conversationally. "However, I have some debts to pay back down below so I want you to actually banish me rather than just let me loose." Okay, I tried not to do the dumb stare again, but this was something new to me.

"A demon can't return to . . . Hell? . . . Without being banished?" I asked in the least dumb tone I could manage.

"Most refer to it as the Below World of Darkness but, as you're a newb, Hell will do." grinned Trishna. Gee thanks for the info after I confirmed my lack of knowledge of all this crap in front of company.

"And, in a sense, no we can't return there unless banished correctly." Mr Vontant continued on, an eager look starting to appear in his eyes. "Yes we can visit, but our powers are bound to this plane of existence unless the right words are used to allow us to move freely between the two."

"And, besides you not ever coming back to hurt or kill me, those I care about or even just make eye contact with anyone near me in the street, nor damage anything around me ever . . . What's in it for me?" Yes, I was learning this whole deal with a demon thing the hard way. Trishna's amused snort didn't help. Rather than look offended, or even glow at the hairline, Mr Vontant open his hands in a friendly gesture.

"Why, besides all that, the crucible of Branwyre of course." Damn, why didn't I guess he'd known why I was there?

"You have the crucible in your possession?" It was Trishna who asked this, but I swear he only just beat me to the question.

"Of course, or I wouldn't be offering it to you." replied Mr Vontant, giving him a disdaining look.

"Show me, then." I requested, before either of them could say any more. "Before I decide to agree upon anything, I want you to show me this crucible and have Trishna confirm it's the real deal. Then and only then will we start to fine-tune our little deal, got it?" Despite the forced pleasant look upon his face, I could tell the little man was not exactly pleased by the way the emblem on his forehead started to glow brighter.

"You doubt my word because I am a demon." Mr Vontant actually looked offended.

"No," I said, trying to calm him. "I doubt anybody's word but my own. You could be the archangel Michael and I'd still want ID and proof before cutting a deal." From his expression, my attempts not to insult him further failed miserably. Oops.

"Fine then." Standing, he straightened his already straight suit and stalked stiffly over to the side cupboard where he went through a rather complicated routine to unlock it. Flinging the low bureaus' doors wide he stood back as if showing me something. Trishna had turned in his chair to watch and started to snicker rather rudely. But he had a point, the cupboard was bare.

"I know I am new to all this," I announced in as level a tone as I could. "But I'm fairly certain the crucible isn't invisible."

Mr Vontant scowled at me for a moment then turned back to the sideboard and ducked to look inside.

"What toe scraping of the lowliest whore has been in my private collection!" he growled, spinning back to stare at me with an expression that put no doubt in my mind he was a demon. He glanced from Trishna to me and then slowly stalked towards us. Trisha and I were on our feet in seconds, back in the fighting stance of before, only marred slightly by my clutching Trishna's box.

"I left you alone in here for only a moment believing, from what I had heard, that you could be trusted to leave my personal possessions alone." seethed Mr Vontant, death clearly in his eyes. "But I forgot the ghost, didn't I? A ghost skilled at lock picking. Why bargain when you can steal? So typical of a newb to not realise the only way to get out of here alive is to deal rather than steal."

I found myself backed up against the wall, Mr Vontant only centimetres away from my face, teeth grinding and spittle at the sides of his mouth.

"Give it back to me, you festering abscess on a mad cow. Don't make me have to search you; I may enjoy it too much."

What was it with this Other World cussing? Couldn't they just call you a shit-faced bastard and be done with it?

"We touched nothing, did nothing to your little stash you bloated tick on a swine's snout. So, just back up a step before I show you what else I can unlock," growled Trishna, though I did note proudly he'd toned down his cursing. He was actually standing just in front of me, making my right side tingle as his back connected to me, offering what protection he could.

"Why the hell would I want to sit down to tea with you and discuss my options if you were just going to fling those doors open and find it missing, you stupid freaked out little shit!" I added quickly, wincing slightly at how lame my insults sounded in comparison to theirs. I was still pinned to the wall, but in one piece, it was a start.

"Then who would dare take something from me? From my own private rooms? Not even those who Earthed me would be so stupid!" Mr Vontant was really getting a good froth up at the mouth now, and had lost all traces of his former trim and precise self. The markings upon his forehead had reached a new peak of searing brightness.

"Who would do it?" he growled the last part and I was at serious risk of wetting myself, I was that scared.

"Well," drawled a voice as the door to the room opened, "That would be me." And there, leaning on the doorframe and twirling a golden cup on the fingers of his left hand, stood Jamal. But boy had he done some work on himself since I'd freed him. I was a little too scared to take in that much detail, but he was definitely several inches taller, as well as sleeker and smoother.

"You ulcerated goat's left testicle!" spat Mr Vontant moving, thankfully. away from me and turning his full attention on Jamal. "I paid you in full," Mr Vontant hissed at Jamal. "How dare you come into my own Earthly domain and take what was mine."

"Well, you see, while you were out getting this little diamond in the rough off the floor, I just couldn't help but have a little look," grinned Jamal, appearing totally unfazed by Mr Vontant's ravening anger. "And imagine, to my surprise, I found exactly what it was I was looking for." He ducked the shorter man's swing and with a flick of the fingers on his right hand, hurled Mr Vontant across the room and into the far wall.

"Now calm your prissy little self down before I really have to get more violent than I had planned," Jamal said as he strode into the room, following Mr Vontant.

"Wait, he paid you for information?" Trishna said suddenly, having appeared more than happy to watch them fight it out without us until this thought struck him.

"Mr Vontant, you puckered rump of a deceased baboon, tell me you didn't make the payment I think you did." Although there was anger in Trishna's voice, there was also a touch of fear. And, as I was already on the brink of complete terror, I was finding it hard to come down and so stayed silent. Yeah, let the ghost speak for me until I could get my voice and breathing back under control, why not?

"Be silent, you filthy shade of a wasted life," Jamal commanded as he actually helped the little Mr Vontant to his feet. "The big boys are talking right now; I'll get to you two in a moment." The demons continued to face each other off stonily until the smaller, Earthed, Mr Vontant looked away in disgust and stepped to one side submissively.

"I do this only because I am not at my full capacity, being tethered to this realm by a mortal as I am." He spat, and gave Jamal another filthy look.

"And what a gosh darn shame the only person nearby able to free you from those shackles, will shortly be unable to, unless I say so?" This last remark snapped me out of my fear induced silence.

"We have a deal, bat breath; you couldn't harm me if I released you." I snapped, my anger for his antics over my car, coupled with him obviously having the crucible in his hand, pushing the fear out of me. Yes I was in a room with two demons and a ghost. I was fairly certain only one of them was able to kill me, and I'd like to think he'd have to get past the other two to do it.

"I wouldn't . . ." hissed Trishna through gritted teeth as a warning for me to stop talking. What did he know now that I so obviously didn't?

"Yes we do have that deal in place," smiled Jamal, leering at me in my barely fitting dust coat, "But nowhere in it did it mention me not being able to bind you to myself." I really didn't like that smile, it was worse than the look Mr Vontant had had when threatening to rip me apart in search of the crucible.

"What sick little twat-licking fart from a leper's backside are you to do something like that?" snarled Trishna, but he was saying it to Mr Vontant, not Jamal. By the level of his cursing he was obviously upset, and as it was concerning me, I started to panic again. What now?

"He promised me freedom," hissed Mr Vontant, trying to regain some of his former demeanour. "I just didn't realise until afterwards how it would come about."

"And how in the depths of hell was it supposed to happen, once he's done what he's going to do? You ulcer on a . . ."

"Oh for Isis' sake, won't someone please tell me what is going on?" I snapped. They were talking about me, and in a way I knew wasn't going to give me a happy ending any time soon. "How the hell do you think you're going to bind me to yourself? I may be new to all this, but I'm fairly certain you need my permission before you can do that. You being a demon and all." I was keeping my voice below a hysterical screech, but only just.

"Not if I get a sample of your blood, freely given by yourself." Jamal grinned and I tried thinking over the past hour or so. Yes I'd gotten a bloody nose, but it hadn't been something I'd wanted. And the dress had been burnt in the fire place. Suddenly my stomach fell to the floor.

"Figured it out yet?" grinned Jamal; pulling the face washer I'd used to clean myself up with, from his jacket pocket. Oh. Shit. And from the expression on Trishna's stricken face, a very big 'oh shit' indeed.

"You absolute little bastard." I turned my anger and attention on Mr Vontant; he stared back with a dispassionate look. "As if I am about to make a deal with you now."

"In a moment, my dear, you won't really have the free will to do anything." he replied coldly, turning back to Jamal. "As you have her, I will allow you free passage out of here with the crucible, if you use her to free me." The little sod was still trying to wheel and deal despite it all.

"Define free passage?" Jamal said, giving him a mildly interested look.

"All binds and guards keeping the crucible here will be lifted and you can just stroll on out. Deal?"

Jamal considered it all for a moment and then nodded. "Deal." He pocketed the cloth again and the two demons briefly shook hands. The act of watching two demons do business made my skin crawl, and wasn't something I ever planned on seeing again, if I had any say in the matter.

"And now, my turn to have a little fun I think." Jamal grinned, returning his attention to me. "I can't thank you enough for freeing me, but it's been dull wreaking havoc all on my own and so it's time I have a plaything to join me."

"You can't have her, she is protected by Isis!" Trishna protested, still standing before me in a protective stance.

"Fustian!" snapped Jamal. "She is neither truly ordained, nor even personally blessed by the Goddess. Therefore she is fair game." He took the face washer from his pocket again and touched his tongue to a spot of my blood. "So nice and fresh and innocent," he said before leaning in towards me, through Trishna, and taking a long, slow inhalation of breath, sniffing my neck and cheek. My heart was hammering so hard with the fear it caused I was frozen to the spot.

"Good, it is indeed your blood. Always best to check." He smiled. "Now, Stephanie Muriel Anders, let's begin the binding, shall we?"

He stepped closer still and the fear in me solidified. "And, just so you don't get any funny ideas like your ghost, when bound to a superior, more powerful being, that being takes control of you, your will and your actions. And, can I just say, we're going to have such fun. I may not be able to enter the Temple of Isis, but you still can, my dear. It's time for another Fallen Church to rise, I think." He breathed this down my neck scenting me, my fear, as he did, obviously enjoying it. Despite being taller and of mildly better appearance, this close to me he was still the slimy little shit I'd dealt with at the nightclub. This bit of anger fizzed in me as the tingling sensation of Trishna's contact to me increased in an unsettling manner. He was stepping fully into me.

'You better be ready to fight this crud filled rotten left testicle, you fluff brained female as I am so not being bound to a human bound to a demon!'

Trishna had somehow spoken these words directly into my mind, without the other two hearing him. Both actually seemed rather occupied with Jamal pawing me into submission. But with Trishna's tingling, rather annoying, power flowing through me, the fear melted and I just got rather pissed-off at the whole situation instead.

"Get off of me you slimy piece of Hell's rectum!" I suddenly spat and, taking a firm hold of Jamal, forcefully shoved him away from me.

I don't know if Trishna had given me some superhuman strength, or that I'd just caught Jamal off guard, as he tumbled backwards and actually fell out through the still open door to the corridor outside. Upon impact I heard the crucible clatter away into the darkness. Putting Trishna's box down on the table as calmly as I could, I gave the startled Mr Vontant my filthiest look, and stalked into the hall to face Jamal once more.

"Why you septic ulcer of a . . ." growled Jamal as he got to his feet.

"Will you all just shut up with your long winded insults? It doesn't make you sound any tougher you know?" I had no idea I could be so angry, nor hold it in in front of Jamal because, as he stood up, he grew in size. He was now a good metre taller than previously and his new handsome looks had distorted into something a lot more ugly.

"How dare you!" he hissed in an unearthly tone. "A mere mortal scum like you."

"Oh, I don't dare." I growled back, "I actually do!" and, not really knowing what came over me I reached up and grabbed Jamal by his shirt front and hauled him down to my eye level and scratched his face with my free hand. Little pearls of blood appeared on his cheek. He couldn't hurt me, we'd made a deal. But he was really, really pissing me off. How dare he feel he could bind me to him? To be able to own my free will? I snatched the face washer from his pocket and shoved it down my front, the only pocket I really had. It must have been Trishna's will giving me the extra strength because I really couldn't have hauled him down like that myself.

As my free hand crammed the cloth between my breasts I felt the vial of purified water I'd been given. Not really knowing, or thinking, about what I was doing, I rubbed some of Jamal's blood onto my thumb and then wiped it onto my own cheek. He didn't stop me, so it was blood freely given. Next I pulled the vial out, tugged out the cork with my teeth and dipped a free finger from the same hand into it.

"You want to be bound to me? You really feel that need?" I hissed at a rather startled looking Jamal. Yes he couldn't hurt me from our previous deal, but he wasn't even struggling. "Then fine. You. Are. Mine." And, with that I wrote ANI upon his forehead and thrust him away from me as he started screaming. He was mine; it was all my thoughts could say. He had wanted to be bound so badly, then fine. Every fibre in my being demanded possession over him. I had no idea if writing that name would bind him as it had done Trishna, but it at least burnt from the way he was now writhing at my feet.

It was at that moment, as I re-corked the vial, that I noticed motion out of the corner of my eye. Mr Vontant and Trishna were standing in the doorway a little down the hall, both with looks of complete and utter shock on their faces.

"How did you get there? You were standing inside me, giving me your strength." I said to Trishna bewildered, suddenly feeling tired.

He shook his head. "I'm afraid not. Yes I stepped into you to break his fear hold, but when you walked out of the room I stayed where I was. Everything after that was all you."

"Oh," I replied, rather light headed and a little worried now. I looked down at Jamal; he was silent now but curled into a ball breathing heavily.

"Oh? All you can say is 'Oh'?" spluttered Mr Vontant. "For damnation's sake woman, you've just bound a demon to yourself and all you can say is 'Oh'?"

It was at this point my knees gave out and the room spun around me as I collapsed to the floor in an ungraceful heap.

Chapter 19

THANKFULLY the faint didn't last long and besides the pain in my head that I put down to the impact it had just received from the wooden floor, I wasn't feeling that spacey any more. I cracked an eyelid and looked about me. Yes, on the floor, and there were the shimmering blue sandalled feet of Trishna, but where had Mr Vontant disappeared to?

"Am I dead yet?" I asked, heaving myself painfully into a sitting position.

"Surprisingly not," said Trishna, squatting down to be at eye level. "But I'll give you ten out of ten for trying to be, you empty headed piece of fluff on two legs." He almost sounded proud as he said this too. Oh God, what had I gone and done this time that was so wrong? That's right; I'd bound Jamal to myself.

"Where's the crucible and Mr Vontant?" I asked, getting to my feet. I suddenly felt rather conspicuous laying there in a barely fitting dust jacket. Yes, I was scared, confused and exhausted. Yes I had just bound a demon to myself and had no real idea of what that really meant. But I just hadn't been enjoying the draft up my scantily-clad thighs.

"I'm here." came a rather reverent and subdued tone from behind me. I turned, still dusting myself off, to find Mr Vontant kneeling on the ground before me, holding the crucible out to me. Not thinking twice, I snatched it up. It felt warm and tingling in my bare hand so I juggled it for a moment before putting it down on the ground. It had been a rather unpleasant sensation like it had been trying to dissolve into me . . . or me into it?

"Guard that." I ordered Trishna. He made a dog noise at me that I chose to ignore as I glanced quickly at the still curled up Jamal and back at the worried little demon kneeling before me.

"And what is your problem? Get up off the floor." I told Mr Vontant, trying to mask my near hysteria of emotions. I was fairly certain I knew what his problem was and it didn't make me feel any happier about the whole situation.

"Just showing reverence where it is due, my Lady." crooned Mr Vontant as he rose to his feet and straightened his suit. Damn, it was what I thought it was.

"What? I bested Jamal and so you're now going to respect me rather than threaten to eat me out of my clothes?" Yes, I was sceptical. My greatest urge right now was to never trust a demon.

"That I see now was a terrible mistake, and one I do apologise most strongly for," he murmured, wringing his hands. I found I had preferred the primly precise Mr Vontant to this little sycophant version.

"Yeah so, I Earthed a Demon. Someone has already done that to you so you should be safe." Trishna spluttered from behind me, and as I glanced at him he also rose to his feet.

"You bound a demon to yourself, you didn't 'Earth' it. I do wish you'd try and remember the right wording frizz hair," he sighed. I was getting nervous now and didn't like having to keep looking in different directions. I was about to tell Jamal to get up off the floor and go stand by Mr Vontant when he went and did it of his own accord. That just freaked me out further and I felt sick to my stomach.

"Isn't Earthing a demon and binding one the same thing?" I asked, eyeing Jamal over nervously as he just stared blankly out into nothing. Mr Vontant cleared his throat.

"When a demon is Earthed, it is bound by its summoner to this plane of existence to do that Master's bidding," he said in his old, precise tones. "When a demon is bound to another . . . person . . . they are bound to their binders will and unspoken commands." He gave me a rather meaningful look as he said this. I glanced at Trishna, his expression wasn't that different.

"Hang on," I started. "I bound myself to Trishna and he is still the same pain in the arse foul-mouthed monk he was when bound to Branwyre. Why is the binding different with Jamal?"

Mr Vontant's expression took on a hard done by look, as if he didn't really want to answer my question.

"The purified water is right here buddy!" I growled at him but he remained silent.

"Trishna?" I asked, he too looked a unsettled at having to give me an answer.

I shrugged; too tired to have to deal with extracting information in his usual twenty question snippets. So I turned to Jamal and, as the question formed in my mind, he answered it. That was more than a little creepy, and stomach lurching.

"A ghost is of little to no substance, its form merely a representation of its captured life force. A force you can control and use as required to enhance your own life force. When not in use, it reverts to its original form," Jamal intoned emotionlessly, staring past me into nothing. "A demon is a beast of substance. Of mind, will and flesh. Such substance must be controlled at all times. As you said, I am now yours, all yours. You. Own. Me. I am bound to you in both soul and will."

I clenched my jaws against the rising nausea his words caused. I remembered thinking those three words, being so angry at him daring to bind me that I beat him to it. Both the demons had said I would lose my will once bound, I had no idea this is what it would have been like.

"Hang on, this has to be some sort of trick." I glared at the two demons suspiciously. "Jamal told me, when bound to a superior more powerful being, that being takes control of you, your will and your actions. So I'm not falling for this little stunt for one moment." The shifty look Trishna and Mr Vontant exchanged made my skin crawl.

"He spoke true, my Lady," Mr Vontant tried to explain politely. "But apparently it appears you were the superior." The world started to swim around me again.

"Trishna . . ." I pleaded. "Please tell me something I want to hear."

"Sorry duck feet." He sounded almost apologetic. "But he's right. That binding you did on Jamal before shouldn't have worked. Being a demon, his will should have beaten yours. But apparently hell really hath no fury like a really pissed-off you."

It was then my knees gave out again and I felt the strong desire to be seated on the ground once more. How the hell was this meant to happen? I'd come for the crucible and got stuck with a demon too?

***

And that was pretty much how Roxanna found me, head between my knees, trying to breathe normally. I had, between gasps, demanded Mr Vontant go get her. At first he had been a tad reluctant, as this area was technically out of bounds to those who walked in the Light. But after I'd used Jamal to pin him against a wall and growled a threat to bind him too, he'd trotted off to find her. Just having used Jamal again without really even thinking, had made me feel even sicker and caused my desire to hyperventilate to increase.

Trishna squatted down by me encouraging me to breathe, in his own dear little way. Calling me all manner of crude names between the simple 'Breathe in, breathe out' urges.

"Isis preserve us, Stephanie, what's happened?" Roxanna demanded, as she rushed forward to help me to my feet. "And what are you doing with all these demons in this place of Darkness? Is that the crucible at your feet?" She bent to pick it up before I had the chance to answer, then dropped it like it was too hot to touch and straightened, looking even more unnerved.

"Please, it would be better for all, if we could conduct this rather unorthodox meeting back in my rooms," urged Mr Vontant, stepping forward and picking up the crucible without seeming to have a problem with how it felt. "It's a nice, out of the way place that such visitors as yourselves won't be seen and, well, set upon." I could see the logic in his request, and with Roxanna taking my arm, we all trudged back into the small room. Without asking, I sat myself back down at the table and kicked Trishna's chair out for Roxanna to sit at. Parking Jamal over in the corner, I then took a few more deep breaths for good measure as Mr Vontant closed the door behind us.

"Should I get a fresh pot of tea and another cup?" Mr Vontant asked, his usual fussy tone returning. Poor guy, from the constant beacon-like glare from his forehead, he was really on edge now. No, actually, screw him. Why was I worried about a demon's feelings?

"You will just sit down and tell me what has happened here Mr Vontant." Roxanna replied curtly, giving Jamal an odd look. She glanced at the expression on Mr Vontant's face, and added, "Please."

Despite his current awe of me, it was obvious he wasn't happy with the High Priestess of Isis telling him what to do.

"I bound a demon to myself," I said bluntly, saving him from spluttering too much.

"You did what exactly?" Roxanna's voice had taken on an icy, suspicious edge. As if feeling she had been drawn into a trap.

"I bound Jamal there to myself," I answered again with a weary sigh. "By accident."

"Yes, I would assume it's not something one does deliberately." Roxanna still had rather a brittle tone, and was sitting rather stiffly on the edge of her chair, poised as if to flee first chance she got.

"Relax Roxanna; I really did bind him to me and not the other way around." I knew what she must have been thinking, me binding a demon? I was still finding it hard to believe and I didn't know half of this Other World stuff.

"She did, you know." Trishna piped up from where he stood behind my chair. "Not that you can really take my word for it as, being bound to her, if he really was in control he could make me say anything too." Damn it, he was enjoying himself. Roxanna had turned pale at the thought of being trapped in a room with two demons and no support, and he was enjoying himself teasing her.

"Trishna." I growled a warning, knowing there was no threat I could make about tea that would shut him up.

"Mr Vontant, please try and explain it to her." I asked, not demanded, and prayed he would.

"Against all the odds, my Lady here has indeed bound that demon to her soul and will," he announced reluctantly. "And may I just add, she has not yet bound me and I am really hoping to play my cards right so that she doesn't." I almost smirked at that, though it nearly became a hysterical giggle, knowing a demon was afraid of me and what I might do to him.

"Can you bind more than one demon to yourself?" I mused out loud, not really knowing where the thought had come from.

"Seeing your stubborn, bossy nature in action, I'd say you can." smirked Trishna, giving Mr Vontant a leer. "Make him 'one of us', go on." I sighed at this and turned back to Roxanna. She was still stiff and still, but her eyes now held a more wary expression than one of fear.

"Look, let me prove it." I said to her softly and started thinking of Jamal. He ran headlong into the wall, leaving a crack in the plaster, and collapsed to the floor in an ungainly heap. I then clenched my jaw at the rising sickness being his will caused in me.

"Isis preserve us, you really have bound a demon to yourself," Roxanna gasped, her fear starting to disappear, to be replaced by awe as she looked at me. "You shouldn't have been able to manage that."

I snorted, I couldn't help it. "Strange how I hear that so often." I said, looking back over to Mr Vontant, standing expectantly by the door. "Sorry about the wall, Mr Vontant."

"Think nothing of it, my Lady," he smiled back. This new subservience of his was really getting on my nerves.

"Okay Roxanna, so now I want you to fix it so that I can leave here one demon less, and get the hell back to saving my sister." What can I say, if I didn't stay focused on my main aim in all this mess, I'd probably me sitting in a corner somewhere rocking myself and whimpering.

"I can't do that!" she exclaimed, sharing the same shocked look that Mr Vontant now wore. "Stephanie my dear, you must realise that I may be able to do a great many things as the High Priestess of Isis, but unbinding a demon from someone's soul and will is not one of them." Damn.

"But, it can be done?" I asked, hating to feel like such a bumpkin. "Without hurting me or damaging my soul, right?"

"You really have no idea what it is that you've done, do you?" gasped Mr Vontant, his prim and precise persona cracking for a moment while his real demon-self showed through. There was naked greed in his eyes that made me very nervous.

"Don't even think about it." I warned him, bracing myself and having Jamal get to his feet and advance on the smaller demon. "I might feel sick to my stomach controlling him, but I'm fairly certain I could still kick your arse with Jamal." Trishna snickered and I swear I heard a near-silent 'that's my girl' but ignored him to focus more on the demon across from me.

"I meant no offence, my Lady." Mr Vontant shielded his true self and returned to the kowtowing little man in a neat suit. "But you must realise the potential you hold in your hands, what you can now control?" Was he urging me to join the Dark side? Isis, I so hoped not.

Roxanna had sat silently through this all, and from her thoughtful expression I hoped she was about to come up with something useful.

"Mr Vontant, no offence, but all I want to do is get out of here, with that crucible you've set down on the table, and get back to killing my undead sister to free her from a vampire." Yeah, no, that didn't sound that crash hot when said out loud, did it?

"But you could take control of this Fallen Church, and make so many more to house your armies," insisted the little man; his emblem glowing with excitement.

"Armies?" I spluttered, "What in the hell do I want with armies? I just want to get a rather painful task over and done with, help this ghost find eternal rest and go home to cry myself to sleep for a month." Anger drove me to my feet. "If I hear the words 'world domination' out of you, I will do more than just bind you to myself!"

"Is that all you really want?" asked Roxanna's now once more calm and controlled voice. "To just free Estella and Trishna, and return to life how it was?"

Of course it was! Why the hell had I been putting myself through all this mess if it wasn't? Then again, knowing what I now knew, the life I returned to after mourning my pain in the arse little sister wasn't going to be exactly normal. As for Trisha . . . how could anything seem normal after I lost them both? In recent years I had led an empty and lonely life — my own choice mind you — but did I really want to go back to it. Really?

"Of course it is." I finally replied, noticing her calculating look as I'd taken my time to respond.

"Normal life!" spat Mr Vontant, "What exactly is there that is normal in the life of a woman who can control demons and bind ghosts on a whim?" Gee, he was really starting to piss me off.

"Wasn't I meant to banish you or something?" I asked him crossly, realising this might be the only way I could shut him up.

He gaped a moment, just opening and closing his mouth. "You . . . You would really do that?" he asked me sceptically, though I swear there was a tremor of hope in his voice. "You have the ability to bind me to you and you would just banish me instead, as we'd originally agreed?"

I shrugged; seriously one less demon in my life right now would be really nice.

"But he tried to sell you out to Jamal." protested Trishna. "You can't reward him for that, turn him into a toad or something at least! Send him back without his power so he can get his arsed kicked down there too."

I hadn't thought of that. I thought banishment was a punishment and it was obviously a reward. Still, seriously, he was a demon. Could I really expect him to have done anything else but sell me out to the highest bidder? And yes I'd be sending him back to hell, so that was one less demon wandering around up here, right?

"That was a mistake. I see that now," spluttered Mr Vontant in response to Trishna's protests. "I will add to my deal that I will never steal your blood and sell it to another demon ever again."

"He did what!'" exclaimed Roxanna, jumping to her feet. I tried to wave off her concern.

"He had my blood on a face washer I'd used to tidy up with," I replied, pulling said item from my cleavage and waving it at her, "He gave it to Jamal in return for information as to who I was in the hopes it would mean I would banish him back down below with his powers. But I got that sorted and got my own back." I pointed to the smear of Jamal's blood I assumed I was still sporting. The look of awe on Roxanna's face was rather unsettling.

"You were about to be bound by blood freely given and you still got the upper hand?" she exclaimed.

"Didn't I say she had power?" added Mr Vontant, that eager look back in his eyes.

"Don't." I warned both of them. "Call it all beginner's luck or being too stupid to know better. I just want to get rid of him," I pointed at Jamal. "Get rid of you," I pointed at Mr Vontant. "And take this little brass cup that makes my skin crawl back to your Temple and get on with it all." I waved at the cup and then pointed at Roxanna. "I really don't care if I am the embodiment of the second fricking coming of Christ, I just want to lay my sister to rest and go home." Oh, great. Now I had three of them gawping at me as if I was an idiot and one just staring blankly into space with a now broken nose.

"Well then," Roxanna finally said, grabbing the sheath of white material off Trishna's box and carefully wrapping the crucible in it. "I think we can just about manage that." It was my turn to gawp.

"But you said you couldn't help me." Yes, I was back to making dumb statements.

"No," she smiled patiently at me as Mr Vontant started to glare. "I said I couldn't fix this. But you can. And I can help you do that." Well that was a relief, right? So, of course, I'd gotten the wording wrong again, but surely it would be nice if one of them would give me a plain and straight answer for once without me having to do all the hard work.

"But the power . . ." pleaded Mr Vontant. "I would be willing to stay Earthed here, my possession transferred to you, if only you would let me help you indulge in the power!'"

I gawped at him again, I really couldn't think of what else to do. The way he was speaking, it was as if I should feel this dark cloud of absolute power and strength welling up in me, tickling my mind and fingers to get up to all sorts of nasties. The truth of it was I was tired, feeling a little chilly in the skimpy dust coat, sick to my stomach from all this binding stuff and getting one of those back of the neck headaches that tended to become a migraine unless I lay down in a dark room with a cold face washer on my forehead.

"Mr Vontant, can I just say you may have been, for most of it, the nicest demon I've met. But if you don't shut up about this whole power thing, I'm going to shove my vial of purified water somewhere and see what else I can do." I had used my best, though strained, 'playing nice with others' voice. If this was his attempt at well, tempting me, it was a miserable failure.

"Now," I continued, turning to Roxanna as Mr Vontant spluttered and fussed, and Trishna snickered. "What exactly is it that I need to do to get me back on track for saving Estella without all this demon nonsense to deal with?"

She gave me one of her bemused, though mildly amused, looks and shook her head slightly.

"Well, if you're happy to banish a demon back to the Below World of Darkness with all his powers intact, then you just add taking Jamal with him as part of the deal," she explained softly.

How on earth could it all be so simple? I banish one, he takes the other and the rest of us walk out of here with the crucible and no regrets? Damn!

"That is, of course, as long as you get the wording right and close all the loopholes," added Trishna smugly. "As you sure as shit don't want one of these two coming back and biting your round and petite little bottom right off . . . or other things."

"From now on I am putting milk and four sugars in any floor sweeping tea I find you!" I snapped at him. He snickered and winked at me.

"Hey, you're the one who wanted me to tell you things you needed to know that were important to your current situation," he pointed out shrugging. Trishna had a point though, and sighing and repeating the mantra 'words are important' wasn't going to fix it all. I needed to think very carefully about what I was about to do and say to ensure I got rid of both demons and stayed rid of them for good. The last thing I needed was for them to be summoned back to this plane of existence and come pay me a visit for old times' sake. But, first things first, and I chose my words very carefully.

"Okay, answer me true . . . well, anyone of you, can a demon bound to you in both soul and will be safely unbound and removed by the act of banishing another demon and making it part of the deal it takes said bound demon with it?" Oh yeah, that was just so clear now wasn't it?

"The only true way to unbind yourself from a demon is to release it from your will and do your best to banish it before it kills you." It was Roxanna who answered, and she seemed a little worried as she said it. "Though, technically, if you happened to have another demon at your disposal that you could make a deal with that ensured it never allowed the newly released demon to ever come back for retribution . . . that might work."

"Oh come now!" protested Mr Vontant. "I refuse to babysit this little arse wipe of a demon, just to get a free ride back to the Below World of Darkness."

"I suppose I could always transfer the possession?" I thought out loud, wondering exactly how possible that was and expecting someone to rather bluntly point it out to me if it turned out to be a rather dumb suggestion. "I mean, if you can transfer the possession of an Earthed demon and all."

Mr Vontant's eyes gleamed at this thought, while Roxanna looked aghast and Trishna looked uneasy. So obviously it was indeed possible, but probably not the best thing I could be suggesting.

"Binding a demon to yourself is one thing Stephanie," Roxanna warned, "And already has you walking a fine line between the Darkness and Light. But if you were to pass that possession on to another, especially a demon, I can't ensure you safe passage in the Light ever again."

Damn, I really didn't like the sound of that.

"Soul trading is never the best way to make friends and influence people in the Light side of the Other World, dumb arse," added Trishna, making me realise exactly how seriously dangerous my suggestion had been.

"Um, okay, forget that thought then." I quickly said, shooting the near drooling Mr Vontant a wary look. He growled his disappointment at me.

"And I don't suppose I can negotiate the release of a bound demon, can I? As in, have him promise not to kill me once released?" Roxanna gave me a sad look that said it all.

"You get all or nothing you silly, naïve ditz." hissed Mr Vontant, his true self starting to show again. "It's like flicking a switch. You're either in control or you're not. So how about you just sign him over to me and we can get on with the finer points of my banishment."

I was so tempted to just be petty and flip him the bird over his statement that I was very surprised Jamal didn't do it for me. Instead I ground my teeth and tried to think this through further. The clock was ticking and I really wanted to get back to Estella before Branwyre got another go at controlling her body for the night.

"Just think of it, removing Jamal from your cares and concerns forever," crooned Mr Vontant, "You and I can come to a deal where I promise to never do harm to you, any you care about or any possessions you may have. You banish me, with my powers, and we both come out on top." He so wasn't helping.

"How about you just shut up and go get me a piece of paper and a pen." I snapped, a plan starting to form in my mind.

"And why should I do that?" he asked stubbornly, obviously wanting to stay and needle me into submission. My stomach lurched before I'd even realised I'd responded through Jamal. He picked Mr Vontant up by his neck and shook him slightly.

"Because I am apparently the person still in control of this situation," I said through gritted teeth. "Now, he's about to let you down and you're about to go get me a pen and paper so I can nut out exactly what it is I want as my side of the deal in this banishment. As, so help me, I am getting really tired of this situation and am currently more than happy to leave you behind as a smear on the wall when I leave!"

Okay, so I was losing it a little, I could see that. Roxanna put a calming hand upon my shoulder and I found myself able to ease Mr Vontant onto the ground and out of Jamal's grip. As soon as he was released, without a further word, he scampered from the room.

I then found a great need once more to be seated, and so returned to the chair I had been in and sat heavily. As I placed my elbows onto the table and cradled my head in my arms I found a strange comfort and strength in feeling Roxanna give my back a gentle rub. Shortly followed by the tingle I knew was Trishna touching me.

"I've just majorly screwed up again, haven't I?" I asked the table. Roxanna stopped comforting me and sat down next to me instead.

"In a way," she said, her voice calm, controlled and oh so soothing. "But you've stopped a badly freed demon from wreaking further havoc, may be about to rid our world of two demons, and have gotten the crucible to help your sister find her final rest."

"And scared quite a few people out of their tiny little minds when they hear exactly what it is you have the ability to do," added Trishna in his usual tactless manner.

I peeped up at him to see Roxanna giving him an admonishing look.

"What?" he shot back at her, "It's not as if she's not on our side or anything."

I went back to staring at the table, trying to ignore what Trishna was insinuating and instead focusing on what I was hoping to nut out as to the whole banishment thing.

"Is it wrong of me to ask how you're meant to banish a demon?" I asked the table. I assumed the snort was from Trishna and the slight gasp from Roxanna, I didn't move to check.

"I was wondering when you were going to ask about that." Yep, that was Trishna's smug tone. I ignored him and looked up at Roxanna again, trying to keep the helplessness and pleading, I so deeply felt, from my expression.

"Words are important. Is there any specific wording I must use to ensure I really do banish them and not just give them an excuse to pretend but really stick around like a bad smell?"

She studied me for a moment before placing a comforting hand once more on my shoulder and smiling gently.

"I will help you with the wording, as will Trishna," she said soothingly. "But judging on your previous actions, I honestly feel you should just do and say what comes naturally to you. So far it's seen you strive forwards in the Light."

Great. I was a natural at all this Other World Good versus Evil stuff. I doubted it was something I could easily work into my CV.

***

It took me maybe half an hour of huddled talk, muttered discussion, and mad scribbling that required so much of my attention that my tongue may indeed have ended up sticking out of the corner of my mouth again. But finally I sat back with relief as Trishna and Roxanna gave it the final once over.

"My, why don't you just sign it in blood and get Isis to kiss it for luck if you must be so precise," muttered Mr Vontant from where I had made him go stand in the corner away from us. This time Jamal did flip him the bird, my only reason for noticing I'd done it was the clenched pain it caused in my stomach.

"Well, now!" huffed Mr Vontant and straightened his suit to make himself feel better. I ignored him and turned my attention back to the other two as they straightened up from reading my scribbled notes.

"And?" I asked nervously. My mind had started filling with all sort of ideas as to exactly what the two demons could do to me if I'd missed the smallest loophole. It made Branwyre's promised retribution pale in comparison.

"I think it may just work," mused Trisha, obviously still thinking it through as I got no insult. "But I don't suppose you could wait until you found a way to release me before giving it a go? I'd rather not be made a ghostly condiment if these two find a way to come back and decide to make a demon and Stephanie sex sandwich, or something." I nearly gagged, that wasn't one of the images I'd conjured up . . . though it sure soon became my top fear.

"I think I need to buy some supermarket brand sweet and sour sauce on the way home and pour it into your box," I told him. He grinned and winked at me, urgh he was annoying. Perhaps life would be much easier once I'd gotten rid of him? Which led me back to thinking of all the things I had to do first, including Estella, and another sigh wracked my body. I stared at Roxanna and she just nodded her agreement to my prose. I strongly got the feeling she didn't want to influence me too much. Not because it would get her into any trouble, more as if she was looking forward to seeing me at work and watching what exactly it was I could do. That did not fill me with a great deal of hope nor positive energy. Damn.

"Okay then." I said, after another sigh, "I'm sure I'm damned if I do and damned if I don't. So let's get this little show on the road." I snatched the paper from the table and turned my attention to Mr Vontant. He wore an odd mixed expression of curiosity, eagerness and distain upon his face. If I got this all right, I'd hopefully not ever have to look at it again in a few moments. I cleared my throat, took a quick slug of the now cold tea, gagged, cleared my throat again and decided to stop procrastinating and just do it.

"Mr Vontant, Earthed demon of Soames and Sons Auction house since eighteen fifty-four, do you agree to be my protector against any and all Dark Forces that may wish me harm, dare harm those I care about or am with, or whom seek to destroy items in my world I'd rather they didn't? That protection commencing from the moment we make this deal, and will include protecting me from Jamal, until time itself forgets about us and our association."

The neat little demon boggled at me — he really did — then spluttered for a moment as it all sunk in. "And what exactly is it you wish to grant me in return for such a hideously outrageous request? I mean, all Dark Forces? Who are you kidding?" he snapped. "I can assure you banishing me with all my powers will not cover all of that."

Having assumed he would try and barter I moved to the next section I had written.

"In return for my stated arrangement, I will not only fully banish you to the Below World of Darkness, I will allow you to regain all your powers once there." He quirked an eyebrow at me, clearly waiting for more carrot to be dangled in front of him.

"I will also grant you the ability to use Jamal's powers for one lunar month and promise that, should anyone once more Bind or Earth you in my life time, I will release you under this same deal and arrangement."

"You? You would ensure I was never trapped in this horrible place again? Never bound to this plain of existence or any who dwell on it?" he was still spluttering, but actually seemed more interested in what I had to say.

"It's the least I could do." I added, ad lib. "So, what do you say?"

"Give me access to Jamal's powers for six lunar months," he demanded primly.

"Three." I growled, not wanting to let him get the final say.

"Four." He insisted.

"Two and you stop now before I just renege and think of something else," I glared. The emblem on his forehead glowed brightly for a moment as he realised exactly how stubborn I was.

"My will, my way." I hissed, in case there was any doubt in his mind that I would sway on any of it.

"Deal," he finally sighed and presented me with his hand. I hadn't wanted to shake it, but Roxanna had assured me that bodily contact was required to seal a deal. And I felt shaking hands was probably the least icky ways of doing that. And so we shook hands; I could feel the little demon's excitement tremble through him as he started to think of all the things he could get up to shortly.

Trying to not look too obvious about wiping the hand he'd just shaken on the back of my dust coat, I took the vial of purified water from my cleavage, once more took out the cork with my teeth and dabbed my index finger into it.

"Mr Vontant, I now banish you from this plain of existence, hopefully never to return. Knowing you will abide to the deal we have just shaken on." I glanced at my bit of paper, now held up for me by Roxanna and started wiping the emerald green emblem from his forehead and thinking hard of how much I wanted him to go away. "You will now, in a matter of minutes, be banished from here to the Below World of Darkness, taking a no doubt very angry and pissed-off Jamal with you. You will not only regain your own powers upon arrival in that World, but have possession of his for the agreed period of time." Sure, this was going well. I then added the last little bit that ensured he actually went. "Be gone oh foul demon from the never ending Darkness. I do so banish thee."

I was expecting a thunder clap or at least a little earth tremor and was sorely disappointed. We all basically just stood there, as we had been. Mr Vontant had water trickling down the side of his face and looked rather pleased. Other than that, nada.

"Okay, Jamal, freed demon and an absolute pain in the arse to be around." I started, turning my attention to Jamal. "I release you from being bound to my soul and will. May we not cross paths again as I am so sure I will kick your arse then too." It wasn't exactly what was written word for word, but the meaning was the same and it suddenly seemed far easier to say.

I wetted my finger again and wiped his blood from my face, then splashed the remainder of my vial into Jamal's face and rubbed the blue ANI off his forehead. "I also banish you back to the Below World of Darkness where, after two lunar months, you too will have your powers restored."

I knew it had worked, as he reeled away from me in a snarl before turning back to me with murder in his eyes.

"You stupid bitch," he hissed. "Two months? How dare you . . ." He lunged for me, and was promptly caught by a rather nasty coat hanger tackle by Mr Vontant. The smaller demon in the nicer suit leaped on top of the now prone Jamal and started banging his head into the carpet.

"So nice doing business with you." Mr Vontant stated between bangs, as a crack appeared in the floor, splitting the room in two. It swirled with darkness and had my skin prickling from the sheer evil emanating from within it. Mr Vontant rolled himself and Jamal into the crack just before it snapped shut, and we were suddenly alone. A little dust drifting down from the ceiling was the only indication that we'd just witnessed a gateway to hell open and close.

"Damn." I snapped, realising something. "I forgot to ask him to ensure us safe passage out of this building." Of all the stupid things to worry about, right?

Chapter 20

———————⊗———————

I SHOULDN'T have stressed, as apparently getting out of the auction house unharmed fell under the part of the deal where we were protected by Mr Vontant from any and all Dark forces. All alarms and triggers we came across where switched off for the period of time it took us to get through them, and we shortly found ourselves back in the main sales room and on neutral ground.

Roxanna had led the way, remembering it from when Mr Vontant had brought her to me. In her hands she held the crucible, still wrapped in the white sheath so the vile metal didn't come into contact with her bare skin. I had felt I should carry it, but found myself too busy feeling overly conspicuous in the dust coat and nothing else. I also felt a greater need to be the one to be carrying Trishna's box. Don't ask me why, as I really didn't want to think about it.

As we tried to slip quietly back into the sales room, the auction now in full swing, the other Priestesses clustered forwards, obviously wanting to ask questions. However, a single look from Roxanna had them swing in behind us quietly as we made our way to the entrance. As we moved through the crowd, however, I accidentally bumped one of the feather-wearing women. She turned to me with a look of distain which turned into a rather nasty lip curl of disgust as she eyed me over.

"Oh, as if someone wearing nothing but feathers has the right to comment on my dress code." I growled at her, giving a filthy look of my own. She looked taken aback a moment, then took in the box in my arms, Trishna and the Priestesses of Isis and started to give it all a thoughtful look. As she turned to get the attention of her fellow feathered folk I yanked her back towards me by the hair.

"Listen, sweetheart." I hissed at her, not fully knowing why I was doing it. "I've already had a rough enough day as it is. What with binding demons to myself and then having to banish a couple of them. One word from you about any of this and I'll not only pluck and slowly roast you, but cram said feathers down your throat until I can use your arse as a feather duster. Do. Not. Mess with me! You saw nothing, you know nothing." I released her and the feathered woman gave me a rather startled look.

"Um, go in peace with . . . Isis?" she muttered before moving away from me and trying to pretend it had never happened.

"Oh, there's so no taking you anywhere to make new friends, is there?" grinned Trishna. "Though I must say, ten out of ten for the feather duster quip. Sheer genius." He stopped abruptly when I turned a similar look on him. I just wanted to get out of the horrible place and get back to the job at hand — killing my undead sister.

"Come now, Stephanie," urged Roxanna, having witnessed it all with her usual cat and mouse expression. "Always good to know the Birdfolk of Wroth don't scare you, but do let's try and leave before we meet any folk who might."

I gave the Birdfolk lady one final death stare, part of my mind wondering why I suddenly felt so on edge and aggressive, as I allowed myself to be ushered out of the auction house and to the waiting van. It was, of course, white. But thankfully its windows weren't all lacy curtain-clad.

***

Parking the van next to the refectory and entering the Temple of Isis from the back area, I had hoped my mood would lighten. In the short amount of time I had known the place, I had come to welcome the peaceful hush that descended upon me whenever I entered the Temple. But not now, my mood barely changed and boy didn't that make me wonder what was next on my daily routine of weirdness. Although we still had a few hours before night truly fell, something just had me on edge. Roxanna thanked the other Priestesses, and sent them on their ways to other duties, before hustling me into her private offices. I started to feel the mood was down to what lay ahead. I had done it. I had found the crucible, gotten it away from the Fallen Church of the Unforgiven and no one had been harmed. Well, I refused to count my blood nose as getting hurt . . . and breaking Jamal's nose didn't count either, nor did the roughing up I'd had him do to Mr Vontant. It was while I trailed down this cluttered path of mild hysteria that Roxanna cleared a place upon her private altar and carefully unwrapped the crucible, always ensuring it didn't come into contact with her bare skin.

All my tension, all my dread seemed invisible to her and I almost envied Roxanna's calmness. Because the thought of now having to use the crucible on Estella filled me with more trepidation than I thought possible.

I mean, I may have been new at all this Other World stuff, but I wasn't a total numpty. I knew exactly what it was I was now going to have to do to Estella, and I didn't know what had me sickened and saddened more. The fact I would have to drain her of what blood she had, into that crucible, or the fact that after that she truly would be dead and gone, forever.

Without invitation, I slumped heavily into a chair by Roxanna's desk as she fussed over the crucible with Trishna's help. It seemed that, although they couldn't truly cleanse it — as that would remove the required Darkness needed to draw Branwyre out of Estella's body — they could at least make it a little easier to use as a tool of the Light. Not that a heck of a lot of that made any sense to me. But Roxanna seemed happy to focus her attention on it, occasionally quizzing Trishna about it, while the ghost seemed more than content to answer her politely. I just prayed he was behaving and telling the truth. He tended to with Roxanna and I was never too sure if this was because she was the High Priestess of Isis, or the best person to help him find his final rest. I was just the dumb schmuck he was bound to after all, no best behaviour needed for me!

And didn't that just send me into another spiral of dark emotions. Soon I would be completely alone. Estella would be at rest and Trishna gone from my life. But I was strong and confident and ridding myself of both of them was what I wanted, right? I mean, I was just itching to get back to my boring old life, and add these little adventures to the other past experiences I squashed right down deep inside me, to do my best to never dwell on again. The fact that so many of those experiences had included Estella just made my stomach twist. She had been a part of my life for so long, caused so much pain, suffering and despair. She had, well she had done something my mind could only ever skitter over, before fleeing to happier thoughts. And yet in the past few days, she had been more the sister I had felt she could have been, rather than the one I had been given. And that just added to my current world of churning emotions and tension. Finally I was getting the sister I should have got, and she was about to die all over again. Just this time, there would be no rising from the dead. And that hurt.

Why was all this strange and unbelievable Other World crap suddenly feeling so much more real to me than my dull old life?

"I said, frizz features, any chance for a cup of tea? The good stuff as I'm being such a help to the High Priestess here." I looked up at Trishna's disgruntled tone and swear I caught a flash of concern and worry in his features for a moment.

"Really?" I asked roughly, wondering if he was deliberately giving me something to vent my tension on. "Is that what it all comes down to? I banish two demons and recover the crucible, but to you I'm still just the tea lady?"

"Well, I could always ask you to dust my box for me, seeing you seem so caught up in keeping that coat," Trishna said, eyeing me over in a way that made me suddenly very aware I was still wearing barely anything at all but the dust coat.

"Oh, crap!" I said, leaping to my feet. "I have to get changed!" Both of them gave me a startled and mildly amused look as I rushed from the room. Had I been so caught up in starting my pity party early that I'd not noticed exactly how much of me was still on display here?

I raced off to the room I had been provided with earlier, leaving Trishna's box behind on Roxanna's desk, knowing my regular clothes would still be laid out in wait for me there.

On my way back some ten minutes or so later, as I just happened to have to pass the refectory on my way, I decided that Trishna's recent behaviour should be rewarded. As I'd left the white tea in my room though, he would have to contend with whatever it was they had in their kitchen. Yes, I could already hear his snicker and the word 'sucker' as I poured hot water from their urn over a tea bag of green tea and ginger.

"Merry blessing to you daughter-sister of Isis," came the perky voice from behind me and I turned to see Jasmine entering the kitchen area with an empty, but obviously used, plate.

"Uh, hi." I replied, trying to use my 'playing nice with those who are not all there' tone and expression.

"I have been tending to your sister Estella," she announced in her airy, happy manner as she approached the sink I was dunking the tea bag next to and started washing crumbs off the plate before placing it into a dishwasher.

"That's . . . nice." I continued, finding if I kept the words simple I could hold the expression and tone a lot easier. Behind it my tense and bitchy mood was still rising.

"Oh yes, she is starting to look so much better," Jasmine wittered on happily as she wandered about the room, frilly white curtained arms waving at this and that.

"The Power of Isis is magnificent, isn't it?" she went on, despite my lack of prompting. "I mean, those nasty autopsy scars are nearly completely gone. And it is just so good to see her finally getting her appetite back."

I stopped jiggling the tea as the hairs on the back of my neck started to rise.

"What did you say?" I demanded, all pretence of being nice dissolving as my fear rose.

"Her appetite is back, blessings be to Isis!" smiled Jasmine, completely failing to notice the change in my tone and expression. "The plate I just brought back, that was all that was left after she asked me for a sandwich. I made her a chicken and watercress one, knowing it was a favourite of hers . . ." I didn't hear the rest of what the silly woman had to say as the cup fell from my hands, smashing wetly on the tiled floor, and I found myself racing for the door.

"Roxanna!" was all I could yell as I started to sprint.

***

"Oh Isis preserve us," was all Roxanna could manage through pale lips as we met in the Temple just outside the doors to her office and the deep cellar. Her hands flew to her mouth and her eyes showed fear as I recounted what Jasmine had told me. The woman herself floated in with her annoyingly serene expression moments later and I was surprised at the roughness in Roxanna's tone as she grabbed Jasmine by the arms and demanded she tell her everything that had happened.

"Estella came to me while I was dusting," Jasmine answered, a bewildered look on her face. She pointed to where a pile of cleaning products rested against the wall, hidden from the main part of the church by wooden screen. "She said she was hungry and that the

Priestesses down by the Pool of Isis were too busy and could I possibly get her a sandwich or something. And so I did."

"And her scars, they had healed?" asked Roxanna, barely able to contain the horror she so obviously felt from the look in her eyes.

"Of course!" smiled Jasmine as if there was nothing wrong in the world. "She had been bathing in the Light of Isis all last night and today so surely that is to be expected?" Something seemed to get through to her cotton wool for brains, however, as a frown creased her brow.

"High Priestess, have I done something wrong?" she asked, her voice quavering a little as if she was on the brink of tears. Roxanna tried to regain control of the look of dread in her eyes as she released Jasmine from her grip and patted her shoulder gently.

"No." she said between a heavy sigh. "No, my child. Please, can I just ask you to go to the front of the church and close and bolt the door? Let no one, and I mean no one out until I tell you otherwise. There's a good girl." Roxanna glanced to me as she said this and my feeling of tension became chilled by her look.

"Very good, High Priestess," the forty-something year old Jasmine with the mind of a small child replied, smiling happily. "Anything else?"

"Pray," Roxanna said. "Go before the Altar of Isis and ask her to give us strength, as we're going to need it." She then turned on her heel and stalked back into her office as Jasmine wafted away, still so unaware of what this all meant, that I just wanted to scream and shake her. Instead I followed Roxanna back in to her office and gathered up Trishna's box.

"This is not good." I said. I had meant it to be a question, but from the hunted look Roxanna gave me over her shoulder as she wrapped the crucible back up, it had become a statement.

"No shit ,Sherlock," muttered Trishna. He had been present at Jasmine's announcement but had remained quiet. That in itself gave me cause for alarm.

Roxanna merely shook her head. "We must go to the Pool of Isis.," she said as she gathered a great book under one arm while holding the wrapped crucible in the other hand. "Let us just pray is it not too late to save Estella and the Temple." Without another word she left her office and I followed, wondering if the nasty on edge feelings I'd had welling up inside of me had been because Branwyre was awake and repairing my sister's body, all before sunset.

As we made our way down the many flights of stairs I suddenly found myself overcome by tears. This was all too much, I had come so close, I had done everything right — and then some — all to fail at the last hurdle.

"It is Branwyre's power," Trishna suddenly said. "Don't give in to it. You need to reserve the power you hold in your anger, stick insect legs, as you are so going to need it." As my Buddhist ghost said these words I felt the strange tingle of him touching me. Whether it was to provide comfort or to start lending me his life force to enhance my own, I really didn't know. Whatever the reason it helped, so I just gritted my teeth, kept going and wished I'd had time to go back to my room for my sword. Hopefully all hell wasn't about to break loose down here as I, for one, didn't want to have to clean up the mess.

Chapter 21

BY THE time we reached the bottom of the stairs I had my emotions back under control, just. They were simmering right below the surface, so strong, I was almost sick from the tension, anger, and fear swirling around within me. I faltered on the final step along with Roxanna, as I realised the chamber was silent of chanting. This was the first time I had ever heard it so silent, and from the frightened look Roxanna flashed me she found it just as unnerving.

Trying to brace myself for every little nasty thing my mind now had me thinking up, I stepped out into the room ahead of Roxanna. Relief briefly washed over me when I found that the place wasn't awash with blood and the bodies of slain Priestesses, nor were there the expected demons pinning said Priestesses down and having their evil ways with them.

Instead there was just a group of white-clad and very scared looking women huddled as close to the Light of Isis as they could get. While in the darker shadows, cutting off their exit to the stairs, paced someone else in white robes, idly swinging my sword about.

"Stephanie Muriel Anders. How very pleasant it is you've finally decided to show up," beamed Branwyre through my sister. If his tones from her mouth hadn't been enough of a giveaway, the sickly feel of evil roiling around her figure certainly did.

"Branwyre, never the gentleman, and never on time." I said in a cold tone, moving further into the room and placing Trishna's box down on the stone slab in the Light of Isis before turning my attention back to Branwyre. The fact I had deliberately turned my back on him to do this task had the desired effect of pissing him off. Glad I was finally getting something right.

"When one is a vampire Lord, being a gentleman is so second class," hissed Branwyre. From the look on his face, it was obvious he was prepared to dislike me even more for being amused I'd upset him. Thankfully he didn't just swing the sword and behead me; I had wondered whether he would or not. Obviously he either wanted me whole, or needed someone to pontificate at for a while.

"Tread carefully Stephanie," Roxanna warned me, as she entered the room behind me "I doubt Mr Vontant can protect you from the Darkness, as promised, when you're in the bowels of our sacred church." I gave her a quick glance of uncertainty. I hadn't even thought of the demon coming to my aid here, despite our deal that he was to protect me from any and all Dark Forces. As I turned back to face Branwyre in Estella's form, I noticed he was glaring at me angrily.

"You sought to deal with a demon?" he said, as he raised my sword at me. "You?"

"She's done more than 'sought', you ruptured pustule," snarled Trishna. "She bound one to herself, Jamal at that. And then made a deal with the other to ensure stains like you don't get in her way again."

Branwyre's face clouded with anger for a moment, whether at what Trishna had called him, or what he had said, I wasn't too sure.

"No demon can enter the Temple of Isis unaided or uninvited," Branwyre finally growled at me, dismissing the rest.

"Oh, I wouldn't be too sure of that," came a familiar fastidious voice that had me turning back to the stairs in shock. Jasmine stood at the foot of the stairs, taking in the situation with a focused and controlled look before turning to me. "It appears my services are already required; I do hope you don't make a habit of this."

"Mr Vontant?" I couldn't help it, despite the tension filled moment; I just gawked at Jasmine as she brushed past Roxanna and came to stand at my side. It was then I noticed Jasmine's usually mud brown eyes were an amazing blue, the same shade as Trishna. Did it mean the demon was also pulling on my aura to possess her?

"How?" gasped Roxanna, "And Isis protect us, please tell me Jasmine is okay?"

Jasmine glanced idly at Roxanna and shrugged.

"The woman's soul is fine. She just happened to be at your door when I arrived to keep my end of the deal. Upon requesting her help, she asked me inside and offered to provide, and I quote, 'Whatever assistance she could provide'. A green light in anyone's rulebook for a quick body possession, don't you agree?" Jasmine sniffed in a very Mr Vontant manner, tried to straighten her robes and turned back to me with a weary look.

"I suppose you'd like me to help out here?" he asked. It was his tone, his mannerisms, but it looked so wrong on Jasmine's wittering foolishness.

"Answer me true, is she really okay?" I demanded, referring to Jasmine. Wittering fool or not, I did feel responsible for her safety.

The demon within her sighed and fussed with the sleeves of her dress. "Of course she is. I simply needed to ensure I kept up my part of the deal. She will be released, unharmed, as soon as you are no longer under threat by Dark Forces." Jasmine shot Branwyre a dismissing look. "It shouldn't take me too long, I promise."

"How dare you!" seethed Branwyre. And can I just say that dealing with two different men in two different women's bodies wasn't nearly as confusing as it may seem at first!

"You should not be able to set foot inside the Temple, dressed in a Priestess or not," spat Branwyre. I almost got the feeling he was trying to buy himself some time to think this all through. I personally felt Branwyre was being a bit like the kettle calling the pot black with this statement . . . but I was still new to all this mumbo jumbo after all.

"I can, and I have. Get over it," snapped Mr Vontant. Turning his attention to the huddled Priestesses he gave a small frown. "And now, as I can assure you I don't do my best work in front of an audience, I feel it's time for you ladies to hurry on up the stairs and start praying. Someone needs to get Isis' attention for what I'm about to do." I fear everyone but Trishna may have gawped at this suggestion.

"You dare remove my blood sacrifices?" snarled Branwyre, moving closer with sword upraised. Mr Vontant just snorted in contempt at this and moved in front of the sword.

"Stephanie." Roxanna, clutched at my arm. "Don't let them hurt Jasmine. Spilling blood and removing the sanctity of the Temple is one thing, but please don't let them harm her. She is far too innocent to be used in such a way." I suddenly felt hopeless beyond measure. I had no control of Mr Vontant, other than the deal we had. And did harming her count as that part of our deal? Or did the 'protecting' me bit counter act it? What was I to do? I had no purified water down my cleavage to try and banish him with and, quite frankly, I approved of his attempt to remove the other Priestesses from harm's way.

"Stop!" I shouted. "I want you all to just stop!" I allowed all my pent-up emotions to fuel the fire in my tone. "Give me your purified water." I demanded of Roxanna, trying to adopt a slightly less aggressive tone. I was still surprised though when she quickly did. I shoved it down between my own breasts and then moved forward.

"Mr Vontant, I appreciate your help, but I would appreciate it all the more if you didn't get Jasmine skewered. Don't make me exorcise you from her body, or I can assure you our previous deal will be altered to exclude the perks you currently have." Jasmine blinked at me a few times then took a few steps back, no longer protecting me from Branwyre or my own sword.

"And you!" I growled, turning to face the vampire within my undead sister. "You have enough witnesses with just me, Roxanna, Trishna and Mr Vontant. The other Priestesses can go free. I command it to be so." I don't know if it was the look in my eye or the final words I had used, after they had suddenly popped into my mind. All the same, the sword wavered and I heard the shuffling of feet behind me as both Trishna and Roxanna urged the other Priestesses up the stairs. My gaze, however, never left that of Branwyre's as he glared out at me through my sister's eyes.

When the sounds all died down, only then did I risk glancing over my shoulder to see the underground chamber now empty, but for Roxanna, Trishna, Mr Vontant in Jasmine, myself, and Branwyre in Estella. How peachy.

I gave Roxanna, who appeared as scared as I felt, a quick glance and held my hand out silently to her. As if reading my mind, she handed over the cloth-wrapped crucible. I ungracefully shook it out onto the dais within the Light of Isis and turned back to Branwyre. He broke my sister's face into a nasty sneer.

"You seriously feel you can use that to stop me?" he spat. "You would truly do that to your sister, your own flesh and blood. Slay her to stop me?"

I squared my shoulders, trying to keep the pent-up mixture of emotion in control and hidden from my face.

"She's already dead; I'm just going to ensure her soul passes onto the correct place." I stated as coldly as I could, somehow hating myself for having to admit openly that Estella really was already gone.

"And where would that be exactly?" hissed Branwyre, starting to smile as if some nasty thought just struck him. "As I am inside her, I know all sorts of things this naughty little girl has done." I refused to rise to his bait. "I also know of the really horrible things she has done too. Especially what she did to you." I fear my attempt at self-control slipped a bit as a look of pure hatred and contempt seeped onto my face. The fact it wasn't all aimed at Branwyre, but also who he possessed, didn't improve matters. His grin widened and, as if expecting me to be caught off guard, he poked at me with the sword, testing my responses.

Surprising everyone in the room, myself included, I dodged the sword as it slid by and stepped closer to Branwyre. With a snarl of sheer anger I backhanded Estella across the face, pleased to see her reel away with a grunt. The blow also made Branwyre lose his grip on the sword and it clattered to the ground between us.

"You stupid, stupid stain from an incontinent demon's undies." I spat at Branwyre as he straightened to glare at me a few steps away. "Do you really think that's the first time my sister has come at me with a weapon, while off her face?" I felt my anger swirling around me now. It had replaced all my unease and fear. He had dared to try and use my sister's past, our past, against me?

"Yes you may know a lot of her dirty little secrets now." I hissed at him angrily, "But I got to experience quite a lot of them first hand. And as they say, what doesn't kill you makes you stronger." I bent down to pick up the sword, too angry to expect the sudden rush by Branwyre as he barrelled into me, and we ended up on the floor in a tangle of limbs.

"You stupid, empty headed daughter of an unmarried leper!" growled Branwyre, using Estella's knees to hold me in place while her arms snaked out to pin my arms above my head. "Never, ever let your anger control you. It lets all the Darkness seep in." A nasty smile spread across Estella's face and I gulped a breath of fear as I noticed her teeth were now elongated in true vampiric style. And up close and dripping with saliva, with a face of pure evil behind them, they didn't look anywhere near as comical or lame as they used to when I saw them in a movie. I felt fear numbing my thoughts as Branwyre leant down to scent me, sniffing at my pulse points and nearly drooling.

"Such a far better host than this shell of a wasted life," he grinned, and dipping Estella's head prised the vial of purified water from between my breasts with her mouth, before throwing it with a toss of her head onto the nearby stone floor, where it smashed. "I do hope you're very afraid right now." purred Branwyre, rubbing Estella's body against me in a provocative manner that made me sick to my stomach. "As it makes the blood taste all the sweeter."

As the fear did indeed ripple through me, I was suddenly aware of two things. One was the growing tingling sensation in my feet, which seemed to be travelling up my body and warming the fear back into anger. The other was the silvery flash of metal I suddenly saw over Estella's shoulder.

"No blood is to be spilt within the Temple of Isis!" came an angry voice from above us. I was surprised to realise it was Roxanna's.

"As much as I hate to disagree with you, however, I do need to stick to my end of the deal," said the voice belonging to the person holding the sword.

Branwyre hissed at the feel of the cold steel of my sword against his neck. I risked a glance between a very angry looking Jasmine who held the sword to Estella's neck, and an even angrier looking Roxanna who stood behind her, book raised as if to use it as a club. Suddenly Branwyre seemed to be undecided as to how to proceed. The tingling heat inside me grew and with it the sudden thought that I acted upon. My knee rose, very hard and very quickly, up into Estella's crotch. She may have been a female, and therefore not as affected as a man would have been, but it got Branwyre's attention all the same. As her body hunched up in pain, I pulled on the strength from Trishna's life force from where he held my ankles, and pushing my arms up, forced Estella off me and scrambled to my feet.

"You fetid ulcer on the left testicle of a syphilitic rapist," muttered Branwyre as he slowly got to his own feet. Behind him, Mr Vontant held Jasmine's arm steady, the sword still at Estella's neck.

Branwyre glanced at me and smiled once more. "And just what is to stop me pressing back a little and spilling some blood onto the oh so precious, but no longer sanctified, floor?" he asked, actually looking like he really planned to do just that.

"Oh, tut tut, my Lord of the Aegean," Mr Vontant said. "We can't have that happening now, can we?" And with that he had Jasmine drop the sword and, in the same fluid movement, snatched Estella's arms and slipping his own arms under them locked them in place behind her back. No matter how hard Branwyre struggled, he was unable to free Estella's body.

"Demon beats vampire any day, you slime," muttered Trishna. Although we had both straightened up his touch had not left mine, his strength and life force still feeding into mine in a way I found both comforting and really quite scary at the same time.

"Vontant!" yelled Branwyre, obviously in pain from the tone in his voice. "Why are you doing this? Why are you helping those in the Light destroy those who walk in Darkness?"

"Firstly, because I have made a deal with Stephanie Muriel Anders. And I can assure you that after seeing her pissed-off at a demon, I don't want her anger directed at Me." hissed Mr Vontant in Branwyre's ear. "And secondly, and more importantly, I don't like you. Any of you filthy little leftovers caused by the destruction of a true being of Darkness. You bring down the name of what it is we are trying to achieve, distracting our worshippers from the true path by the appeal of your lesser, deviant natures."

Somehow, I found this some rather interesting information to know and, something I felt I might just use if I ever had to call on Mr Vontant again. I physically shook myself from that horrid thought. No, once the hell in front of me was over, there would be no more Mr Vontant. There would be no Trishna, Roxanna or Isis. And there would be no Branwyre . . . or Estella. There would just be me, back in my own safe, sane little world, licking the wounds the past few days were going to leave me with for years to come.

Trying to move myself from those dark thoughts and get back into the verbal fray going on, I turned to Roxanna and found her kneeling by the stone slab within the Light of Isis, the thick book now open as she quietly recited the words she was reading. Branwyre must have followed my gaze as he let out a yell of fury and started writhing against Mr Vontant's steel grip once more.

"You blackened soul of mass murdering whore!" he bellowed, "Let me go! That leprous castoff is reciting the Words of Cleansing. Help me!"

Mr Vontant held Jasmine's face in a grim look as her grip tightened on Estella, Branwyre continuing to struggle within her.

"I will make a deal!" Branwyre yelled. "I will make you a deal so great, that the one Stephanie Muriel Anders holds you to will pale in comparison."

My stomach lurched as I saw the calculated look spread across Jasmine's face.

"I'm listening . . ." Mr Vontant replied, lips pursed hungrily.

Next to us Roxanna's voice raised slightly and she started to hurry, carefully, through what it was she was saying.

"Let me live, help me make this a new Fallen Church of the Unforgiven, and I will become your servant. What is mine, who is mine, will all become yours. Think of the souls I can give to you: the pure and clean virgins, the newly born and freshly slaughtered babies. All can be yours." Branwyre sounded as eager as he did desperate.

"And all a bunch of lies from a worthless Skid Mark." declared Trishna angrily from by my side. "A promise incapable of being delivered. Hollow words from a fading Lord trapped in a weak female."

"You traitorous, lying scum sucking wretch!" screamed Branwyre, struggling again, this time to get at Trishna. "I should have just drained you of your life force, and eaten you as my breakfast all those years ago! You were a wasted life and an even greater wasted stored life force!"

The tingling of my connection to Trishna increased to an almost burning sensation as the anger rose in Trishna at my side.

"You made me what I am, you parasite." Trishna hissed. "I may have briefly strayed from the path of enlightenment in the days before I met you, but no one deserves the punishments you have put me through, the things you have made me witness since that time. I wish you had just killed me, even being reborn as a slimy maggot that feasted on my own body, would have been better than witnessing what you have done!" There was real pain, anger, and I swear almost tears in Trishna's voice. He would not let me to look at him though, turning his head away, but still stayed connected to me.

"I may not reach enlightenment for millennia." Trishna finally muttered, "But these last few days freed from you will feel like it, in comparison to what you put me through."

"Silence!" bellowed Mr Vontant from behind Branwyre. "I haven't decided whether the deal is worthy of my consideration yet. Shade of a man, you say our Lord of the Aegean here has promised me something he cannot fulfil, how do you know this?" He glanced at Roxanna, who had been doing her best to ignore all of us and was still reciting what sounded like a remarkably long prayer to Isis.

"Before I was bound to Stephanie Muriel Anders, I was bound to him for almost a century." Trishna replied softly, seeming to be in control of his emotions once more. Poor guy, he really deserved some more white tea if we ever made it out of all this alive.

"And?" Mr Vontant prompted. An eager gleam had appeared in Jasmine's eye and it unsettled me. We were so close, if we could just stall things a little longer.

"And he is next to powerless. His minions are nearly depleted, his lands and fortunes long gone."

"Lies, all lies!" screeched Branwyre, struggling harder against Mr Vontant's grip.

"Then explain why it was that not one but two, of your Possession ceremonies were interrupted by the Priestesses of Isis? Yes they pack a wallop, but their strength is still limited compared to those with real power in the Darkness."

All struggling and discussion seemed to suddenly stop except for Roxanna's low murmuring. I held my breath as to what was going to happen next.

"Stephanie Muriel Anders, I am sorry to have doubted our deal. I do hope you don't take it personally. As you can see; I didn't waver from my support of you, even as I considered this stain's empty proposition," Mr Vontant finally said in his usual precise voice. I was too stunned to respond. Was it really that easy for a demon to keep switching its allegiances?

"You fetid hellspawn's reject!" growled Branwyre, obviously too emotional to come up with a more colourful curse. Whether he had been speaking to Trishna or Mr Vontant was quite unclear.

"And by Isis do I now bind your soul to this crucible, ensuring the letting of our innocent child's blood will release her from your possession. Amen." Roxanna said loudly before turning to look at us all, as if remembering we were all still there.

"No!" hissed Branwyre, struggling once more. "This cannot be how it ends. I am the great Lord of the Aegean!"

"Meh, I'll send them a postcard explaining what's happened." huffed Roxanna, much to my surprise. Having never seen her act in such a casual and sarcastic way, I almost laughed despite it all.

"Stephanie, blood sister to our beloved Estella, it is now time," she added, giving me a look that captured all my attention. Then, surprising me further, she pulled a long, silver dagger from within the spine of the book she had been reading. She handed it to me intoning: "The blessed dagger of Isis, used to release even the most wicked of souls to their final resting place."

Suddenly, feeling I was all nerves and emotions, I dumbly took the dagger from her. This was it and I suddenly so very much didn't want to be there, nor be the person who was about to do what I knew I had to do. I was struck speechless, even my long suffering sarcasm had dried up.

"It is time." Roxanna urged me quietly as pinpricks of tears started in the corner of my eyes. For all the hate and loathing and anger and pain Estella had put me through. For all that she had taken from me and destroyed . . . I didn't want to do this. I shouldn't have to do this.

"I . . ." I began as the tears grew fatter in my eyes and a few escaped.

"Oh put on your Big Girl panties and get on with it!" spat Mr Vontant. "I have better things to be doing with my time you know."

I turned a glare on him, how dare he be here, how dare he be witness to this? I felt a soothing, warm tingle shift into the left side of my body.

"You have the blessing of Isis." Trishna told me calmly. "You are not killing her, as she is already dead. You are freeing her soul from its path to purgatory. You are giving her that one last chance to walk in the Light and be a better person in her next life." His voice and words warmed me as much as his ghostly touch, but still I felt a horrible chill deep in the pit of my stomach.

As Mr Vontant shifted Jasmine's grip to hold Estella's head back, exposing her throat, a string of filth and curses started to spill from Estella's fanged mouth. Her face twisted into an ugly mask of hatred and I then knew what I had to do. Of all the horrible and tragic things she had caused to happen in my life, even she didn't deserve to end up like this.

All my emotions seemed to drain away, leaving the chill to bloom within me and give me the strength to do what I had to do. I grabbed the crucible from where it sat within the Light of Isis and approached what was left of my sister. The crucible no longer held the repulsive tingle it once had. Or if it did, I could no longer feel it in my numbed state.

"Through the blessing of Isis and the strength of her Light and Power, Branwyre, eighteenth vampire Lord of the Aegean, I do banish thee from my sister." I touched the tip of the knife to Estella's neck, right on the pulse point, and with a breaking heart, dug it into her. "I purge your sick and disgusting soul from her body and into this crucible." I had no idea where the words were coming from; they were just there, being said. And as I spoke them, the dagger seemed to move to where it needed to be and I felt Estella's jugular give, and the slow throb of her congealed undead blood press against it.

As I removed the knife, the tirade of abuse from within Estella also stopped. I pressed the crucible against her neck as the sluggish black blood started to ooze out. I suddenly realised I was staring Estella straight in the eye, no longer certain as to who was staring back at me.

"Forgive me, Ella." I whispered as fresh tears gathered in my eyes and the black blood filled the cup.

"Be gone, Branwyre, allow my sister to now lie in peace in the Light of Isis." I finally intoned and the eyes staring back at me softened as the blood stopped flowing.

"I forgive you, Ani," came a feeble reply before the eyes then closed and her body slumped limply in the arms of Jasmine.

Chapter 22

"WELL, this has been a pleasant and interesting day to possess a dull little Priestess." Mr Vontant's prim, voice suddenly broke the stunned silence as I held the blood filled crucible before them. "But now I simply must be off to see what Jamal has been up to. Try to not need me again anytime soon." He hoisted Estella's lifeless form onto the stone slab, and with a wave started back up the stairs.

"What in the—?" I finally managed to splutter, just standing there, dagger in one hand and blood filled crucible in the other. Was that it? Was it all now truly over?

"To be able to release Jasmine properly, Mr Vontant will need to be out of the Temple and free of Isis' protection." Roxanna replied, slowly taking the dagger from me, cleaning off its tip with the white material the crucible had been wrapped in, before ramming it back into its sheath within the spine of her book. She closed the book with a snap, and started to lay Estella out in a more comfortable looking position.

"And Jasmine?" I asked dumbly, I really don't know why I cared. I assumed it was to keep my mind off the fact I had just killed my sister, and still literally had her blood in my hands. Before Roxanna had a chance to answer there came the sound of many feet upon the stairs and several of the Priestesses burst into the room.

"High Priestess?!" one of them asked in a fearful tone.

"It is done." Roxanna sighed sadly, finishing neatening up Estella. I still just stood there; I had no idea what I should do next and feared moving in case I spilt the blood. "Please send someone to assist Jasmine; she will need help and some very strong, sweet tea any time now."

"Priestess Helena is already with her." The leading Priestess replied, coming closer with an awed look on her face.

"You really did it?" she asked and I suddenly realised it was me she was talking to. Somehow this broke through the numb state I was in, and I started to shake as the emotions came rushing back. Roxanna quickly grabbed the crucible from my hands and placed it gently on the stone slab at Estella's feet within the Light of Isis as I crumpled, tears burning through me, and crunched myself up into a ball. All those days of drowning in Other World craziness, as I sought the crucible while trying to keep Estella safe. All the turmoil, stress and tiredness of it all suddenly engulfed me and I sobbed. I sobbed until I could barely breathe from it all. My sister was dead, she was really dead and I had made it happen. She had been a thorn in my side; she had used and abused our relationship for so long, it had been easy to hate her for what she had done. But she was now dead and I felt so tired, so alone and so lost without her.

"Oh Ani, please don't cry," came a weak voice from above me and through all the shock and tears I found the ability to look up and see Estella propped up tiredly, looking back.

"But . . ." I asked as kindly arms helped me to my feet and I could once more feel the comfort of Trishna tingle down my back as if he was trying to hold me as well.

Estella smiled softly and then turned her head towards the pool in the centre of the room.

"I'm going to have to go soon," she said softly. "I just wanted to thank you for saving me after all the dumb shit I've ever put you through."

"How?" I asked, searching the faces of those around me, but they were all turning to the pool with an expectant look, as mist roiled from it and the light above it grew brighter.

"As she has now been cleansed of all her sins, Isis is ready to take her into the next world to await her rebirth." Roxanna explained soothingly, providing some of the comfort I so sorely needed. And, before I could say any more the Priestesses around me started one of their melodious chants. As we stared towards the Pool of Isis the mist rose higher above us before slowly drifting back down. Suddenly, through the settling mist, the head of a woman appeared at the edge of the pool.

My breath caught at the sight of her. Although her hair was so long it nearly trailed to the floor, although she was robed in wispy material that almost looked as if the mist itself had turned into clothes, she was beautiful. And not in the way of a supermodel or how modern culture expected us to see a woman's beauty. She held the flawless beauty that a young child only sees, through eyes clouded by love, in its mother and giver of life. Her warm, kindly eyes looked about the room as she smiled and my heart sighed happily, especially when her eyes fell upon me.

"Blessed be of Isis. Mother and creator. Giver of the Pure Light in which we try and live our lives," intoned Roxanna reverently and I almost felt the need to kneel before the dazzling woman in front of me as the love and joy rolled off her, and filled the room as much as her Light did.

"No child of the Light need ever kneel before me, Stephanie Muriel Anders." Isis spoke softly, gently and I felt as if I was the safest I had ever been. I didn't even feel freaked by the fact that a Goddess I had felt was imaginary a week ago, was smiling at me. We all watched, transfixed by the Lady of Light as she moved over to Estella and bestowed a loving smile upon her.

"Peace be with you, my child." Isis whispered happily, as if greeting an old friend. "I see your brave and strong sister has rescued you for the very last time. May our thanks guide her softly in her path through life." Estella looked up at the Goddess with sheer devotion, and I no longer felt jealous she never looked upon her own mother in that way. After all, Isis was the mother of all. Before Estella had a chance to reply, Isis moved to the crucible and a frown marred her beauty for the merest of moments. She placed her hand over the cup and intoned deep and warming words that I couldn't quite understand. The cup, and its horrible contents, shook for a moment before dissolving into dust under her hand. She blew on the dust and it swirled before her for a moment before wisping up into the air and spiralling up into the light above her pool.

"And so we save the world of Light from one more creature of Darkness." She smiled to the room in general, before turning back to Estella.

"Is it time, oh Goddess?" Estella asked, almost nervously. Isis smiled at her again and then sadly shook her head.

"I am sorry my child, but it is not," the Goddess replied, and this was obviously not the news everyone expected as the room suddenly went quiet.

"But, she has been freed of the Darkness and her soul is free to join you in the Light." Roxanna pointed out. Yeah, she was the only one in the room with the balls to question their Goddess. Obviously why she was the High Priestess, right?

"There is a bond that still ties her to this plane of existence." Isis replied calmly, not offended by Roxanna at all. "Until that tie can be severed, she is unable to move onto leave this life and pass onto her next."

"Oh please, what now?" I had thought the annoyed question had come from Trishna, but was stunned to realise it had actually come from me.

Isis turned her smile towards me, still not offended by my tone before looking down at Estella and giving her a meaningful look.

"I feel, my child, that you know what it is that keeps you here." Isis said. For a moment Estella merely looked ashamed before slowly nodding and looking over at me.

"She needs your forgiveness." Isis went on, when it appeared Estella was at a loss for words. "Her remorse and regret for actions in your past need pardoning before she is truly free."

I suddenly felt very sick. It was as if a great hole had opened up behind me and I was about to fall into it. All the feelings of beauty, peace, and love in the chamber fled as I realised what it was they were talking about. The history Estella and I had had was not pretty. Most of it I had just put up with over the years, ending up accepting it as what life was really like. But the sickening feeling was coming from the pain she had caused that ran even deeper within me.

"She was what she was; I accept that and have moved on." I stammered, trying to avoid the dark and painful memory that was slowly opening up within me. The reason I had been so reluctant to come to the original funeral, to want to help my sister.

"Accepting who she is one thing Stephanie, forgiving her is another," Roxanna said softly, almost reproachfully. I shared a look with her and realised she knew! She knew the pained truth I kept hidden to allow myself to actually get up in the morning and get on with my cold and lonely day. She must have known all along, when asking me to help find the crucible on that very first day. She had known and had still asked me to help? Of all the gall!

"I . . ." I stammered again, the long hidden emotions choking me and preventing the words from coming out. Why were they doing this? I had helped save my sister from purgatory. She was free to walk in the

Light and be a better person in the next life. Wasn't that enough? I had been reluctant, but it had been my duty to do it. Even after everything else in our past. Even after what Estella had done to cause our final estrangement. Even after she had destroyed my world.

My stupid little sister and her wayward ways. It had cost me not just my friends, my husband and quite a bit of the carefree freedom and love I had had for life . . . it had cost me my very reason for living. My baby.

"Ani!" pleaded Estella, her eyes welling with tears for the first time since she had become undead. "I am so sorry. I . . . I was wrong to have been driving drunk, I was a stupid, stupid fool who never deserves your forgiveness. I know that." I could hear the sincerity in her voice, so unlike the sister I knew. She looked helplessly at Isis, "I am sorry Mother Goddess, I can't go with you," she whispered sadly as her apology pierced my very soul and I sank to my knees as the hidden memories and linked emotions finally burst through from the deep, secret place within me and it felt like they were crushing my very soul. My baby, my beautiful, sweet Heather. My reason for living, my hope for a future, my unborn butterfly. How I had hated Estella for it all, hated the world for going on as if nothing had happened.

Although the pain had never ever left me, I had found a way to squash so much of it down into the darkest depths of my soul, I could go through life and function almost as if I was normal too. All my inner Darkness. I had held it deep enough down, the only person it truly hurt was me. But the memories of it all, of Estella, drunk and arguing with me while I drove her home from another bailout, snatching the wheel and causing us to crash, causing me to lose my baby at thirty weeks pregnant . . . I couldn't face those memories every day. It caused too much pain, too much anger, and too much hate for my little sister. Too much Darkness for the person who had ruined my life.

I suddenly felt so alone in this room full of women, so very alone as the pain that had driven away a husband unable to understand or cope with my loss, my friends who were unable to sympathise with me losing something they felt I had never had. The pure hatred and disgust I had for my sister who hadn't even visited me in hospital, but instead disappeared from my life for several years until she turned up dead . . . It all just hurt so much to finally release it, to finally allow myself to morn openly. My baby, my sister, both now gone. My life as a carer for those I loved now at an end. I was a no one, a nothing now the pain filled Darkness burned through me. It blackened my sight so that I could thankfully no longer see them all staring down at me in my misery and loss. In a pain so deep I could barely breathe any more, nor did I actually want to.

And then the tingling enfolded over me, the comfort of the sharp spikes of needle pricks that I knew to be Trishna seemed to find me and pick me up, carry me from the Darkness I had fallen into and place me back in the chamber where the Pool of Isis was.

"You are never alone; those you have lost will always walk with you in the Light, mere shadows not often seen by the dazzling brightness of the good you create." It was Trishna's voice, though lacked his usual sneering tone. His words comforted me, giving me the strength to look up at everyone. To look Estella in the eye as I released my Darkness, let go of it to embrace the Light. Everything I had done in the last few days, the struggles and fears and danger I had gone through, I had done it because I loved her, despite the pain she had caused, despite the careless person she had been. In the last few days, she had been everything to me once more, reminding me of what it was to be needed, to be her protector.

"I forgive you." The words were weak, wavering and it took me a moment to realise it had been me who had said them. Slowly I got to my feet, approaching Estella within the light. "I don't know how, but I do forgive you Estella. I don't want to keep you from the Light you so rightly deserve." I said in a stronger voice. "You have changed, you are a better person since becoming a Priestess of Isis, and I want you to be free." I then looked to Isis with her dazzling smile and then to Roxanna and was amazed at how free and whole I suddenly felt. My sorrow and loss were still there, dampened once more, but the near-constant nagging of hate was finally removed. I felt . . . light. Where there had been Darkness, there now glimmered Light.

"But do you really mean it?" asked Roxanna, a shared sympathy of what I had gone through showing in her eyes. "Please be sure you're not just saying it to finish all the hard work you've been through. It doesn't work that way."

Isis then laid a gentle hand on Roxanna's shoulder and smiled at her.

"She means it," the Goddess stated calmly. "The tie is now severed and we are free to return to the Light." Isis then looked at me across the stone slab, her eyes taking on a studying expression, not unlike that of Roxanna.

"It has been a pleasure to see you enter the Light, Stephanie Muriel Anders," she announced quietly. "I do hope you will walk with the Priestesses of this Temple for years to come." She laughed at my expression, being able to see my fear of becoming one of the white robed wonders. "No Stephanie, you are not of Priestess stock," she said, her beautiful smile widening even further. "You are a Protector, a rescuer of souls from the Darkness. It is a blessing given only to those with the greatest of hearts. Use it wisely and walk with my blessing." Moving around the stone slab she embraced me, and I felt like I was a small child again, surrounded by the joy, love and comfort of a mother's hug. She took from me some of my pain, my sorrow, my uncertainty. But not all, as even I knew we all needed to keep some for when we needed the power to do what was right. Isis kissed me on the forehead and moved back to Estella.

"We must go, my child," she urged, helping Estella from the stone dais and to her feet. Even as the other Priestesses started chanting again, and the mist started to froth and thicken once more, Isis guided Estella towards the pool. Just before Estella reached the pool however, she turned to me one last time and I felt the pain of it all again, just below the surface.

"I promise to try and be Heather's Protector until you can be with us once more in the Light," she said and my heart suddenly soared. She knew her name, she acknowledged my baby as a real person in a way so few others ever did.

"Thank you." I whispered, unable to say more without the tears flowing again. Turning again, she took Isis' hand and moving into the mist of the pool with her, disappearing into it.

Slowly the mist cleared to reveal the pool once more, and for a moment it was nothing but a still blackness beneath the Light. Then slowly, the lifeless body of Estella floated up to the surface, a serene smile upon her dead features. I knew at last she truly was dead, truly was at peace and walking in the Light with our beloved Isis. I had done it; it now finally was all over.

Chapter 23

TIME after that was a bit of a shocked blur. I really don't know how long I spent at the Temple of Isis. I'm fairly certain it was only a couple of weeks at the most, but at the time it seemed more like months. A lot of it was spent in the room they had given me, crying, staring at the ceiling and trying to come to grips with it all. All I had seen, all I had done and all I now had to come to terms with. I wasn't a pretty sight, let me tell you.

I hadn't wanted to go home. I would eventually, but there was nothing there for me and I would have truly been alone. At the Temple at least, I had caring souls who fed me, washed me and in general mothered me just enough to get me back on my feet.

I wasn't pampered, more poked in the right direction to ensure I ate, changed my clothes and wasn't allowed to dwell on it all for long periods of time.

And I had had a lot to dwell on. It had been several years since I had allowed myself to mourn so openly and let such raw emotions out. Add to it the final goodbye of Estella and, well, I had gone through a lot of tissues and even a bit of their red wine.

Trishna had been with me a lot of the time, but often had his box removed by Roxanna under the pretence she needed to discuss his release with him and a Lama. Though sometimes I felt it was to give him and me a little time away from each other as he wasn't the most sympathetic of people to be around, and our yelling matches only stopped from coming to blows because he didn't have the physical form for me to hit or throw things at. He had however, had a few things thrown through him.

Despite admitting to now believing in Isis and the power of her Light, I wasn't encouraged to join in the daily prayers of the Temple or even forced into the flowing gowns. Instead, I was left to my own thoughts. Though one of them had gone shopping and I spent my time slouching around the Temple in tracky-dacks and sloppy t-shirts. It was when I started laughing at being addressed as 'Protector' by a passing, well-meaning Priestess that I realised I was going to be okay. As, looking like I did, I didn't feel I cut the best 'Protector of souls' mould. Even if you'd given me my sword, and yes it was now most definitely my sword, I would still have looked like a messy haired, depressed and miserable nobody.

The day I eventually had the energy and will to dress neatly, and look like I could blend back in to the real world and go home, was the day Roxanna approached me to tell me it was time for Trishna to go too. She and the Lama had discovered a way to release him and, being bound to me, I was once more required to get the ball rolling.

I really don't know if she had only just found out about it on that day, or whether it was something she had been holding back until I appeared to be back to normal. Whichever was true, the end result was the feeling of my stomach falling into my feet and I was very nearly tempted to just crawl back into my oh so soft bed and hide again. However, the look of eagerness and joy on Trishna's face prevented me. He had the right to be free. He had eventually turned out to be a really nice guy to know and had been more than willing to help out with all the 'walking in Light' side of things. And I felt fairly certain this wasn't because he was bound to me, but because he had originally been one of those who walked in the Light, before Branwyre had killed and trapped him.

Despite Trishna mentioning it during our final confrontation with Branwyre, I had never asked what he had done to stray from the path, allowing the vampire to do what he had done to him. It was personal and if he wanted to explain it to me, he would have. Yes we had gotten into a few arguments over me feeling sorry for myself and needing to snap out of it, but not once had we gotten into the deep and personal secrets I knew we both held. I had Heather; he was allowed to have whatever it was he had. And now I was going to be free of him. That was a good thing, right?

***

I don't know why I did it, and admittedly did feel foolish enough without Trishna snickering at me, but I brought all our remaining collection of tea with me as a token of thanks to the Buddhist monks who were about to help us. Despite the puzzled look I received, they accepted it politely enough and even served some of it for us as we sat in the Buddhist temple's garden with the Lama as he explained things to us.

Apparently they had gotten hold of a Bardo Thodol, or Tibetan Book of the Dead from the Temple Trishna had lived at in the foothills of the Himalayas, that dated from before the time he had been there. Which somehow meant it held the right sort of words to release him, when combined with a spoken ritual Roxanna had come up with, that would banish Branwyre's powers binding Trishna to the contents of his box, and therefore setting him free.

I tried to listen with interest as I had the Book of the Dead explained to me, it seemed that when a monk died, one of his family, or fellow monks spent some days reciting the book to them until it was time to burn their now empty earthly remains, the soul having moved on to the next life, or enlightenment if good enough.

As with any and all of the heavy religions, Isis now included, it seemed to wash over me and I only seemed to absorb the bits I needed to know. As Trishna's body was well and truly gone, his life force now bound to the box, this ceremony would be altered slightly. The Lama and other monks of this temple would take a few days to read through the book to him and his box. I thankfully wouldn't have to be present for all of it, but would have the final word, so to speak, to send him on his way.

It all sounded so simple, I did wonder what the catch was going to be. However, I was informed that the worst thing that could happen was it wouldn't work and Trishna would still be bound to me and the box. Secretly I felt I could live with that, as I had deep wardrobes if he really started to piss me off. But I still hoped it would work. Especially when I looked at Trishna and saw the look in his eyes as it was all explained to us. Half of me didn't see the problem with being in his situation, but the other half kept reminding me of how important the sense of touch was. Not just the ability to touch and hold things for himself, but the ability to be touched or comforted by others. This was something Trishna had been without for a century now, and despite him saying all he really missed was being able to drink the tea as well as smell it, I felt I had gotten to know him well enough to know he missed the tactile responses of life. And not in a crude way either, or at least I hoped not. He was a monk after all!

And so after this was all explained to me, I found I had to agree with it all, due to Trishna being bound to me. I agreed to it all wholehearted- ly, receiving a rare grin from the ghost himself. I even offered to sit and stay for the first few chapters to be recited.

"It is probably best if we just leave them all to it until we're needed again." Roxanna advised me gently. "So as not to distract them from the task ahead. As for you Stephanie, maybe you would like me to take you to your real home for a while?" It hadn't been a suggestion, no matter how kindly it had been worded. Obviously it was time for me to move into the next stage of getting back to my normal life. Sister gone, Trishna being sorted out, what was there really left for me amongst the Other World now?

Reluctant to leave Trishna alone, despite him being in an obviously safe place, I slowly got to my feet and allowed Roxanna to lead me to her car. It was now time for me to face some of those theoretical demons, rather than the real ones.

Chapter 24

I FELT conspicuous standing in my living room with Roxanna just behind me. It wasn't as if the place was a mess or anything, just neatly cluttered, but I felt it was not a real place any more. It was small, currently stuffy from having been closed up for so long, and normal. Flat pack furniture, to assist in keeping my clutter at bay, mundane prints on the walls, factual more than fictional books in the shelves. It looked more like we'd stepped into a display at Ikea than a real home, and sadly this was the first time I realised just how drab my life had become, hiding for so long from all the bad stuff.

"This is . . . nice." offered Roxanna, as she gave one of my now dead pot plants a sad look. I was just so glad I'd not been a pet sort of person as I'd hate to have come home to what would have remained, after so long. The kitchen and fridge alone was going to be a nightmare.

"It's a shell," I suddenly said, as if seeing it all for what it really was for the first time in the seven years I'd been living there. "A shell I've been living in like a hermit. Getting on with my life as best I can and then hiding away in the emotionless, lifeless shell. Oh God, I mean Isis, I'm a hermit crab!"

As my sarcasm fought against the rising hysteria, I plopped down onto my couch, not knowing whether I should be fighting the welling up of emotions or letting them all wash over me. It had taken a mere week of being active in the Other World, a week of my sister teaching me things I never knew or wanted to know were real, for all the life that had come before it to become a sham.

Rather than saying anything, as I struggled with my emotions, Roxanna sat down calmly across from me in the arm chair. Her familiar look of cat and mouse barely hidden on her face as she watched me, waiting to see what I would do or say next.

"I don't want to be here anymore." I finally said, realising just how drab and alone I was going to be without the Other World in my life, and without even having Trishna there to annoy me into living again. "I mean, I don't want it all thrown out or anything, but I really don't want to live here anymore Roxanna." I tried to keep the pleading from my voice. "I'm not going to become one of your lace curtain acolytes, but I can't be this person anymore. I am more than that. I know that now." Actually, I didn't know that. I didn't really feel like I knew anything. Except I knew I didn't want to be here, and I didn't want to keep living in the Temple of Isis. So where did that leave me?

Roxanna, finally giving up on her need to study me like specimen, cleared her throat and looked me right in the eye.

"There is a small stone house half a block away from the Temple," she announced slowly, watching me for any response. "It belongs to the Temple, and was used in the past as a lie-in hospital for new mothers with nowhere else to go." Flinching herself at the pain that briefly crossed my expression at the mention of birth and motherhood, she pressed on quickly. "But it has been empty for over a decade now, and in need of a tenant that up-holds the beliefs of Isis and truly walks in the Light . . ." she trailed off, waiting for me to take the bait. I just sat there, too afraid to say anything or agree to anything as I was waiting for the catch. It wasn't just demons or people of the Darkness who did deals. I'd learnt that much.

"I should explain that the house has been vacant for so long because it has been waiting for the coming of someone predicted by Isis. This person is special, someone to take up the tasks of fighting the Darkness so the Priestesses of Isis could return to a life of peace." Ah-ha! I knew there had been a catch; I could stay there until that lacy curtained freak turned up, right. When was that then, I wondered.

"That person," continued Roxanna, seeing I was still not rising to the bait, "Would be known as the Protector, rescuer of souls from the Darkness. Blessed by Isis and welcomed by her with open heart to walk with her in the Light for all days."

I broke down. I hadn't meant to, but as those words sank in I found my slowly repaired hard and sarcastic shell shatter as I sank to the floor and sobbed onto Roxanna's knees. Whether it was the reopened pain of it all, the relief of not being alone, or the memory of love and welcoming Isis herself had given me, I don't know. All in all I felt rather embarrassed when I finally finished, as such behaviour was so not me and so not the tough, sarcastic cow I strived to be in life.

Without looking at Roxanna, as I accepted her proffered fresh tissues, I eased myself back onto the couch and took a moment to think it all through. I wouldn't be at the Temple itself and therefore not technically a Priestess in bed sheets. But I would be close by if I was to need them. Or, more importantly, if they were to need me. Slowly it all sunk in, Roxanna wasn't just offering me a place to stay, she was offering me a new life and a job, a place to be me in the Other World.

"Do I get paid?" I asked, finally looking back at her. Hey, I found it best to always get to impolite questions out of the road first.

"There is a small salary that comes with the responsibility of Protector." Roxanna replied lightly, her cat and mouse gaze back. "But it will also be your responsibility to maintain the upkeep of the house itself, walk in the Light and be there to help whenever you are needed. The call may not come from Isis, and may not be one that appeals to you, but it will be up to you to respond willingly and quickly. The Priestesses of Isis were never meant to slay vampires. We simply did it out of need until you came along to work in our name in our fight against the Darkness."

"Do I have to become a regular church goer to the Temple and start being a good little devoted worshipper?" Yes, I had a thing against any organised religion; that should have been obvious by now despite my opening myself up to Isis' Light.

"We all worship and show our devotion to Isis in our own way," Roxanna replied cryptically. "Yes the occasional appearance at worship would be nice, but not attending won't get you fired . . . unless you are straying from the Light."

"And by fired, that's not a literal thing now is it?" Words were important, and I didn't always trust in the use of a smoke detector. Roxanna stifled a smile.

"No, it just means you will be removed from your position and the house," she replied, still in that light tone while studying me. "Though, if you were to slip into the Darkness, there's always the possibility of the literal meaning." She winked at me as a look of horror flicked across my face. That was something I was beginning to realise with not just Roxanna, but a lot of the Priestesses at the Temple. They might appear silly women in lace with a rather aimless attitude to life, but they could really pack a wallop when needed and definitely weren't someone I would want on my bad side.

"Please tell me there won't be a uniform," I said resignedly, finding I had little else to question her on. Roxanna's smile returned as she saw she'd gotten me to agree to the job without me actually saying I had.

"Not us such," she said. "But we would rather you didn't do a lot of your work in track-suit pants and overly big t-shirts." Another smile, this time matched by one of my own. "Oh, and you're not a superhero so there's no need to go get kitted out in tight leathers and a cape either. Just be yourself, it's seen you through so much and kept you and those with you safe."

And that, really, was all it took. Despite me still not knowing about a lot of the Other World ins and outs, I had found my place in it. As a result I planned on spending a significant amount of my time actually writing the books for dummies on demons and what not I'd been muttering about, rather than just keeping it all in my head.

***

And so, with look-ins to check on Trishna and the recital of the Book of the Dead, I suddenly find myself moving into my new life. I also learnt the Temple of Isis had both laymen and woman. People who weren't Priestesses, but still somehow fitted into the whole scheme of things. A lot of the laymen were actually the husbands of the Priestesses. Not because they needed a man to get on with their lives, but because they had found someone suited to be by their side in their worship. Isis' religion within this Temples wasn't one for celibacy, being the Mother and Creator; she liked to see these attributes used to their fullest by her followers.

The reason I learnt about the laypeople of the temple was because they descended en masse to my apartment, and quickly and efficiently emptied it. A lot of the things I found I had accumulated to keep me in my hermit-like state, but not really needed, were freely given away to charities and people who really needed them. Though there were some personal items and pieces that needed to be kept, including my hidden stash of photos and memories of Estella from happier days. All of these were moved into the well-maintained and homely house I had been given to start my new life. It still all seemed unreal, while also feeling right. So I suppose it was meant to be.

My non-Other World affairs were put in order, including quitting my job as a hermit-like accountant, contacting my parents to let them know it was all okay, and selling my apartment. At first I was sure I would be expected to hand over all my money to the Temple of Isis, but Roxanna boggled at the thought, and told me to keep the money safe for when I needed it. I had been amused, however, when she mentioned she now knew who to turn to the next time the roof needed repairing. And this was all okay. I still felt odd to be caught up in it all after Estella was well and truly dead and buried — well, cremated and returned to the Pool of Isis actually — but I no longer felt out of my depth. It was weird, they were a bunch of lacy curtain wearing oddballs, and vampires, ghosts and demons were real. Go figure. Somehow it just all had started to make sense, even when I still felt out of my depth and having to madly learn something new every day.

Still, I accepted my new place and with it, my new title. And we celebrated with a feast in the refectory of Isis. Knowing the next day my final task on entering this world was to happen. It was time to say goodbye to Trishna.

***

Thankful I hadn't enjoyed as much wine the night before as I had wanted to, I found myself sitting in the garden of the Buddhist temple early the next morning, watching the sun rise over the Eastern wall and relishing the warmth it brought to my chill mood.

I don't know why I felt so upset over what was about to happen. In the week it had taken the monks to read the book to Trishna, who I am told just sat there patiently as long as there was a hot cup of tea in front of him, I had done so much more with my life. Moved on, literally from everything I had known and into my new life. It was just that, during that time I seemed to have missed his presence even more than I missed Estella. I couldn't really explain it, despite having tried to with Roxanna, but there was just something about him I was going to miss. And I was certain it wasn't the paint peeling insults.

"Don't pout, frizz head." Trishna smiled at me, noticing my expression as the ceremony came to an end. "I'm sure there will be other people who you can flip off in the days to come. And just think of what perverse things the next ghost you bind yourself to may want to smell."

I tried to hide the smile he had caused, feeling I should be sombre at this time. But his teasing manner caught me out again and I started to wonder if that was what I would miss: A talking second consciences to say out loud the things I tried to avoid even thinking.

It was then, finally, my turn to speak the words Roxanna had written, the words that should allow Trishna to be freed from the binding Branwyre had used to tie him to the items within the box.

I stood, not really knowing why I did this, as everyone else was still sitting in the cushion strewn grove, and cleared my throat. I had read over the words from Roxanna a few times already that morning and still wasn't too sure if they sounded right.

"Trishna Duhkha, brought to an untimely end by Branwyre, eighteenth vampire Lord of the Aegean, your life force captured to be used as his tool, I free you from your binding. Having banished Branwyre from this place, his powers over you have also been banished. Be free to move into the Light and continue on your path towards enlightenment." That was it, all she had written. I looked around at the small group expectantly, but was met by blank faces. To me, there was just something unfinished in it all.

"Trishna, so wrongly trapped and abused beyond measure, I wish for you to find peace as you return to your point of death and find freedom and harmony there, rather than the pain and anguished you met through Branwyre." I added, suddenly feeling it was the right thing to say. His expression changing, Trishna suddenly rose to his feet and stood before me, his blue shade shimmering and changing to a yellow colour I somehow knew was his own true aura. And having started to have read up on aura colours, I somehow wasn't surprised to see it was that shade either. It suited him.

"Be free, Trishna." I then said quietly, suddenly feeling tears prick my eyes as I realised I was saying goodbye for the last time . . . again. "Be at peace, find enlightenment and, for Isis' sake, behave yourself. Thank you for all your help. It has been . . . interesting." We shared a smiled as he nodded.

"Thank you for keeping your promise," he said in as polite a tone I'd ever heard. "And for the cups of tea. For a white woman, you weren't so bad at making them." He grinned again, and before I could find the right witty comeback he stepped into me. Face to face he merged into me in his version of a ghostly embrace. The usual pinprick tingles quickly turned into a sensation so warm and filling and near exquisite, it took my breath away. It was like a passionate heartfelt kiss goodbye that surged through my whole body and, as he stepped out of me, left me tingling in places I was fairly certain he shouldn't have been able to touch.

"Oh you are so not reaching enlightenment any time soon for being able to do something like that!" I said breathily. He broke into another of his grins and winked at me.

"Maybe," he replied cheekily, "But I felt it was well worth the risk. Goodbye Stephanie Muriel Anders, and thank you." And then, as I was still getting my breath back, he was gone. He just dissolved into the morning sunlight and I was left standing in amidst a ring of rather shocked looking monks, and a rather amused looking Roxanna.

"Well, here's hoping not all freeing of ghosts has such an interesting ending." I tried to say it lightly, but was still rather rattled by it all and desperately trying hard to not think over the fact I was never going to see Trishna again. I was now, also, thinking it was probably a good thing too, if the bugger could do that!

***

The ceremony ended shortly afterwards with the burning of Trishna's box, and all its contents in a fire especially lit for the occasion. I had been half tempted to ask to keep the box, now it was just a box, but something inside me stopped me from asking for it. It had been a torture device, binding Trishna to this world for one hundred years and making him a witness to who knew what. It was right to burn it all, remove all trace of his prison.

Then, as we were leaving, the ageing Lama came to me and handed me a small porcelain tea cup, explaining to me it was the one Trishna had used in his time with them. I had felt a little uncomfortable when faced with the Lama's knowing look, but politely accepted the cup. In a way, I could see it reminding me of the foul-mouthed monk, I just hoped I didn't so clearly remember his magic touch.

Epilogue

WHILE it had looked like an old Christian church sold off due to lack of funds and taken over by a bunch of new-age loonies, it had turned out to be a Temple of Isis. A temple built for that very purpose, but dressed like a church of God to hide it from those who just didn't get that there was more to life than what they were told to believe.

It was part of a greater community, part of other places of belief and worship of those who walked in the Light. A place of peace, a welcome haven to those who had become lost in life and needed to find themselves and, most importantly, the home of a Goddess.

In the days leading away from saying good bye to Trishna, I often found myself just standing out the front of it and staring up into its great grey stone walls and welcoming façade. I didn't want to admit — or get too soppy in feeling — that I too had been one of those people who had become lost in life and had needed the guiding Light of Isis to set me on my way. And while I would never agree to being a worshipper of any single organised faith, slash religion, it was pretty cool to be on first name basis with a Goddess. And not that bad being known as a Protector of the place either.

So far that hadn't amounted to much, as it appears souls lost to the Darkness don't just come knocking on your door asking to be set free. I had, however, already had to free Mr Vontant again from the auction house when they attempted to summon and Earth him once more.

I won't go into exactly what I did to those who felt they could summon a demon willy-nilly, but you can be assured they got a firm talking to. Yes, I had then been banned from ever attending one of their auctions again, after having thrown a fae cup — while wearing gloves — at the senior partner and cracking him on the side of the head with it, but shit happens. When you're a Protector and walk in the Light, there is no Darkness you can't penetrate. Gah! That still sounds lame when I say it; I really did need to get myself a new ghost sidekick or something.

Still, this little lost soul who had been living with her own personal Darkness stewing away inside not only found the Light, but jumped into it, boots and all. And, despite having lost the sister I had always wanted — but had only had for the briefest of moments — I had no regrets. Life went on, it always did, even when you asked it to just stop and leave you alone so you can get on with a good cry.

I was me, I had accepted it. And now it was time to move on.

The End.

Thank you for reading
ISIS, VAMPIRES AND GHOSTS — OH MY
we hope you enjoyed it.

If you would like to be kept informed of further releases in the Other World series, or other new books from Hague Publishing, why not subscribe to our newsletter at:

www.HaguePublishing.com/subscribe.php

And if you loved the book and have a moment to spare we would really appreciate a short review.

Your help in spreading the word is gratefully received.

About The Author

JANIS grew up in and around Darwin and its rural surrounds. As a child, she spent a lot of time around 'science geeks' at the Darwin University, where her father was a lecturer for many years. It took her a long time to realise that not everyone got to grow up like that or could relate to all the Science Labs scenes in the old Dr Who.

Janis now lives in the Adelaide Hills with her husband and three children, lovingly referred to as the 'Demonic Hordes'. She is a semi-retired ICT Support Officer who, when not writing, takes pride in her work as a Haus Frau while dabbling in the art of translating century old cookery books into modern recipes to experiment on her family with.

For more information visit https://janishill.wordpress.com/

Hague

Publishing

www.HaguePublishing.com

PO Box 451 Bassendean
Western Australia 6934

www.ingramcontent.com/pod-product-compliance
Lightning Source LLC
Chambersburg PA
CBHW071355100726
47908CB00004B/1002